MW01489685

PAINTED IN LOVE

MAVERICK BILLIONAIRES
BOOK TEN

BELLA ANDRE

JENNIFER SKULLY

PAINTED IN LOVE

The Maverick Billionaires, Book 10
© 2025 Bella Andre & Jennifer Skully

Meet the Maverick Billionaires—sexy, self-made men from the wrong side of town who survived hell together and now have everything they ever wanted. But when each Maverick falls head over heels for an incredible woman he never saw coming, he will soon find that true love is the only thing he ever really needed...

After years of working with artists to build their careers in a world where fame can exact a terrible price, billionaire Clay Harrington's number one priority is to foster creativity and nourish artistic dreams through his innovative video platform. So when he agrees to mentor a former foster kid with raw talent, Clay is determined to find the young man's hero, a legendary street artist named San Holo. In his wildest dreams, Clay never thought it would be so difficult to uncover the real identity of this elusive superstar. Until he discovers that the key to unlocking the artist's identity might be sexy, brilliant Saskia Oliver.

When Saskia opens her door to the tall, handsome, and sexy-as-hell stranger, she can't fight their immediate electric and irresistible attraction. But even after passionate kisses and seductive nights, she still can't give Clay what he wants. She's sworn to keep San Holo's identity a secret no matter the cost... even if love is on the line.

When their two hearts and bodies collide like shooting stars, is there any way they can create a love that will last forever? Or will the cost of keeping secrets destroy any chance at having the love they've both craved for so long?

A NOTE FROM BELLA & JENNIFER

We're so thrilled to welcome you back into the world of the Maverick Billionaires! Your love for the Mavericks and Harringtons means so much to us, and we're endlessly grateful for your support, your enthusiasm, and your loyalty.

We especially loved writing Clay and Saskia's story—two hearts that were meant to find each other in the most unexpected way. We hope you fall head over heels for them just like we did.

And can we please take a moment to raise a glass to our most beloved scene-stealer, Fernsby? Oh, how we *adore* our fabulous, unflappable, and often hilarious British butler!

Thank you for laughing, swooning, and sighing with joy right alongside us. We couldn't do this without you.

With love,
Bella Andre and Jennifer Skully

P.S. Please sign up for our New Release newsletters for more information on new books. www.BellaAndre.com/Newsletter and www.JenniferSkully.com/Newsletter.

PROLOGUE

*P*eople think the night is darkest at midnight. They're wrong. True dark comes just before dawn, when the temperature drops and the fog rolls in. I pull my hoodie over my head to keep my ears warm. A streetlight shines through the fog, giving me just enough light to work by. This alley in San Francisco's Mission District is perfect for my next masterpiece.

Night is when I work, with the foggy halos around the streetlights. This isn't commissioned work, but a piece for myself. I've been dreaming about it for weeks now, but I've been too busy to get out here. My best work is always the stuff I paint just for myself. Don't get me wrong—commissions are good, my bread and butter. I'm not ashamed of that. But this work, it's special.

The narrow, dingy, stinky alley—I've painted in places far worse than this—is off the beaten track, definitely not an attraction on the street art tours. Most likely, no one will ever see what I've painted, let alone realize it's my work, unless they look closely. But no one will. Because it's street art, and the next artist will paint right over it. I don't care. All

I care about is getting the images out of my head and onto the wall. That's how I stay sane—by painting the pictures out of my head. Until another one comes along from some deep secret place inside me.

Out here, no one tells me what to paint. No one judges it. Under the veil of night, that's when I feel most creative.

As dawn breaks through the dark and the fog, I step away to survey what I've done. "Yeah," I say aloud. "This is good."

I've got to remember to get out here more often, to work in the middle of the night. Because these are my roots. This is where I came from—the dark, the cold, the loneliness of the middle of the night.

I look behind me. Yes, the street is lighter than before. The dawn is coming. I need to get away before the light hits me. I add my last flourish, then escape down the alley, leaving behind the tools of my trade. Some other street artist will need them.

By the time I make it back to the place where I sleep, the sky is lightening. Fog still shrouds the city by the bay, but in a little while, it'll be gone, just as I'll be gone.

Like a vampire, I climb into my bed as the sun spills its rays over the city.

CHAPTER ONE

*C*lay Harrington looked at the kid beside him. Pretty soon, Dylan might be taller than him, though Clay was well over six feet. "If you want to do more street art," he said, "this is a great place for it."

They'd come out early on a Wednesday morning, before Dylan had to get to school, to San Francisco's Mission District, famous for its street art. Early April could be cool in the Bay Area, but neither of them minded.

A lanky kid three months shy of his eighteenth birthday, Dylan Beck pushed his longish hair back from his face. Clay would have called its color *dirty blond*, but since Dylan was a foster child, the term felt demeaning.

Dylan shrugged. "I don't know." They stood in front of a mural resembling a robot made of small buildings melded together into its robot parts.

"But you've already done a lot of street art," Clay reminded Dylan.

Again, he shrugged. "That's just stuff."

Clay knew what he meant. Dylan got out his frustrations

3

by throwing paint at the wall. But Clay wanted to see the kid put his best work out there.

He'd mentored Dylan since Rosie and Gideon Jones's wedding six months ago. It started out as a favor to Gideon, who'd met the kid through his foundation, Lean on Us. Dylan would soon be aging out of the foster care system, and he'd been getting into trouble tagging in places where he shouldn't. Since Clay worked with a lot of artists, Gideon had asked him to help out, claiming Clay understood the artistic temperament.

Clay had come to appreciate the brilliant young street artist. He'd given Dylan a studio in his warehouse, among the other artists Clay assisted. While the kid's tagging was good, the stuff he created in his studio came straight from the heart.

Instead of telling Dylan he needed to put his real work out there, Clay had brought him to the Mission District, home to some of the most amazing murals in the city, maybe even the country. Many of these wall paintings weren't strictly street art, because the nature of street art was that it could be painted over, sometimes the same night it was created. These commissioned murals would remain for all to enjoy, but there were plenty of nooks and crannies where street artists could make their mark.

This morning, they'd studied incredible murals on their walk-through, the Maestrapeace mural on The Women's Building, the Carnaval mural, plus all the street art along Balmy Alley and Clarion Alley. While not all of the murals they saw had been paid for, street art was still far from tagging. It was big business, and despite its transient nature, it had spawned mega street artists like Banksy, who was rumored to be worth millions, maybe even a billion, as well as rising stars like San Holo.

Clay wanted the same glory for Dylan. The kid was that

good. But he had to put out some of the art he worked on in the studio.

Clay's downtown warehouse, only blocks from where they stood, housed the studios of many of the amazing artists Clay had come across since art had taken over his world. He gave equal opportunity to painters, sculptors, mosaic layers, potters, jewelry makers, dancers, writers. His warehouse included all art forms.

Their meandering walk brought them to an alley beyond all the famous works. Dingy, dank, and slightly ripe as the morning sun rose in the sky, its walls were relatively tag-free.

Clay stood at the mouth of the alley. "How about trying something here?" He pointed to the left. "You could do something that takes up this entire wall."

Dylan wrinkled his nose. "It stinks."

"It can be cleaned up." Clay could have a team on it within a couple of hours.

But again, Dylan shook his head. "I don't know."

Clay recognized the boy's fear. He was fine tagging when it was totally anonymous and good working in the confines of his studio where he controlled the invitations to view his work. But out here, everyone would see it. Clay had witnessed that kind of fear firsthand back in university, when he'd roomed with one of his best friends, Gareth Tate. Gareth used to be a painter, but now served as Clay's lawyer.

Clay said almost forcefully, "You don't have to worry about being trashed. I'll make sure that doesn't happen."

Dylan looked at him, his head wagging on his narrow neck, his body otherwise immovable. "You can't really stop that."

But Clay assured him, "Yes, I can."

That's what his new video platform, Art Space, was all about, providing a safe place for artists where they were never demoralized by cruel or vicious comments. He had the power to make sure Dylan never suffered what his friend Gareth had.

He went back to Dylan's earlier comment. "Once it's sanitized, this is a good place to start."

But still the kid repeated his refrain. "I don't know."

Clay walked into the alley despite its eau de garbage. Dylan followed more hesitantly. Until they both made out a mural at the end of the alley. Though slightly obscured by shadow, there was definitely a painting there. Street art. As he closed in on it, Clay saw materials on the ground beside it, spray paint cans, regular paint cans, even a stepladder to reach the uppermost parts of the mural.

Suddenly, Dylan overtook him, almost running. He stopped at the base of the mural, staring up as if he were looking at a religious icon.

"This is him." Dylan's voice dripped with awe, his gaze reverent.

"Who?"

"San Holo." Dylan looked back at Clay. "It's him. I know everything he's done, and this is totally new." The boy's voice had taken on the worshipfulness of a postulant.

Clay stared with him. He knew about San Holo, the famous street artist Dylan always talked about. When the kid first mentioned the artist, his voice had been full of adulation. "San Holo is the *best*. This is what I want to do. I want to be just like him."

Clay had immediately researched San Holo and studied his art. He'd talked to Cal Danniger, too, since he'd heard the story about Cal coming across San Holo's early work in London. In fact, that was the trip where Cal had first met Clay's brother Dane. Cal had spoken highly of the artist and owned several first edition prints.

San Holo, like Banksy, sold canvases of his murals and

limited-edition prints. That was where the money came from. He also did commissions. But what made San Holo almost as famous as Banksy was right here in front of them. His street art.

Despite having studied the man's art, Clay still had to ask, "Are you sure this is his work?"

The kid narrowed his eyes mutinously. "I know it." He put a hand to his chest. "Don't you feel its power?"

Dylan obviously wanted them to experience that power together, as he stepped away, hand on Clay's arm, pulling him back to gaze up at the mural. Breathlessly, he said, "Isn't it totally amazing? Everything he does is mind-blowing." His voice dropped low to that reverent note.

Clay stared up at the painting. A ladder reaching all the way to the clouds was peopled with an array of climbers: a Native American woman, an Asian man, a Black man with a child's hand in his as he helped her climb. A Black woman held out her hand to a white woman on the rungs below. People of all diverse cultures climbed into the clouds together.

Dylan pointed. "Look. There's even a little green man."

Sure enough, a green alien with bulging eyes held out a three-fingered hand, helping the people of Earth reach for the sky.

Dylan murmured, "Do you feel the power?"

Clay did. Much of the work had been spray-painted—the clouds, the sky, the grass and flowers surrounding the ladder. But the expressions on the individual faces were rendered with perfect brushstrokes.

"Could he have done this overnight?" Clay asked, not so much of Dylan, but of the universe.

"That's what he's famous for," Dylan expounded. "His paintings appear overnight." He squeezed Clay's arm in his excitement. "Let's find the fleur-de-lis."

7

The fleur-de-lis was part of San Holo's signature. Once they found it, they would also uncover the small initials *SH* that went with it. San Holo was known for making his acolytes search for the symbol. If Dylan found it now, that would be the real tell that it was one of the artist's new pieces.

They searched every inch—the flowers, the people's clothing and faces, the trees, the ladder, until the sun crept up the wall to banish the last of the shadows. Dylan set up the stepladder, climbing for a better look.

"I found it." His cry echoed with joy as he pointed at the alien. "I told you this was San Holo." Then he took his phone out of his back pocket and snapped a picture.

Once on the ground again, he pushed Clay to the ladder. "You have to see."

Clay climbed beside the people ascending their ladder, until he was level with the alien's bulging eyes. There it was, right in the eye, a fleur-de-lis and the initials *SH*.

Dylan was right on the money.

After Clay had descended, Dylan grabbed the stepladder and put it back against the side wall where the artist had left it, almost as if he didn't want anyone else to consider climbing up.

His hazel eyes glowed with flecks of amber. "This is how a gold miner must have felt when he found a vein of gold." He slapped his hand to his chest. "We're the first!"

Clay had to correct him. "*You're* the first. I never would've known." He was so impressed, he'd forgotten the stink in the alley. Or maybe the beauty of the street art banished it.

Dylan stepped back to take another photo. "I'm putting this on my social media." His fingers moved like lightning over his phone screen.

Since he followed Dylan's social media, Clay heard a ping on his phone.

"You really get it, don't you," Dylan finally said.

Clay smiled his agreement. "Since you introduced me to San Holo's work, I've been captivated. But this one…" He opened his arms to encompass the artist's latest. "It blows everything out of the water."

"I mean you really get us artists." Dylan looked at Clay as if he walked on water. Which Clay knew was far from true. But Dylan went on, "That's why you find places for all of us in your warehouse. Even though you don't make art yourself." He shook his shaggy head. "I really don't get why you're not an artist yourself, but maybe that's because you give it all to us."

Clay had a hundred studios in his San Francisco warehouse, with a total of five warehouses in the US and plans to expand internationally. He understood that artists spoke a different language, that their thoughts were in colors or shapes or ideas, wherever their artistic endeavors led them. He appreciated that language and knew that when inspiration sparked, there was no stopping them from jumping into it. Many went to sleep dreaming of their next artwork, or their next novel, or their next piece of music. Their ideas could not be leashed and couldn't be slotted into someone else's formula. That's what his warehouses and Art Space were all about, allowing artists to dream their dreams the way they needed to be dreamed. They could post their works, their thoughts, talk about their process, whatever.

It pleased him immensely that Dylan understood how Clay felt about art and artists. The kid, not even eighteen yet, was perceptive, and that would make him one of the greats.

A fervent light gleamed in Dylan's eyes. "If I could talk to San Holo—" He sucked in a breath, blew it out harshly. "It would be my dream to ask him even one question. He wouldn't need to be creating art at that moment. Just to stand next to him would be the best thing that ever happened to me in my whole life."

Clay's heart turned over for this kid who'd lost his parents when he was only ten years old, his father into the prison system and his mother to a drug overdose. He'd bounced from one appalling foster home to another. Until a couple of years ago, when Gideon found him. Now the kid was in a decent foster home, and Clay had given him the artist's studio to work in.

In the face of this kid's hero worship, Clay couldn't help committing himself. "You know what, Dylan? I'll make this happen for you." Even if he had to commission a massive piece of San Holo's artwork, he would get it done.

The malodorous alley no longer mattered. There was only the bright light of zeal in Dylan's eyes. "It's impossible," he said on a gasp. "It can't be done."

Clay shook his head. "I can do it. And I never break a promise."

Dylan dug his fingers into Clay's arm. "If you think you can…" His eyes were like fire. "OMG, man." His voice trembled. "If I could meet him, life could never ever get better than that."

"I'll make it happen," Clay vowed to both Dylan and himself.

Then Dylan was bouncing through the alley like he was at a rave. "I'm so freaking inspired. I have to go paint now."

Not wanting to tamp down his enthusiasm, Clay still had to say, "But you've got school."

Excitement rolled off Dylan in waves. "Would you call in for me? Just this once? I'll never ask again, I promise."

Both Clay and Gideon had been given the privilege of dealing with the school on his behalf, rather than his foster parents. Dylan had never abused that. But Clay knew that if he didn't let Dylan dive into it now, the kid might lose the inspiration that had struck him as he stood before San Holo's latest masterpiece.

"All right," he agreed. "This one time."

"Thank you." Then Dylan took off running, punching his fist in the air. The warehouse was only a couple of blocks away.

Clay made the call, standing just outside the alley. Once he was done, he strolled back in, gazing up at the great man's work. He still couldn't believe this had been accomplished overnight.

He'd considered commissioning a mural for the exterior of the warehouse. Just as he'd commissioned a lobby sculpture from Charlie Ballard. She might be Sebastian Montgomery's fiancée and part of the Maverick clan, but she was an amazing metal artist, and the art she'd created was magnificent. Now he'd promised Dylan he'd find a way for the kid to meet the great San Holo. The two things dovetailed perfectly. He wanted a mural that spoke of his love for art, of his respect for artists, and his gut told him that San Holo was the right artist for it.

While he commissioned the piece, he'd find out the artist's true identity and fulfill his promise to Dylan.

Alone in the alley once more, he pulled out his phone. Since Cal Danniger had shown him those first edition prints, Clay knew what it would mean to Danniger to see this new work.

Cal answered, saying, "What's up, dude?"

With no preliminaries, Clay laid it on him. "You need to get down here right now. We've found a new San Holo. And it's freaking incredible."

Cal didn't even question him. "Where are you?"

"I'll text my location."

Cal was gone without even saying goodbye.

Cal and Lyssa, Daniel Spencer's younger sister, had a

handsome baby boy together—Owen, who was now nine months old. A billionaire in his own right, Cal Danniger still managed the Mavericks' joint ventures. That now included the projects the Harringtons pulled together with the Maverick Group, especially the new resort Clay's older brother Dane was building for special needs kids and adults. Cal managed the cash flow and investments.

The Harringtons and the Mavericks had begun doing deals together more than a year ago. They'd all just... clicked. Maybe it was their backgrounds. The Mavericks had been raised in a seedy Chicago neighborhood, dragging themselves up with the help of Susan and Bob Spencer, who acted almost as foster parents to the scrappy group of boys. The Harringtons had lost their parents just about the time Clay started high school. They'd had to drag themselves out from under the mountain of debt their parents had left behind.

Now the two groups, Mavericks and Harringtons, were like family.

It didn't take more than half an hour for Cal to get there, but already a massive crowd had formed. The info could only have come from Dylan's social media post. The kid was probably gaining thousands of followers.

He spied Cal's head above the throng as the man pushed his way through. Reaching him, Cal said, "The whole freaking art world knows about it now."

Clay clapped him on the back. "I swear, it hasn't even been a full hour since we found it. I can't believe how fast the news traveled."

But Cal wasn't paying attention, starstruck by the great man's latest work, the detail, the message. "Wow," he said in a low, awed voice that resembled Dylan's when he'd first seen the mural.

Finally, his gaze still on the masterpiece, Cal said, "To

think it was only eighteen months ago that Delic told me San Holo was an artist to watch."

"Delic?" Clay asked.

Cal smiled as if it was a fond memory. "He was our guide on that street art tour Lyssa and I did back in London."

Clay suddenly understood why the man was smiling. He'd heard the tale from the Mavericks, how the two had known each other for years, Cal twenty years her senior. On that trip to London to see Dane, Cal and Lyssa had fallen for each other. The rest was history. Now the two families were inextricably entwined.

"It was only a couple of months later," Cal explained, "that San Holo did the London mural on Brick Lane—" A famous spot for street art. "—and suddenly the guy's art went viral." He pointed. "After seeing this latest piece, I think he's going to be almost bigger than Banksy. He'll certainly be bigger than Lynx."

Clay had researched all the big street artists, Banksy being the most famous. Lynx, whose real name was Hugo Lewis, had also been an amazing street artist a few years back, although his work over the last five years wasn't anywhere near as good as his early stuff. Lynx had lost his edge. Unlike San Holo, whose work showed more brilliance with every new piece.

Cal's canvases and first edition prints would rise in value after this latest piece. San Holo's work might even start to rival Banksy's, some of which went for as much as fifty thousand pounds for just a print. There were even Banksy museums in New York City and London. Street art wasn't just tagging anymore; it had become one of the most lucrative art forms.

Now San Holo's street art had solidified *him* as an uber artist.

Cal was saying, "I've already tripled my investment. I

really appreciate the art." He turned to Clay. "I've got to have this one too."

Clay searched for clues as to the artist's real identity. "You think the guy's British? Since he got his start over there?"

Cal shrugged. "Probably. But his stuff pops up all over the world. He could be from anywhere."

The whispers rose in volume all around them.

"San Holo has made a new one."

"There's no one like him."

"It's amazing."

Still staring at the mural, Clay asked, "Do you know who his agent is?"

Cal snorted. "Got her on speed-dial."

"I want to commission a mural for the warehouse," Clay told him.

Cal was already scrolling through his phone contacts. "I'm sending her info."

A moment later, Clay's phone pinged. Then Cal elbowed him lightly in the ribs. "But don't you try buying the canvas of this work out from under me."

Clay laughed. "I want something that's specifically for my warehouse. Something no one else has seen."

And he would have it. Along with the artist's true identity.

CHAPTER TWO

*C*lay had set up the meeting with Adrian Fielding, San Holo's agent, for the afternoon. Her downtown office in a Market Street high-rise had no waiting room and no receptionist. When he knocked, the door opened to reveal a pretty woman, thirty, maybe a little older, blond hair curling over her shoulders.

Her curvy figure made him think of Gareth, because this woman was exactly his friend's type.

She held out her hand, shaking with a strong grip, her voice smooth and very British. "You must be Clay Harrington. I'm Adrian Fielding." They exchanged business cards.

So, the agent was British. Another clue to the artist's origins?

She beckoned him into the large office overlooking the bay, with an oversized desk holding a computer and two monitors, a conference table, a couch with two wing chairs, and a sideboard holding a coffeemaker, fridge, and microwave. Nice digs, but it was the view of the bay that made the space impressive.

"Please, have a seat," she said. "Then we'll discuss how I

can help you." He'd given her no idea over the phone. "Can I get you some coffee? Or water?"

"Water would be great, thanks."

She poured him a cup from a water cooler next to the sideboard.

Instead of getting directly to his mission, he made small talk. "Where are you from in England?"

She smiled. "London."

"I enjoy London," he told her. "The city has a marvelous art culture. I'm surprised you could leave it. How long have you been in San Francisco?"

She shrugged nonchalantly, as if she didn't suspect he was fishing for information. "About five years."

San Holo had come on the scene big-time about eighteen months ago, from what Cal had told him. His first works showed up in London, and he had a British agent. Had he come from London to San Francisco and searched out Adrian Fielding, a woman who was probably the only British agent in town? Like sought like. It made sense. He'd be willing to bet that San Holo was British.

He eased into what he wanted. "I've been watching San Holo's work, and it's brilliant."

She smiled like the cat that ate the cream. "I totally agree. San is brilliant."

"Cal Danniger is a big fan of his work."

"Yes," Adrian said. "Mr. Danniger is a very good client."

"I also have a young friend who's in love with San Holo's work. In fact, Dylan was the one who found San's—" He used Adrian's familiar abbreviation. "—mural down in the Mission District. He discovered the trademark fleur-de-lis."

Adrian raised an eyebrow. He could have sworn the pupils of her blue eyes grew larger. "I didn't know he'd done another mural right here in San Francisco." She made it sound as if San Holo didn't live in the Bay Area. Maybe he still resided in London, and the latest mural was just a pop-up.

It gave Clay the perfect opportunity to build up Dylan. "I have a warehouse close to the Mission District where I provide space for artists' studios." He didn't tell her he housed almost a hundred artists. "Dylan is one of them. We were searching for virgin territory where he might try out his street art. That's when we found San Holo's newest work. Dylan swears he's never seen this one before." He smiled, drawing her in. "He is all-knowing about anything San Holo."

Adrian returned the smile. "Your friend even has one up on me."

"He's a foster kid three months shy of eighteen. He's a brilliant artist, in my humble opinion." There was nothing humble about it. "But he was going downhill for a while, stuck in a bad foster home and getting in trouble tagging in the wrong places. Gideon Jones helped him." He paused a moment, then added, "I'm not sure if you know anything about Gideon. His nonprofit foundation, Lean on Us, gives aid to veterans and foster kids. He asked me to mentor Dylan, and we're both giving the young man every opportunity."

Clay hated to think about what the kid's life had been like before Gideon came along.

"I've heard of Gideon Jones and his foundation," Adrian said. "He's the one who sold that Miguel Fernando Correa painting a couple of years ago for sixty million dollars." Her lips seemed to pucker around the incredible amount. "Instead of pocketing the money," she went on, as if she had to tell Clay, "he opened a nonprofit foundation with the proceeds."

Clay completed the story for her, the part she probably didn't know. "Gideon was given the painting by a comrade who was killed over in Afghanistan. He carried it around for years, not knowing its true value. When he did find out, he sold it at auction to my brother Dane."

"I'd heard that too. Now your brother is loaning the painting to the Tate in London and other museums and galleries so everyone can see it." Her smile stretched wide. "I'm even more glad to hear Gideon is doing good things for your young friend. What did you say his name was?"

"Dylan Beck."

"A foster kid," she repeated, as if cataloging the fact.

Adrian Fielding seemed suitably primed and the timing right. "Let me tell you why I'm here. After seeing San Holo's work today, and also having studied it extensively—" He wanted her to know he was a serious collector who'd done his research. "—I'd like to commission a mural for the ware-house I mentioned. Since I have so many artists with studios there, I want something that shows we're like an art colony."

If she knew of Dane Harrington and Gideon Jones, then she probably knew of him, but she eyed him as though she didn't. "Exactly what would you like?"

He gave her his vision. "I want a mural depicting artistic endeavors around the entire warehouse." Dollar signs flashed in her eyes. As the agent, she would get a percentage of the commission. With a mural this large, that commission would be ginormous.

But she said casually, "How large is your warehouse?"

"A full city block."

"That's an immense project," she said noncommittally, but oh yes, dollar signs definitely glinted in her gaze.

"San Francisco is host to a great selection of street art. That's why I thought of San Holo for this."

She studied him a moment, her gaze sharp. "You do realize how street art works, right?" After a short pause, she added, "Even if San agrees and you're willing to pay the exorbitant fee for something like this, the ethos of street art is that anybody can come along and paint over it at any time."

"I'm well aware of how street art works." Then he laughed. "I wouldn't put it past one of my own artists to paint over it." Though he knew none of them would dare make a mark on San Holo's work. No one would.

"It will be an astonishing amount of money," she said with a smile like a cat ready to pounce.

It was his turn to smile. "I don't care how much it costs."

"Oh, the beauty of being a billionaire," she said flippantly.

So she did know who he was. Obviously. She probably knew about his warehouses for artists too. "I admire his work." He leaned forward, elbows on his knees. "I'd love to move ahead with this as soon as possible. Of course—" He prepared her for the kicker. "—I need to meet the man. Mostly for Dylan's sake. He'd love to speak with his idol." He waited a beat, and just as Adrian opened her mouth, he added, "It's part of the deal."

She was silent for perhaps fifteen seconds, which, in a quiet office with barely a street sound reaching the high-rise's windows, was a very long time. Finally, she said, "I could possibly convince San to do the work. But I can't guarantee anything. It's a massive project that could take months. I don't know that he'll want to give up that much of his time to one project."

"I understand there are no guarantees."

"In addition," she went on, "San works only in complete anonymity. No one sees his work until its completion. You'll need to provide lighting, because San usually works at night. As well as security to make sure no one peeks inside. Not even you." She waited another beat of silence, then added *her* kicker. "But I can tell you right now, the in-person meet you want will never happen."

With the amount he was willing to pay, Clay was sure

he'd get what he wanted eventually. But for now, he said, "I can provide security to protect his anonymity. I understand that's an important part of his mystique. No one will see the mural until it's done." He smiled, meaning it. "Not even me." Then he stared her down. "But whether you make this introduction happen or not, I will find out who San Holo is." He didn't want to be an ass about it, nor was he threatening. But his mind was made up, and nothing would deter him. "I made a promise to Dylan that I'd make sure he meets his idol." He held up a hand before she could speak. "It's not why I want this commission. I'm doing that because I find San Holo's work incredible."

She wasn't cowed, and she smiled as she stood. "All right. Let's end the meeting here. I'll present the offer to my client, but no guarantees."

He stood and smiled in return. "You should know that when—" Not *if* but *when*. "—I discover who he is, Dylan and I will keep that secret. It's only for the two of us."

She actually batted her eyelashes at him. "I'm sure you have immense resources, Mr. Harrington. But then so does San Holo." She stepped aside to let him precede her to the door before her final word. "I'll let you know what my client says."

"Thank you."

He wouldn't back down on his promise to Dylan. He was sure he could make the great man see that Dylan was worth his time.

CLAY PUSHED OPEN the door of Adrian Fielding's building, stepping out on the San Francisco street bustling with businesspeople, shoppers, and tourists.

His gaze seemed to zero in on only one woman. A gust of

wind blew her long black hair across her face, and she swiped it back as she sipped from her coffee cup. She must have just left the café next door. A tall woman, she was probably around his age, in her early thirties. Her long flowery dress fell to her calves, and her black tunic sweater combatted the blustery April afternoon, all the high-rise buildings blocking the sun from reaching Market Street below. She wore black leggings and heavy Doc Marten lace-up boots, but the flowery dress tipped all that black into elegance. Or maybe the elegance simply shone off her, her hair reaching to the middle of her back, its strands like silk floating in the breeze. Her pouty lips pursed to take another sip from her cup, and he made out her high cheekbones and long eyelashes as she drew closer to him.

Her body was like one long drink of water.

Standing in the middle of the sidewalk, people flowing around him, Clay found himself entranced. He had no shortage of women in his life, most of whom were far more interested in his money than in him. It was mutually beneficial, each of them getting something out of the short-lived relationship. They received beautiful trinkets, and he got, well, what every red-blooded American male wanted. When it was over, everyone left satisfied. Anything more than casual wasn't in his game plan. He had too much to accomplish to let a relationship get in the way. Relationships, and especially love, were all-consuming, taking a person's eye off the goal. So he'd steered clear.

But looking at her, this woman he didn't know, would probably never know, he felt the first flutter of desire. Not just for sex, but for something more.

The thought was almost enough to make him walk in the opposite direction. He might have done just that if he hadn't seen her sidestep a gaggle of giggling teenage girls. Maybe she was concentrating on her coffee, enjoying that next sip, or maybe she was daydreaming, because she veered close to the curb. The girls fanned out, pushing her even nearer the street, and to avoid them, she made a move to step into the road.

The oncoming car didn't slow down, even with a pedestrian nearby.

He was about to shout a warning, but she never would have heard him over the city's cacophony.

Clay ran, his heart pounding with fear that he wouldn't make it in time. His vision narrowed to only the sight of her in the street, the car bearing down on her, and her complete lack of awareness.

Grabbing her arm, he hauled her back onto the sidewalk, the whoosh of the vehicle whipping her hair around her face, her coffee cup falling to land with a splat in the gutter.

Only then did she register the rear of the car as it raced past, and her words came out in a rushed, panicked wheeze. "Oh my God." She slapped a hand to her chest. "That car. I could have died."

Clay was still breathing hard from the fear, from the near impact. From his touch on her arm. "It was one of those damned AVs." As the car flashed by, he'd seen the empty driver's seat through the passenger window.

She looked at him, dumbfounded. "AV?"

"An autonomous vehicle," he translated.

She was breathing fast, a pink tinge rising to her cheeks. "Like one of those robotaxis from that old movie *Total Recall?*"

He nodded. "Only this one was going a lot faster."

She glanced down the street after the retreating car. "I'd heard they were testing those things in the city. But that's just crazy. Aren't they supposed to sense when people are around?"

"Supposedly," he scoffed. "But this one didn't. It didn't even have a passenger."

"Maybe it was racing to pick up its next fare." Then she laughed—that could have been nerves—and the musical sound reached down deep inside him.

The thought of her crushed beneath that driverless car sent his pulse rate into the stratosphere. "Are you sure you're all right?"

She glanced at his hand on her arm. "I'm fine. Except for the bruise I think you're leaving."

He immediately let go. "I'm so sorry. I grabbed you because I didn't think you'd hear me over the street noise."

She smiled. It was like the sun and the moon and the stars shining all at once. "You're right. I'd have looked around like a deer caught in the headlights instead of getting out of the way." Then she went up on her toes and kissed his cheek. "Thank you."

It was a kiss like no other. He barely registered her words, feeling only the tingle of her lips against his skin. He thought of her Cupid's bow mouth leaving red lipstick marks all over his body, even if she wore no lipstick. Her fragrant skin fogged his brain. Something sweet and fruity. Like peaches, and as delectable as her skin.

Then her lyrical voice broke through the delicious fog. "So, like, where can we report that car?"

He answered with complete honesty. "I have no idea. I didn't even get a plate number." Holding her chocolate-brown gaze, he added, "But I'll find out."

"Thank you for saving my life." Her West Coast accent was as melodic as her laugh.

Had he been terrified she'd have a New York twang or a Southern drawl? Though there was nothing wrong with those accents, neither would suit her.

She laid her hand on his arm as if she had to hold on just

to stand up. "I need a stiff drink after that close call. Will you join me?"

His heart rate ratcheted up once again, not with fear but with need. "I will. Because if I hadn't grabbed you—" He shuddered dramatically instead of saying that she'd have been flattened in the street.

That would have been the worst thing imaginable, to lose her before he even knew her name.

CHAPTER THREE

That was crazy! She hadn't been paying attention, and that wasn't like her. Saskia Oliver knew how fast people drove on San Francisco streets, trying to make the next light before it turned. She'd never run into one of those AVs before, literally or figuratively. But she'd slept so late, and now it was midafternoon, and missing her first coffee of the day messed with her system. Maybe she was addicted to caffeine. She'd been steeping herself in that heavenly aroma when she stepped into the street to avoid those girls. No self-respecting San Franciscan ever stepped into the street without looking first.

But *he'd* rescued her. Her reaction to him was even crazier. He was just so... so... delicious. She wanted to lick him like her favorite ice cream cone. And she just did not think about men that way. Not normally. She should have thanked him profusely, then gone on her way.

But this man had saved her life. And he was just so... so... *everything.* Then she'd suggested a drink. Another thing that wasn't like her.

Her appointment could wait. Because there might never

be another opportunity like this with a man as drop-dead gorgeous as this one. If not for him, she'd be dead, for God's sake!

She looped her arm through his. "I know a great place. The cocktails are fabulous." She assessed him a moment. Was he a cocktail guy, or…? "They also have good draft beer, if you'd prefer."

Clay Harrington said, "Draft beer or cocktail, either one. Because we need to celebrate that you're still in the land of the living."

And she led this exquisite man to her favorite bar.

Of course she knew who he was. She'd worked for years in the art world, and she'd seen Art Space, his new video platform, watched interviews about how innovative it was, how perfect for artists who wanted to put their work out without a lot of hassle and criticism. Though how he'd accomplish that, she had no idea.

Outwardly, he seemed like a good guy. And he *had* saved her life. Based on her past experience, though, she didn't trust him or his new platform. He could be luring unsuspecting artists, taking advantage of them because they were unknowns. Really, no one could promise an artist that they wouldn't be hassled once their work was out there for everyone to see. And to judge.

She'd read the articles, watched the interviews, and knew his history. A highly successful entrepreneur—not to mention to die for in the looks department—he came across well on screen, the perfect combination of dark hair, startling blue eyes, and a body that made her pant.

Several years ago, he'd developed an exercise and nutrition app, then sold it for a whopping half billion dollars. His Harvard degree was in business. What could this man possibly know about exercise and nutrition? It was just a way to jump on the app craze and make money. Now a billion-

aire, he'd moved into the art world, starting this video platform where artists could showcase their work, create
podcasts about their process, their inspiration, and sell their
art in virtual galleries. But what on earth could he know
about art? Businesspeople cared only about the value of
something. They didn't understand art or artists.

But the man was so handsome he actually made her heart
stop. That hadn't been the car. No, it had been the sight of
him. *Before* she'd recognized him. When she'd been gazing
into those sexy eyes and getting hot and bothered. Then
there was his voice, the deep tones like fingers playing all her
strings.

He hadn't been smarmy, as if she owed him something for
saving her life. She didn't want to believe he was like the
other rich art patrons out there preying on struggling artists.
She'd had her fill of that type.

But a man that devastatingly handsome could make
people believe in him. He made *her* want to believe in him.

He made her want other things too.

Plus, he'd pulled her off the street before the car could
mow her down. Would a smarmy user have done that?

It was time to find out. Okay, it was also time to breathe
in his delicious male scent, to gaze into those beautiful
eyes, to—

Whew! Get hold of yourself, Saskia.

She backed away as they entered the bar. "Why don't you
get us a table? I have to make a call. I had a meeting. But it's
more important that I buy a drink for the man who saved my
life."

"Shall I order for you?"

"That would be great. A Toasted Almond. The bartender
will know what it is." She craved the sweetness of amaretto
and the coffee taste of Kahlúa. Then she shook her finger at

him. "But don't you dare pay for it. This is on me." She pulled a bill out of her tunic pocket.

"You don't need to pay me back." He stared her down, his eyes seeming to touch every part of her without actually moving. "I couldn't stand there and watch such beauty get creamed by a robotaxi."

She narrowed her eyes. "What about an ugly guy?"

He laughed, a soul-touching sound. "Or an ugly guy either."

"Let me pay anyway," she insisted. "Because I want to."

Gazing into her eyes for a long moment that seemed to steal the very breath out of her lungs, he finally took the money and headed to the long mahogany bar with its rows of bottles reflected in the mirror behind it.

The place wasn't full, since it wasn't even close to five o'clock, and she headed to the back by the bathroom hallway and tapped her phone, making her call. "Hey, I know we had a meeting. I swear I was on my way. But I need to postpone till tomorrow."

The answer was just as rushed. "But I got this huge offer I need to tell you about."

She looked at Clay Harrington's backside as he leaned on the bar. "Let's table that until tomorrow."

An exaggerated breath huffed air on the other end. "Okay. But I really need to talk to you. Call me ASAP."

Clay had a table and their drinks when she finished, and she slid into the seat next to him rather than across from him, their knees touching. "Isn't this place great? The owners recently refurbished the upstairs, turning the place into a funky hotel, with dark wood paneling like down here in the bar, and super-cool artwork." She'd asked for a tour and found each room decorated uniquely, the paintings all having a different theme. "I love that they put as much thought into the art as they did the accommodations."

Clay looked around him at the polished hardwood floors, the long, elegant bar, the old-time San Francisco photos on the walls. "I like it."

Then he slid her drink to her. She sipped before saying another word, the sublime taste of Kahlúa, cream, and amaretto hitting her tongue and tingling in her toes.

Or maybe that was him. Oh yeah, it was breathtakingly him.

Spreading her arms, she tipped her face to the ceiling, eyes closed as she relished the moment. "Oh my God. I'm alive."

He saluted her. "Thank God, you're alive." He slugged back his draft beer without getting a trace of foam on his upper lip. "I'm Clay—"

She raised her hand, cutting him off. "My name is Saskia. And you're Clay. That's all either of us needs to know. Right?"

Something flickered in his magnetic blue eyes, as if he wanted to say they needed more. But he agreed. "That's fine with me." Then he asked, "What do you do for a living?"

"I don't want to talk about *work*." She gave the word a disgusted little twist, not wanting to get into any arguments about what *he* did. That would only piss her off, and she didn't want to lose last night's really great high. Or the adrenaline rush of having narrowly escaped with her life this afternoon. Or the sweet thrill of sitting across from the most gorgeous man on the planet, who smelled delectably spicy and whose deep voice strummed her nerve endings and excited all her cells.

"Fair enough," he agreed. "Then what would you like to talk about?"

"Don't tell me work is the only thing in your life. Are you married? Do you have kids?"

The articles she'd read hadn't mentioned his relationship

status, as if that part of his life was a closed book to the media and his hungry audience.

He answered as if she was something different. Something special? "No girlfriend. No kids. Not even an ex-wife." He smiled, one eyebrow raised. "What about you? Single? In a relationship? Married? Divorced? It's complicated?"

She laughed. "That sounds like a social media questionnaire."

His eyes seemed a little hotter, a little deeper, as if a flame were lighting them from behind. "Which is it?"

Suddenly, it didn't matter who he was. She wanted those beautifully sculpted hands all over her. She wanted to taste the yeasty beer on his tongue. She just plain *wanted* in a way she hadn't for five years. She wanted *him*.

"Single," she whispered, unequivocal and uncomplicated.

The atmosphere around them turned damned near steamy.

CLAY LET HER LEAD, and they talked about everything, except work. About their favorite books, TV shows, movies, actors. His favorite books were mostly business or theory or art history, even things like *The Art of War*. Hers were all fantasy authors and fantasy series. His movies and shows were mostly spy thrillers with intricate plots. Hers were things like *The Hunger Games* and *Buffy the Vampire Slayer*, even if the latter had first aired when she wasn't more than a toddler.

They found so much in common—not *what* they liked to read or watch, but that they both loved books and movies.

On his third beer—and her third Toasted Almond—Clay was nowhere near drunk. But he was nicely lubricated. He suspected she was too.

She raised her half-full snifter. "I'm not sure if I've thanked you enough for saving my life."

He smiled, letting his gaze dance over her beautiful face, her cocoa eyes, her silky hair. "I couldn't let anything happen to such a beautiful woman."

"Or an ugly man," she said, harking back to their earlier conversation.

What he didn't say was that he couldn't let anything happen to a woman he was already falling for, from the moment he'd seen her on that sidewalk. Even before he'd seen the car. It was the craziest thought. Because he didn't do love. He didn't even do relationships.

But there was something about her that made him want to.

She leaned close, elbows on the table, her glass near her lips. "If that car had taken us both out, what would be the three things you'd regret not having done?"

The question took him totally off guard. His first thought was that he'd regret not having fallen completely in love with her.

But talking about love or relationships or work—or even their last names—was off the table. What did that leave?

"I'd regret not having bought a sports car and driven it across Europe."

She stared at him, wide-eyed. "You mean you don't already have a sports car?" she said, tongue in cheek.

He laughed, feeling the corners of his eyes crinkling. "No. I've never driven across Europe either. That's why it's on the list of things I'd regret not doing." Then he added more seriously, "I'd have to let someone else take the reins while I did it. I wouldn't forget all my responsibilities."

She ran her gaze over him. "You don't look like a man who would ever forget his responsibilities. You look like someone who has a goal and doesn't let anything stop him. Nothing. Ever."

He marveled that she could see him so clearly after just a couple of hours.

"That's why you want to let go for a little while as you drive your luxurious sports car across Europe." She blinked, smiled. "For how long?"

The answer was immediate, as if he'd already planned the trip. "Two months. Long enough to relax, but not enough to neglect my life back home." Then, for some inexplicable reason, he didn't want to talk about it anymore, didn't like how edgy it suddenly made him feel. "What's number one for you?"

She rolled another sip of her Toasted Almond around her mouth. Christ, he loved how she savored that drink. He imagined that was how she savored everything, from food to sex.

"I'd also like to take a break," she mused. "Not two months, maybe just two weeks. I want to lay on a beach somewhere and let my brain explore all the possibilities about what my life could be like."

He grinned. "Sounds like we're pretty similar in our first things."

She raised an eyebrow. "What's the second thing you'd want to do?"

To be on that beach with you. Somewhere tropical with warm waters, where I could swim out into the waves, take you in my arms, and touch you everywhere under the water.

His thoughts were becoming decidedly erotic.

What he said was completely different. "I'd like to take a week and just read. No business books. Just fiction that lets me escape real life for a little while." He'd recently come across an interesting article. "I read about this group in

England that sponsors reading retreats. That's all you do. Read."

She gaped. "You don't even eat?"

He shook his head, laughing. "Oh yeah, you eat. The best food. But you're even allowed to read at the table."

"Do you hear yourself?" She leaned forward. "You picked two things that suggest you need to relax more rather than doing and going."

He considered her. She was right. Both of his wishes suggested he wanted to get away from it all.

Especially if he could get away from it all with her.

He admitted only, "Yeah, but I actually love what I do." He jutted his chin at her. "What's your next thing? Or let's call them wishes. What's your next wish?"

She totally surprised him by the depth of her answer. "I'd like to learn to trust more and fear less."

Her words struck him so hard, the only thing he could say was a nebulous, "Wow."

But she made him think about himself. It was true he didn't trust when it came to love. Because love meant giving everything, your whole being. Which also meant expecting too much. And having too much expected of him.

His parents had loved with everything in them. Their love had been all-consuming, causing them to neglect their children, leaving Clay and his siblings with a series of nannies who never filled up the well of love that kids needed. They'd died in an avalanche while skiing in the Alps, just after he'd started high school. Even in death, they'd gone together. For him, loving meant giving over everything to that love. But that would mean losing sight of all his goals, all the things he wanted to accomplish. Losing part of himself.

Yet he'd thought of falling in love with her.

What the hell did that mean?

He would have liked to probe her answer more, but he didn't want her probing him in return—at least not his heart.

Instead, he jumped into his third wish, his eyes on hers, drinking her in. "My last wish is to kiss you."

———

SASKIA COULDN'T HELP LAUGHING. Wasn't that so billionaire-ish? Just flat out saying what you wanted.

Yet her skin heated with a full-body flush. She imagined his lips on her—not just her mouth, but every part of her. And her lips on him, all over him.

She'd have to start fanning herself if she didn't get her thoughts under control.

His answers, though? She loved them. He couldn't possibly be as bad as she'd thought when she'd read about him and watched his interviews.

He hadn't told her much of anything that was truly deep —she'd revealed far more—but he'd still given her a few insights, especially that he was dying for a breath of fresh air, for a chance to step away from his responsibilities, if only for a couple of months.

She liked his goal-oriented reading—maybe she needed to do more of that too—his favorite movies, his favorite shows. Maybe she should take a break from her supernatural shows and try one of his.

Maybe she should try *him*.

The idea was crazy. Totally unlike her. Yet today was unlike any other. Being with him was unlike being with any other man.

This day, this man, this chance at something fresh and sweet after near death…

She upped the ante. Maybe she wanted to shock him. Or maybe she just *wanted* him.

With a sensual smile that felt so right, she murmured, "My number three is going to bed with you." The words sounded so nonchalant he might have taken them for a joke.

Except his eyes blazed like a raging fire. She knew exactly who he was. But she didn't care right now. Because he was so damned hot. Because it had been such a horribly long dry spell. Five years. Her ex-boyfriend was such a creep, she hadn't gone near a man since.

Not until Clay Harrington.

Just for one night. She'd never have to see him again. But more than anything she'd wanted in five long years, she wanted this one night with him.

So she asked, "You want to go upstairs?"

CHAPTER FOUR

*H*is eyes going wide, Clay said, "You mean…?"

Saskia didn't hesitate. She hadn't eaten all day, and maybe she was tipsy, but she'd made up her mind. Nothing would stop her. "Yes, I mean…"

She leaned over, fisted one hand in his shirt, and pulled him close, until she could see each individual eyelash. Then she gave him his third wish, her mouth on his, teasing him as she ran her tongue along his lower lip.

He groaned, opening his mouth, and she slipped inside, tasted him, a delicious combination of yeasty beer and her sweet amaretto. Their tongues tangled in a few luscious strokes, and with his next groan, he thrust his hands in her hair, angled her head, and took control of her mouth. And control of the kiss.

She wasn't a virgin. She'd had lovers. She'd had Hugo, who did actually know his way around a bed despite being an ass. But there'd been no one since, the scars he'd left too deep for her to want another man.

But there had *never* been anyone like Clay Harrington.

He kissed the breath out of her, stole a moan rising up

from her throat. After that, she didn't care who he was, didn't care about his artists' platform. She cared only about his lips on hers, his tongue in her mouth, and his hands in her hair.

Until finally he pulled back, his breathing fast. "Holy hell."

Saskia stood then. She didn't hold out her hand to him. She said only, "I'm just going to use the restroom. I'll be back."

She was, as promised, then she led him to the hotel stairs almost as if she'd grabbed his shirt again.

The hotel entry lay opposite the bar's front door, up a narrow set of wooden stairs, reminding her of the stairs to a garret above a bar where Charles Dickens might have written *Great Expectations*. Reminding her of another garret too. But she wouldn't think about that now.

Clay's footsteps followed her up.

At the top, the lobby walls were filled with vintage posters from French circus acts. The reception desk could have come out of a French chateau, too, delicate and ornate, and the standing lamps resembled Tiffany. The lady at the desk looked vintage as well, somewhere in her seventies, in a matronly dress that reached well past her knees.

Though Clay was behind Saskia, the concierge glanced at him. "Can I help you, sir?"

Saskia answered, "We'd like a room with a king-sized bed. The one with the van Gogh prints." She looked at Clay. "You'll love the prints. They aren't his famous stuff, but more like imagined works that would have been in the crates of paintings van Gogh's mother supposedly tossed out after he died. Although that could be an urban legend." She turned back to the gray-haired woman. "Is that room available?"

"Yes," the concierge replied. But her gaze was still on Clay's truly impressive physique.

A woman was never too old to appreciate a gorgeous man.

Reaching into the pocket of her tunic, Saskia pulled out her credit card. Those deep pockets carried everything she needed.

But Clay was already pulling out his wallet. "I'll get it."

Saskia stepped between him and the concierge. "I'm taking care of this," she insisted, even as she felt Clay's credit card poke her in the back.

She wanted him to know this was her decision. With her retaining control of the entire adventure. He hadn't seduced her. In fact, she'd seduced him. And she loved that.

The woman returned her credit card along with two keys. Not cards like a regular hotel, but two ornate skeleton keys. Saskia handed one to Clay. The woman called out the number on the key tag and said, "Down the hall, to the left, the second door on the right."

At the door, Saskia inserted the skeleton key, feeling him right behind her, so close she could smell his masculine cologne. Or maybe his pheromones. Maybe hers. Maybe both.

He laid his hand over hers before she unlocked the door, bracketing her with that magnificently toned body. She couldn't help a shiver of need, as if the sex goddess she'd kept under lock and key for five years was about to be unleashed.

His breath tantalized her ear. "Are you sure about this?"

She turned the key, pushed open the door with her foot, then turned and met his flame-hot gaze.

"You don't even know me," he said.

She pressed close to his body, his hardness. In her boots, despite his height, she didn't feel petite. But she did feel womanly. Her voice came out in a husky whisper. "You don't know me either. I could be a succubus luring you to my lair so I can drain you of your essence."

He laughed. But his breathing was harsh, his chest rising and falling rapidly. "Doesn't the succubus sneak into the victim's room in the middle of the night?" His nostrils flared as he breathed her in.

"She comes to men in their dreams. Maybe this is all a dream."

Then she grabbed his shirt and backed into the room, pulling him with her. When he was inside, she kicked the door closed. The sun, not yet obscured by fog, lit the room. "I have only one rule," she told him.

He seemed to be begging when he asked, "What's that?"

"This is only for one night."

His lips curved, this time with a cocky smile that turned her heart over in her chest. Damn, he was so dangerously good-looking. "What if you want more?"

He had the looks of a beautiful devil, a smile that promised glorious sin, and eyes that could devour her soul. But she smiled right back at him. "I won't."

He ate her up with those eyes. She was so very hot, wet, and ready to jump him right this moment, before they even made it to the bed. Especially when he asked, "Doesn't a succubus keep coming back?"

She trailed a finger from his chin down his throat to the neckline of his shirt. "When I'm done with you, there won't be anything left to come back for."

HIS ENTIRE BODY seemed to go up in smoke. She was so gorgeous, and he'd never wanted a woman more. His chest to her breasts, her scent rose to his head, clouding his brain like the San Francisco fog starting to roll down the hill. That's what she was like—a whisper of fog, or a ghost, something that couldn't possibly be real.

But he scented how much she wanted him.

Like a predator, he took hold of her hips, jerked her close, let her feel how badly he wanted her in return.

"Don't you want to look at the van Gogh prints?" she murmured.

"Screw the prints."

Like animals, they tore at each other's clothes, fabric flying. He picked her up, strode to the bed, her combat boots bouncing against his backside. Then he laid her on the bed, her legs parted. She was amazing. Her breasts were perfect, not large but rose-tipped, begging for his lips, his tongue, his teeth.

Her flowery dress and black tunic lay somewhere behind them. So did his shirt. Now he toed off his shoes and shucked his slacks while she watched. Her eyes widened as he stripped down to nothing, and he teased her a moment just by standing there, letting her look her fill.

He squatted to untie her boots, yanking them off, throwing them with a thud against the wall, then peeled off her socks. She wore no bra, and that was even sexier than a scrap of lacy lingerie. Thrusting his fingers into the tops of her leggings, he yanked them down. Her breathing ratcheted up. Then she was gloriously naked before him.

"Christ, you're beautiful," he whispered with the awe he would have felt gazing at van Gogh's *Starry Night*.

He didn't know her. She didn't know him. While he didn't have relationships, he'd never moved on a woman quite this fast. He'd wooed a little, given gifts, spent money on jewelry and dining and shows. But this woman wanted no trinkets. In fact, she wore no jewelry and not even a speck of makeup. Yet her lips were a luscious red that beckoned him.

He fell on her, kissing her, taking her mouth as if he'd never tasted a woman before, as if she could fill up every empty nook and cranny inside him. He was the incubus, taking everything he could and needing more. She tasted so damn sweet, like Kahlúa and amaretto and something so much more. *Her.*

Pulling back, he whispered, "I have to taste all of you." Then he started to glide down her body.

But she grabbed his shoulders. "I want you inside me. Right now. As deep as you can go." Her beautiful brown eyes were now like dark amber, mesmerizing him.

Until rational thought flooded in. "I don't have a condom."

She laughed, a sparkle in her sexy eyes. "I thought all men carried a condom in their wallets in case they got lucky."

An answering laugh rumbled up from his chest. "I don't. But if I'd known I'd rescue a woman like you from a robotaxi, I'd've made sure I had one."

She wrinkled her nose, a smile twinkling in her eyes. "Luckily for me, I think ahead. When I went to the restroom downstairs, I slipped into the men's room. Guess what kind of machine they had hanging on the wall?"

He gasped. "No."

She nodded wickedly, stirring him to greater heights. Then she pointed past him. "Check my tunic pocket."

She was freaking incredible.

He dove off the bed, swiping up her tunic, feeling in the pocket where she'd stowed the credit card. He came out with a strip of three condoms.

"They didn't come in singles." Then she held out her hand. "Come here. I'll put it on for you."

Like a teenage boy, he could have lost it just at the sound of her voice.

THE FOG HAD ROLLED past the window so quickly that it was as if nothing else existed but them, together, in here. He stalked her like the predator she wanted him to be. A graceful panther, with dark hair and gleaming skin.

He stole her breath and made her heart beat a thousand times a minute. Her mouth watered for a taste of him. She should have been self-conscious; it had been so long. But this man doused every ounce of embarrassment, because she had to have him.

Grabbing the strip of condoms from him, she tore one off and threw the rest on the bed. While he was standing, she crawled to the edge and took him in her hand for the first time.

His groan was pure pleasure, his growl pure predator, his fingers in her hair like the claws of the beast she wanted to release. Still stroking that silken flesh, she ripped the packet open with her teeth and drove him crazy with her touch.

Then she growled like his lioness. "Get on the bed and lean back."

She wasn't submissive, but then, she'd never been dominant either. But for this, she wanted him under her complete control. When he threw himself back on the bed, his erection standing straight and tall and ready for her, she slowly rolled the condom down, stroking him through it.

Until he gave another guttural groan. "Christ. I can't stand anymore. Do it. Now. Please. I'm begging."

She gave him exactly what they both wanted.

Climbing on top of him, she caressed him as she guided him to her entrance. Then slowly, so slowly, she slid down onto him, sensation shooting through her, his heat making her a little crazy.

She savored the feel of him inside her. It had been so long. As she seated herself on him, she realized for the first time in five years how much she'd missed a man filling her up. And this man was better than any imagining.

Then he thrust upward, going impossibly deep, impossibly perfect. She moaned her pleasure. "So good."

She thought about taking him for a slow ride, but there was something about the burning glow of his eyes, the rigid feel of him inside her. She couldn't think slow. She could only think fast and hot.

Resting her hands on his chest, she rose, then took him deep inside her once again. And again. He put his hands on her hips, pulling her down on him, guiding her. The intense friction filled her body with heat, her skin turning hot and pink.

She rode him, taking him hard and fast, as if he were a stallion and they were galloping across the moor. Closing her eyes, she clenched her fingers against his skin, her nails biting into him, her body milking him.

He swore. "Christ, you make me nuts. You're so damn good."

She didn't have the breath to speak smoothly; he'd stolen it with his devilishly handsome face painted beautiful in the dim room. Words fell in pants from her lips. "So good. Need this so bad."

She reached for the peak—almost there. Then he put his hand between her legs, touched her hot button. A wave crested inside her, taking her higher, higher, until it crashed through her. She didn't simply cry out, she wailed. Not caring who heard. Not caring what he would think. Because it had been so long. Because he was so good. Because he felt so perfect between her thighs.

Her climaxing body worked him, and she felt him throb deep inside, knew he was close. She tensed her muscles around him, and with one more growl, followed by a deep groan, he pulsed inside her, filling her.

That brought a second wave crashing over her, and she lost herself to sensation. To the exquisite feel of him deep inside her. To everything she'd missed over the last five years.

He made her wonder how she could live without this for the next five.

SHE LAY atop him while he throbbed inside her. Her hair was like silk across his chest, her skin hot against him. Her body contracted around him with an aftershock, and he groaned softly against her ear.

She'd been so beautifully vocal, crying out her ecstasy. Many women were careful about the sounds they made, careful with their makeup, their hair. But she'd taken him with complete abandon, not caring how she looked or sounded.

That made the sex all the hotter.

As she lay against him, her breath fanned the hairs on his chest. "I only had one orgasm. I need more." Her chin on his chest, she grinned at him.

He laughed. "I love how insatiable you are."

With a too sexy smile, she admitted, "It's been a long, long time."

He needed to know more. "How long?"

"A very long dry spell," she added dreamily.

He rocked inside her, feeling her body flex around him. "How long?" he pressed.

"Five years."

He put his hands to her face, lifted her to look at him again. "You're kidding."

She shook her head. "No. But you've certainly made up for it tonight."

He couldn't believe this exquisite woman hadn't made love in five years. "But why me?"

She snuggled down against him. "Have you looked in a mirror recently?"

That didn't answer the question. The Harrington brothers were a handsome lot, especially his older brother, Dane. Troy was up there too. Not to mention his two sisters, Ava and Gabby. But there were a lot of good-looking hunks out there. Yet she'd chosen him. After five years. "Was it because I saved your life?"

She shook her head against his chest, her hair caressing him. "It was more about your answers."

"My answers?" For a moment, he was mystified.

Until she said, "To the three wishes."

She'd made him forget everything. "Because number three was about kissing you?"

Again, she shook her head, the silk of her hair across his chest causing him to pulse inside her.

"About wanting to read books for a week." Her laugh vibrated through him. "Like a little boy whose mother had taken away all his favorite books. You wanted to spend a whole week reading them all over again."

He didn't tell her that his mother had never read to him. The nannies had done that. But that would be revealing too much.

"And the sports car," she added. "I even saw myself driving beside you, the wind blowing through our hair."

He wanted to hug her so tightly she'd never get away. "You never know," he said softly.

Without even looking at him, she murmured, "Remember, just one night."

Just one night. He couldn't bear for it to end. Not before he'd pleasured her until he exhausted her. Not until she'd drained him too.

He wasn't done with her yet, especially since she'd bought a three-pack of condoms. One down, two to go.

Plus, there were all the other things they could do without one.

CHAPTER FIVE

When Clay returned from the bathroom, Saskia lay sprawled on the bed, the sheet covering one leg and half her body, leaving a breast bared to him. Like a satisfied succubus, a sweet smile curved her lips.

She opened her eyes when the bed dipped as he knelt on it. "That was hot and quick," he murmured. "Now we'll slow everything down." He grinned, pulling the sheet aside until her beautiful naked body lay before him, her spread legs inviting him. "You said you needed more orgasms."

She smiled as he came down on top of her. "I could definitely use another. Maybe two or three. Or four or five."

He laughed. Then he kissed her, tasting her sweetness, losing himself in that kiss for long, glorious minutes before he trailed kisses down her throat to the swell of her breasts. "I'm sure we can make that happen."

Closing his lips around the tip of her breast, he sucked hard, swirling his tongue around the tight bead. She moaned, and her arousal scented the air, her skin heating. He was suddenly so hard, he wasn't sure he could take it slow.

He'd never felt this needy for a woman. Not that he'd ever been an insert-tab-A-into-slot-B kind of guy. But he'd never felt like this, entranced by the fragrance of her skin, the sweetness of her in his mouth, the silky feel of her against him. He'd always striven to leave a woman satisfied. But this was more. This was wanting to taste every inch of her, to mark her indelibly, to be able to wake up at night and hear her moans in his ears.

Sliding a hand down her body, he traced her quivering skin until he dipped between her legs. She was so wet. He could take her now, and she would want it. But he needed to make her come over and over before he took his pleasure.

He played her lightly, felt her squirm beneath him, and relished her one word. "Please."

He played, slowly stoking her fire. She moaned and arched, pushing her breast deeper into his mouth as her body dragged his fingers deeper too. With his stroke across her G-spot, she quaked against him, but he was out again, caressing that sweet, hot button between her legs.

Until finally he crawled down her abdomen, kiss after kiss, taste after taste, lick after lick. Then he lay between her spread legs, her body open and begging for him.

She cried out the moment he put his mouth to her. He sucked, swirled, made her writhe, and slipped one finger, then two, inside her. She shimmied and rolled, tossing her head on the pillow, her hair flying across her face.

That was what he wanted. To make her forget everything but this.

Licking, stroking, circling, he felt her body heating around him. She raised her legs to lock them low across his back, holding him close as she rocked into him.

Little pants puffed from her lips, and her legs tightened around him, her muscles quivering. Then her body clamped hard around his fingers, and she cried out, thrashing beneath him, her climax rolling through her and into him.

This was how she'd felt around him, dragging him in, squeezing him hard. If he'd been inside her now, he would have come right along with her. His instinct was to rear up and slam into her. But not yet. She had to come a few more times.

She had to come screaming his name.

SASKIA COLLAPSED ON THE BED, her body still firing with little explosions. Now *that* she'd never experienced before. And Clay wasn't done yet, she could tell. He lapped at her lightly, keeping her needy and close to the edge. Her body wanted to come again. Her lips wanted to beg. But her mind needed to collect itself.

She touched his thick, silky hair. "Come here."

He crawled up her body like a predator. Clapping her hands to his cheeks, she pulled him down for a kiss, tasting herself on his lips, his rock hardness probing between her legs.

She whispered, "Wow," against his mouth.

"Good?"

He didn't need affirmation. He damn well knew he was good. Maybe he wanted to hear her beg for more. She would, but for something else she wanted just as badly.

"Very good," she told him. Then, pushing his shoulder, she rolled him to his back and climbed on top of him, straddling his legs. "Now I want this."

She wrapped her hand around him, stroked him. He was thick, hard, ready. Spreading his legs with her knees between them, she curled over him, licking him like a lollipop.

He growled. "I need to make you come several more times before you do anything to me."

She didn't say a word, just took the very tip in her mouth, sucked hard, circled him with her tongue. Then backed off to say, "I'll stop just before you come."

He half groaned, half laughed. "You really are going to drive me crazy."

She smiled. Like a succubus. "Maybe just drive you." Then she dipped over him once more, taking just the tip, driving him insane with her whirling tongue.

His groan told her how much he liked it.

Her fingers around his shaft, she pumped him gently as she worshipped his crown. Reaching between his legs, she squeezed him. His body arched off the bed, his words a garbled groan. "Christ. Please. Don't make me come yet."

His legs tightened around her, and he rocked in time with her movements. Then she took her hand away, slid all the way down, taking all of him, and he gasped for breath. Again, then again, until he throbbed in her mouth. Only then did she back off. "Are you ready to come?"

He laughed, the sound strangled in his throat. "You do know how to tease a man."

"It's only a tease if I don't intend to follow through."

He leveled a look on her. "Do you?"

She smiled, its wickedness filling her. "Oh yeah."

He moved quickly then, flipped her to her back, came down on top of her, their bodies at an angle across the bed. His fingers between her legs, he played her until she was the one going crazy. He swallowed her cries with his mouth, kissing her, his tongue delving deep the way she knew his body wanted to.

With both hands, she pushed on his shoulders, because she couldn't breathe, because she *needed*, and another blissful wave rolled through her body.

She thought he'd enter her then, but he only rocked between her legs, letting the sensations flow through her.

Then he said softly, "This is how we're going to do it now. Slow and sweet. Making it last forever."

Saskia trembled, knowing it would be better than anything that had come before.

He grabbed a second condom packet, tore it open, and rolled it on.

"I'm going to make this so good for you." The gleam in his eyes echoed the promise.

Then he draped her legs over his haunches, his erection rising between them, beckoning her.

He slid inside her, slowly. Just when she thought he'd slam deep and hard, he stopped. Smiled. And rocked gently right there at her entrance.

It was mind-blowing.

She moaned, looked at him through her lashes, her voice like gravel. "Oh my God. That's too good." He rocked over her G-spot, the slowness of it driving her crazy. Her body quaked, and her legs tightened against his sides, quivering. "What are you doing to me?"

"I told you." His words were a low growl. "Slow and sweet and good."

She sucked in a breath, arched her body, grabbed the pillow beneath her head with both hands. "So perfect."

His eyes glittered. "Do you want me to make it even better?"

Her words came out in a gasp. "You can't possibly make it better."

But he smiled, like the devil she knew he had to be. "Oh yeah, I can."

Then he put his hand between her legs, stroking her with his thumb. Everything inside her went up in smoke. Because yes—God, yes—this was so much better.

She stopped looking at him, stopped thinking about him. There was only the feel of him inside her, the caress of his thumb on her, and the sensations rolling through her.

She tossed on the pillow, her movements somehow making everything better. Fisting her hands in the covers, she wrapped her legs around him, tried to pull him deeper.

But his body resisted. There was just that slow, seemingly endless stroke across her G-spot and his thumb making her utterly insane. He was so right. This was so good. She'd never felt anything like it with anyone ever.

She panted, she wailed, she begged. The climax built inside her, quaked through her body, and burst like an imploding star. She screamed, her body bucking. Cried out his name.

Then he slammed home, taking her hard and fast. It was so good, so perfect. *Don't stop, please don't stop, I need it bad, so bad.*

She didn't know whether she said the words, or they just rolled around in her brain. His relentless pounding somehow kept sensation flying through her, on and on. Tears leaked from her eyes, and she dug her fingernails into his arms. She grabbed his butt, pulling him deeper, forcing him to a relentless, pounding pace.

She opened her eyes to see him rear his head back as he growled and groaned and came hard inside her. It felt as though he were filling her up. Despite the condom.

They came together. Endlessly. Blissfully.

Until he collapsed on top of her, his body still quaking, hers still quivering.

She whispered against his ear, "You're right. That was good."

Better than good. The best ever.

WHEN CLAY CAME TO, he lay flat on his back, Saskia cradled against him, one leg over his thighs, her foot tangled between his calves. The room was steamy with sex.

His body buzzed in the aftermath. She'd said it was good. He couldn't remember it ever being better. Maybe it was the adrenaline from that near miss out on the street. Maybe it was the beers he'd drunk without eating lunch.

Or maybe it was just their off-the-charts chemistry.

Her breathing didn't have the rhythm of sleep, so he asked, "Are you hungry?"

Her groan rumbled through his chest. "I'm starving." She looked at him, her eyes dark and expressive. "I haven't eaten all day. I was working so late last night, then I slept almost until I went out for coffee."

"I wonder if they have room service here."

She grinned. "I happen to know they do. I'm dying for a hamburger. With French fries." Then she laughed. "I can never eat the whole thing. Will you share with me?"

He was ravenous enough to eat two burgers, but he said, "I can share."

She scrambled out of bed, naked but not self-conscious about it, her skin the pearly pink of good sex. While she grabbed a menu off the desk, he strode into the bathroom, cleaned up, and was back before she'd finished perusing the menu.

He flopped down on the bed beside her. She hadn't even pulled up the covers, as if her nakedness didn't bother her at all. He liked that she wasn't embarrassed about what they'd done.

And they still had another condom.

It was dark outside, but he didn't glance at his watch. He didn't want to know how much time he had left with her.

He'd called her insatiable. But she'd made *him* insatiable.

Her eyes glowed when she looked at him. "The half pounder with extra pickles."

He'd take it any way she wanted it. "Absolutely."

She called in their order, then grinned at him. "They said fifteen minutes." She waggled her eyebrows. "What can we do in fifteen minutes?"

He loved the way she thought. "I could make you come again."

"Let's see if you can," she challenged, her eyes glittering.

He met the challenge twice over, and in less than fifteen minutes.

When their meal arrived, Saskia ducked beneath the covers, and he pulled on a robe from the bathroom. The waiter laid the tray on the desk as Clay fished in his pants for the tip.

After the young man left, Clay carried the tray to the bed, setting it between them as Saskia sat cross-legged, the sheet draped over her. Dipping a French fry in ketchup, she popped it in her mouth, moaning as she chewed.

Holy hell. The sounds this woman made.

Instead of cutting the burger in half, she took a bite, then handed it to him. It was so damned intimate, sharing bites, handing the burger back and forth, feeding each other French fries. Until the plate was empty.

She flopped back on the bed. "I needed that so bad."

He needed the taste of her, the feel of her. It was still dark. Maybe not even past midnight. They had all night.

With the plate scraped clean, he carried the tray back to the desk.

"I'm going to use the bathroom." Jumping from the bed, she closed the door. He heard water running. Not the sink but the tub. He waited. Then she opened the door, steam billowing out, her body wrapped in a towel.

"They have the biggest tub in here." She crooked her finger. "Let's take a bath."

He'd do anything she wanted. The water was almost too hot, but she sank into it as if it were the sweetest luxury she'd ever known. She squeezed shampoo from the minuscule bottle, and bubbles rose in the water.

Climbing in, he slid down behind her, pulling her flush against his chest.

She stretched. "I do so love a bubble bath after a long, hard day."

"I love a bubble bath after good, hot sex." Not that he'd ever indulged.

She laughed. "I like it then too. But it has been a long, long time."

He still marveled at that. How had the woman gone without sex for five years? He wanted to make sure she never had to go without it again.

Then he remembered. Only one night.

He had to make it so good she'd change her mind.

Starting his campaign right then, he smeared bubbles over her breasts, gently tweaking the tips between his fingers, sliding his hands down between her legs, until she writhed against him.

They played with each other, her taking him in hand, stroking him, bringing him to the edge but not pushing him over. He repaid her in kind, making her tremble and beg until he pulled away. They teased, touched, stroked, licked, sucked. And kissed. Such slow, delicious kisses.

Until neither of them could stand it a moment longer.

Standing, water streaming down his body, he pulled her up with him, then stepped out of the tub. He dried them both with the big, fluffy towel, and she moaned as if it was foreplay. Then he hauled her up, drawing her legs around his waist, and carried her to bed. Letting her slide to the mattress, he came down on top of her, spread her legs, and tasted her, loving the sweetness of her skin, the fragrant scent of her, the way her body quivered when she was ready to come. This time, he didn't stop, instead taking her over the edge, feasting on her as she cried out his name.

He would make this last all night.

And hopefully far longer.

CHAPTER SIX

*H*e was so good at finding the most sensitive parts of her. As if he knew her body inside and out. He made her world implode. She didn't know if she could survive an entire night of this. He was just too, too good.

She'd turned the clock away so she wouldn't have to think about when this would end. By God, she would enjoy every moment until the sun shone through the window.

He licked his way up her body until he lay on top of her, kissing her with the taste of herself all over his mouth. It was so erotic, so sensuous.

"I should've bought more than one condom pack," she moaned.

He laughed. "We can send out for more." Then he swiped his tongue across her lips, tantalizing her. "Or we can save the last condom for the finale. And do every other thing we can think of until then."

His thoughts were so sexy. "I like that." She pushed him to his back, crawling down his body until she could take him in her mouth. "Do you want to come?" she asked. "Or do you want to wait?"

He looked out the window at the halos of fog around the streetlights, then back at her. "Make me come again. I'll still have more left for later."

He was young, he was virile, he could go forever, she was sure. She took him in all the way, licking and sucking, holding him in her hand, squeezing him. Over and over until he trembled. She'd never had sex all night long. But everything was different with Clay.

When his body bucked and he shouted her name, she took every drop. And loved it.

They spent the next few hours in play, mouths and tongues and hands and fingers. He made her come so hard, tears leaked from her eyes. Her voice grew hoarse with her cries of pleasure. Her body had never felt so worshipped. And she became intimate with the timbre of his groans and growls.

She couldn't say whether she fell asleep or passed out from pleasure overload.

But she dreamed of featherlight kisses on her neck and tender caresses across her breasts. Then a hand pulling her leg back over his thigh, spreading her for his sensual touch. Long, delicious minutes of play took her to the edge.

But this was no dream. Unless Clay was her dream man.

He nudged at her entrance, and she mourned the feel of the latex he'd donned. She wanted skin to skin.

Then she forgot all that as he teased her, seduced her. She loved the intimate angle, her back to his chest as he slid slowly inside her, her ankle hooked behind his calf, holding herself open for him. His fingers played an erotic melody on her body as he caressed her G-spot. He touched her everywhere—kisses against her neck, breath across her ear, his hardness inside her.

He killed her with pleasure. She panted, moaned, cried out. Still, he took her with that slow, relentless stroke that never went deep enough yet somehow drove her to the edge of madness.

He withdrew, rolled her to her belly, stuffed a pillow beneath her stomach, and seated himself fully between her legs. Then he drove fast, he drove hard. Burying her face against the pillow, she screamed out her pleasure. She'd never wanted it this hard, but with him, it was so sweet, so good, so necessary to her whole being that tears pricked her eyes. Her body clamped down on him, and her release catapulted her into ecstasy, going on and on in delicious waves.

He stiffened, pressed tight against her, his back arched as he braced on his arms. She wanted to see him, but she couldn't turn her head far enough. A guttural cry fell from his lips as he climaxed against her womb, the feel of him vibrating through her chest and gripping her heart.

Finally, he fell prone on top of her, his weight luscious.

No man had ever been as good as Clay.

Maybe no man ever would be again.

HE'D USED THE BATHROOM, and when he returned, Clay wrapped himself around her. He couldn't say exactly when he fell asleep, but he woke to the foggy light of dawn. Saskia hadn't moved. He couldn't move either. The sweetness of her in his arms was too much to give up.

She'd said only one night. But one night would never be enough for him. Would she tell him her full name? Give him her phone number?

She held all the cards. Because he was the one who wanted to beg for more.

But she must have felt how extraordinary their night had

been. She must feel that once would never be enough. He wanted to send out for more condoms. Maybe he could sneak down to the bar's restroom and get another three-pack out of the machine.

Then he could seduce her into staying with him.

Maybe forever.

SASKIA WOKE to the feel of him covering her like a warm blanket, the soft, crinkly sensation of his hair along her legs.

The sex had been ridiculously good. Amazing. Incredible. How many superlatives could she come up with? She'd enjoyed learning more about him last night in the bar, his list of three wishes so unlike a man who was only out for what he could take from other people.

Yet he was running a business she didn't trust. The entire art world was full of greed. She'd seen it. She'd been a victim of it.

If only he wasn't who he is.

He must have felt her stir because his breath brushed her ear, turning her liquid inside as he whispered, "That was amazing." He stole the word right out of her mind. "When can I see you again?"

Her body wanted to say, Y*es, yes, yes*! But her mind cried, *No, no, no*. In the time it took her not to answer, he said, "You are the most incredible lover I've ever known."

A man like him must have had many lovers; she didn't begrudge him that. It was his artists' platform she wasn't sure of. It was the way he could potentially use artists.

But after talking with him, after making love with him all night long, she wondered if he could actually be that kind of man. Of course, men like him could be deceptive. They told you what you wanted to hear. Just as he was telling her now.

"I know you said only one night." He seduced her with a light caress down her arm. "But don't you think what we had last night was too good to experience only once?"

She wanted to beg him to take her again, right now.

But that way lay madness. She couldn't entangle herself with him. Not only because of who he was, but also because of her own complicated life. Pulling away, she climbed off the bed, reaching for her clothes where they lay with his in a mismatched pile on the carpet.

"It really was only for one night," she said over her shoulder.

She pulled on her panties and leggings. Her nakedness didn't embarrass her. But clothes were a fortification, and she pulled her flowered dress over her head before she looked at him.

He lay naked on the bed, covers pushed aside. They'd steamed up the room to the point where blankets and sheets were unnecessary. Lying there, he was like a statue by Michelangelo, the lines of his body perfect, his face sculpted like that of a Greek god.

"You don't really mean that," he said, his voice taking on a cajoling note.

She stuffed her arms into her tunic and tugged it down her thighs. She admitted the truth as she met his beguiling gaze. "I'm not saying it wasn't great. I enjoyed every minute. Like I said, it's been a long time. You certainly lived up to all my expectations." She sat on the desk chair to put on her socks and boots.

"Can you really say no to at least one more time?"

"I can."

He looked at her as if she'd lost her mind. Maybe she had. But he was Clay Harrington. She absolutely could not get involved with him. It didn't matter how he'd roped her in with all his talk down in the bar. She couldn't let herself be tricked and couldn't let him add another complication to her life.

She stood as he rolled to the edge of the bed.

Oh, how beautiful he was. How badly she wanted to touch him, taste him, take him. For five years, she'd had a rule not to get involved, especially not with an artist and, even more, not with an art *dealer*. Everything about him violated her rules.

He strode toward her with the sinewy grace of a jungle animal. "Don't leave yet. Let's talk."

If he touched her, she'd pick up the phone and have the concierge send out for another twelve condoms.

Instead, she backed to the door, put her hand on the knob, twisted it, and realized they hadn't even locked it. Then she gave him her parting shot. "One time only." She opened the door, hoping there was no one in the hall to see that he was completely naked, and slipped out.

Before she closed the door behind her forever, she said softly, "Believe me, that was the best one time I've ever had."

———

CLAY STRUGGLED INTO HIS CLOTHING, almost tripping as he tried to get one foot into his pants. He felt like an idiot. Why hadn't he dressed the moment she had?

There had never been a woman on earth who hadn't said, "When can we see each other again?" It was programmed into their DNA.

Especially after a night like that. Clay had always been the one to put an end to things. He didn't treat women badly; in fact, he gave them exactly what they wanted. He could gauge when a woman wanted something more permanent, and he steered clear, stuck to casual. He didn't want to break hearts, but he'd never allowed a serious relationship to take his eyes off the goal. Relationships—and worse, love—were uncontrollable.

But no woman had ever said, *Loved it, but it was one time only.*

He'd thought their lovemaking would speak for itself. But now, he sat staring at the door, completely dumbfounded. In less than twenty-four hours, she'd become the woman of his dreams. And now she was gone? Just like that?

He sat there in just his slacks, his zipper still undone, his mind reeling. *What the hell just happened?*

He'd felt something for her when they had sex. He was positive she'd felt something too. Even if she wouldn't admit it.

He needed to find her again.

But if he did, what would happen to his goals? He didn't want to be like his parents, so besotted with each other that there was no room for anyone else in their lives, not even their children. They hadn't planned for the future, leaving behind crushing debt when they died. It had fallen to Dane and Ava to bail out the family. The two of them had given up their university educations to go to work—Dane at a resort and Ava as an aide in a nursing home. Of course, Dane had turned that job into a resort empire, and Ava had loved working with older people so much that it became a calling, providing eldercare with more than a hundred facilities in the US and internationally. And now they'd both found love.

But Clay wasn't sure he could split himself between his goals and a relationship. He wasn't ready for an intense love that would devour his life. He had so many things to do.

But there was something special about Saskia. It wasn't only the sex. It was the connection he'd felt as they talked. It was how she'd exposed herself to him by revealing her trust issues. There was so much more to her than what they'd done last night in this room.

It didn't matter if he wasn't ready for a relationship or a woman in his life. Or even love.

He had to find her.

But first, he called the robotaxi company and blistered them for almost running over the woman with whom he was completely infatuated.

CHAPTER SEVEN

*A*drian's office was almost next door to the hotel where Saskia had last night's tryst with Clay. Seated at her desk, Adrian was alone, and Saskia walked right in.

Before she could ask about this big deal Adrian had mentioned, her friend *and* agent said, "First, the word is out about the new mural in the Mission District. The art world is going nuts for it." Adrian arched one eyebrow in a practiced move designed to get the upper hand on anyone she was facing down. "But I had to hear about it on social media rather than from you?"

Adrian's imperious eyebrow never worked on Saskia. "It's been little more than twenty-four hours. I was going to tell you, but I slept most of the day." How could the street art possibly get so much notice in just one day?

Remembering all the years when her art was barely seen, she was gratified that someone had found the new piece.

Adrian drummed the end of her pencil on the desktop. "Your work *was* noticed." She rolled her eyes. "By someone big."

Big or small, Saskia didn't care. She just liked that people saw her art. Especially the stuff she didn't do on commission. Those were the pieces that came straight from her heart.

Adrian was an excellent lawyer and an even better agent, and Saskia spotted the twinkle in her blue eyes. In many ways, they were complete opposites. While Saskia was tall, with dark hair falling to the middle of her back, Adrian was blond and petite. And curvy. She attracted men like flowers attracted hummingbirds. So far, no man had caught her.

"I can see you're dying to tell all," Saskia said. "So spill."

In her precise British tones, Adrian said, "The guy who told me about it came here for a commission. He's willing to pay just about anything. I mean *an-ee-thing*," she stressed with bared teeth. "He wants a mural around the entire exterior of his warehouse. He's a mega fan of your work."

Saskia might prefer her street art to commissioned work, but commissions paid her bills. And Adrian's.

"Tell me more." Saskia slid into the chair opposite.

The high-rise office on Market Street overlooked the bay, and today the view was stunning. Now that the fog had burned off, the sky glowed bluer than anything she could find on her paint palette, and sailboats dotted the waters out by Alcatraz. She wasn't a landscape painter, but this view was almost worth trying it.

Adrian leaned back. "Here's the kicker. He wants to meet the great man himself. I, of course, didn't reveal your identity." Her lips curved in a cheeky grin. "Imagine. He thinks you're a man."

Saskia draped her forearms over the armrests in a disgusted gesture. "Why is it that men are always drooling over another guy's art? There's tons of stealth female street artists out there who use male-sounding pseudonyms because of the inherent gender bias in the field." Just like she did. She'd chosen San Holo as an homage to the famous character.

"Sister, you are preaching to the choir." Adrian leaned her elbows on the desk, the cream color of her crisp silk blouse accentuating her skin tones. "But since you want anonymity, if they think you're a man, it plays right into that." With a shrug, she added, "Especially since you don't want to do interviews."

Saskia had never wanted that kind of notoriety. She just wanted to make her art without interference.

Now some rich dude wanted to know who she was.

"You'll never guess who." Adrian said, almost deadpan. She'd been waiting for this big buildup.

Saskia let her have it. "Who?" she asked mildly.

"Clay   freaking-billionaire-who-will-pay-anything-for-your-art Harrington."

Saskia smacked her forehead, almost giving herself a headache. "Of *course* that's why he was here. It was about my *art*."

She should have seen it. But then, she'd so enjoyed talking with him and the sex had been so damn good, she'd barely thought about anything else.

Adrian was looking at her, eyebrows knit. "What?"

Saskia simply said, "I can't do it."

Adrian burst out with a yell of dismay. Adrian was her agent and whatever Saskia made, Adrian got a percentage. But even more, Adrian wanted Saskia's career to grow, wanted her art to be seen by everyone, because her friend believed it was absolutely brilliant.

Mouth still open, Adrian demanded, "Why on earth would you not do this?"

She had to be blunt. "Because I slept with him last night."

They weren't just agent and artist. Adrian was her best friend, the person she'd counted on. Saskia trusted her implicitly.

They'd been best friends since they were sixteen—half

their lives—when Saskia was living in a dingy London garret with some artist friends. While creating her street art—which would always be her first love—she'd supported herself by selling caricatures to tourists. Adrian bought one. They'd been besties ever since, even moved to San Francisco together five years ago. But while Adrian cultivated her British accent, because Americans thought it was posh, Saskia had worked diligently to get rid of hers so she wouldn't stand out in an American city. Her accent was Anywhere USA. It facilitated her anonymity.

Adrian dramatically pushed her mouth closed with two fingers. "Let me just wipe up my drool." Then she sighed. "He is so hot. Was it as incredible as I imagine?"

They usually shared intimate details. Not that either of them had much to share recently, and Saskia, not for five years.

She closed her eyes and exhaled a long, satisfied breath before looking at her friend again. "Oh. My. God. It was like… take amazing and multiply by a thousand," she said just as dramatically. "Fireworks and everything you ever dreamed of."

Adrian fanned herself. Then she rushed to the water cooler, pouring two cups and handing one to Saskia. "You must be parched after a night of major fireworks." Seated again, she drained the small cup. "It wasn't all about him and his needs?"

Saskia shook her head, once to the left, once to the right. "It was all about me. About *my* fireworks." She widened her eyes, "Not to say that he didn't get his."

Adrian let out a sigh. "You held out for five years until you got the very best."

Adrian knew everything about her, especially why Saskia hadn't been with a man in that long. Hugo, the awful ex. He'd been Saskia's everything. But all the while, he'd been screwing her over. He'd stolen her pseudonym and claimed her art as his, which meant he'd stolen her whole life. She'd had to start from scratch, building her name all over again.

Adrian had seen her fall into a dark pit of despair. "I know how hard it was for you back then."

But Saskia had to be honest. "If Hugo hadn't claimed my early work, I might not have made the style switch to stuff that's truly me."

"Didn't Taylor Swift say something about making your best stuff even when your heart is broken?"

Saskia nodded.

"That's you, baby," her friend said. "You got even better after Hugo broke your heart."

Yeah, Saskia thought, she had. She'd always felt a lot of her early work was derivative of famous street artists like Banksy and his girl with the balloon, using symbols and hearts and butterflies and lots of blank space. Though she'd put her own spin on it too. But now she was all about bold colors and diversity and filling up every space with imagery.

Hugo Lewis was an ass, and she'd never forgive him for what he'd done. But she was a better artist for having struggled through the madness he'd brought into her life.

Then, Adrian being Adrian, she got down to business once more. "Okay. You slept with him. Had amazing sex. How do you want to deal with this situation now?"

Saskia pinched the bridge of her nose and closed her eyes a moment before she looked up. "You know who Clay Harrington is. And what he does. I don't agree with his new artists' platform. There's got to be something off about it. I totally shouldn't see him again."

Adrian set her lips in a prim line. "After you blew me off yesterday so you could have amazing sex multiplied by a thousand with an incredible hottie, I did a deep dive into what the man is actually doing in our artistic community.

Honestly, it might be not only aboveboard, but also a really good thing for budding artists."

Saskia snorted. "Come on. He cherry-picks who he wants on his platform. And he won't allow anybody to criticize? There's just something wrong with that."

But Adrian shook her head. "I didn't find a single artist who said he or she was used by him. In fact, I saw only praise."

Saskia narrowed her eyes. "There are companies that scrape the internet and remove anything negative. It costs money, but he has a lot of that."

"You didn't hear him yesterday talking about your art."

"You mean San Holo's art," Saskia said for her.

Adrian tossed that away with a flick of her wrist. "That's because you want to remain anonymous. I'm telling you, he truly appreciates the art. You should give him a chance."

Saskia was adamant. "We'll just have to agree to disagree for the time being."

But she had to consider what Adrian said and compare it to her time with Clay. If he was the kind of man who screwed over his artists, would he have been so unselfish with her in bed? The night truly had been all about her. And hadn't she liked everything he said while they talked over drinks? About wanting to go on a reading retreat? Hugo had never even cracked a book.

Having stared Adrian down for a couple of seconds, Saskia finally said, "It sounds like it's time for me to do some research myself. Rather than just making the blanket assumptions I have so far." Because she hadn't *researched* the man. She'd read a few articles, watched some YouTube videos, and listened to a couple of podcasts. But there seemed to be so much more out there.

Adrian raised her imperious eyebrow again, and Saskia said, "I know that look. I'm not interested in him. It was a one-night thing. But I would like to learn more about what he does, since you've become an insta-fan."

Adrian smiled wide enough to crinkle her eyes. "It's more accurate to say that *you* became the insta-fan. In his bed."

Saskia had to laugh. That was how they were with each other. Lighthearted teasing. Yet there were some serious feelings beneath it for Saskia. Sure, there'd been pleasure so great that her body still vibrated with glorious aftershocks. But also fear and curiosity. If he learned who San Holo was, he could blow up her entire world.

In a way, hadn't he blown it up last night? Because what they'd done was just too good for one night only.

The truth was, though she wanted to learn more about his platform and whether it was damaging to artists, she was dying to see him again.

Not as San Holo, but as the mysterious Saskia in his bed.

Adrian swiveled her chair back and forth with her foot. "There's a foster kid involved in all this too."

Saskia leaned in, almost without thinking. "How so?"

Adrian sweetened the pot. "He's why Clay wants to know who you are. The kid is your biggest fan, and he wants to meet you. In fact, it was the kid's social media post that brought your latest mural to light."

Saskia closed her eyes. A foster kid who loved her art. And wanted to meet her. That changed things up.

"His name is Dylan. Clay thinks he's a brilliant street artist. He's almost eighteen and close to aging out of the system. He needs guidance. The way I understand it from Clay, he and his friend Gideon Jones are providing that guidance."

Saskia bent forward, setting her elbows on her knees and clasping her hands between them. She hadn't grown up in foster care, but her parents had kicked her out at the age of sixteen. They'd hated her art. When she wouldn't stop, they'd cut the cord. She'd found a place to live with some of her street artist friends. Even if it had been a dingy, overcrowded garret, at least she had a roof over her head. But that didn't mean things had been easy.

She'd bet things hadn't been easy for Dylan either.

Saskia pointed an accusing finger at Adrian. "You knew this kid's situation would resonate with what happened to me."

Adrian gave her a wicked grin. "Yeah. But don't tell me the *only* thing resonating is the foster kid. Admit you want to see Clay again too."

But Saskia was already shaking her head. "This has nothing to do with last night. I'm thinking about the kid. I can pose as San Holo's assistant with Clay, the way I do with everyone else. That would give me a chance to help the kid too."

Adrian only looked at her with that all-knowing gaze until Saskia had to admit the truth. "Okay. Maybe there's a part of me that wants to see Clay again. If only to find out whether the sparks blowing up like crazy last night are still there in the light of day."

Adrian shot her with a finger pistol. "Bingo."

Saskia pointed her finger and shot back. "I still want to meet this kid."

After all the gunplay, Adrian turned serious. "Despite what happened between you and Clay, even despite his desire for you to meet Dylan, it's a great opportunity. Think of it—an entire building." She spread her arms. "You've never done anything like that. It'll become part of the San Francisco landscape. You're big already, but this could make you mega. Let's talk seriously about how we'll make it work."

Saskia shrugged. "Like we always have. I go in as San Holo's assistant, talk to Clay about what he wants, tell him the rules about anonymity."

Adrian nodded. "I already told him, and he agreed to guard your anonymity." She smiled. "Even from himself, for the time being."

Saskia had to smile too. The Clay she'd slept with last night would never let it go at that. "After I get an idea of what he wants, I'll give him the usual spiel, that San will keep in mind his general theme, but then the artist's imagination and creativity will take over. What comes out is what Mr. Clay Harrington gets."

Saskia had always vetted clients this way. Adrian was a good judge of character. Saskia was, too, especially with the way she'd grown up. Okay, Hugo had been the exception. Major screw-up there. But when she met clients, just as they judged her work, she was judging them. If she got a bad vibe, she didn't take the commission. It hadn't happened often, especially after the client had gone through Adrian first, but there'd been a few.

Honestly, she'd already vetted Clay last night. Now she just had to see exactly what he wanted San Holo to do. And make sure he understood that meeting San in person wouldn't happen.

She slapped her hands on her thighs. "All right. Let's do it. Set up a meeting."

Before Saskia could even stand, Adrian picked up the phone and punched in numbers. "Let's strike while the iron's hot." She chuckled. "No pun intended."

Saskia would have laughed, but her stomach sank. Whether it was a good sinking or bad, she couldn't be sure. She hadn't thought to see him again, especially not so soon. Especially not in her assistant's disguise. How would this go down?

She keyed in to Adrian's half of the conversation. "I'm glad I reached you, Mr. Harrington... Yes, San has agreed to consider the commission. I'd like to set up a meeting... Sure, today would be great... That time sounds good. At your warehouse in the Mission." After another pause, she added, "But you won't be meeting with San Holo himself. He'll send his assistant, Miss Oliver, as usual." She shook her head at whatever she heard. "No. Absolutely not. The first meeting is always with Miss Oliver. I will remind you, San has not agreed to reveal his identity." She paused again, then said, "Yes, that's how we work. You tell Miss Oliver what you're looking for, she'll relay that information to San Holo, then he'll decide whether or not to take on the project. Do you still want to go ahead with the meeting?" Adrian's blue eyes sparkled brighter than the sun glittering on the bay. "Take it or leave it, Mr. Harrington. It's your choice." She winked at Saskia. "Good. You can expect Miss Oliver at two o'clock. Goodbye."

Barely a moment later, Adrian jumped from her chair and did a happy dance around the room, punching the air. "Clay Harrington. Do you know what this means?"

Saskia couldn't get out of the chair. She knew exactly what it meant. She would see him again. She would breathe in his spicy, seductive scent that made her crazy. She would remember every kiss, every touch, every lick, every taste.

Would he be angry when he saw her and throw her out?

Or would he want to do it all over again?

Because if he did, there was absolutely no way she could resist.

ADRIAN WATCHED her best friend leave as if she had a fast-moving zombie on her heels. Were there any fast-moving zombies? Whatever. Saskia had raced out of Adrian's office, probably wanting to dress up before she met Clay for the second time.

But wait, this was Saskia. *Dressing up* wasn't in her vocabulary.

Adrian strode to the sideboard and pulled out a glass and a bottle, pouring a finger of whiskey. Best day ever. It deserved a celebratory drink. Crossing to the bank of windows, she gazed out at the bay, Alcatraz, the Golden Gate, and sipped. Moments later, she saw Saskia bounce out onto the sidewalk below.

Adrian had never seen her friend glow like that, as if she were lit from the inside. Even though this affair could end in utter disaster, Adrian had seen that spark. Not just a spark, but a blaze. It was time for Saskia to get over everything that had happened with her ass of a boyfriend. Hugo Lewis wasn't worth it. Saskia needed to come out of isolation. Maybe she didn't have to come out to her adoring fans as San Holo, but she *needed* to get out, to stop working only in the middle of the night like a vampire. As San Holo, she was always wrapped in that anonymity. It was time to move on.

Maybe it was time for them both to move on. Because Adrian hadn't been doing much in the outgoing department either, unless it was work-related. Growing up, she'd had it far better than Saskia, with loving parents who supported her life choices, her Oxford education, her desire to get her law degree, even her move to the United States.

Everything had been different for Saskia. She came from a privileged background, just as Adrian had. Until she was sixteen, when all that privilege had been torn from her. When Adrian found her, Saskia had been as thin as a rail, staying with a bunch of artists in a barely livable garret. She'd loved Saskia's artwork from the moment she'd bought that caricature. But she couldn't walk away, afraid the waiflike Saskia was starving. She'd taken her to lunch that first day—and often after that—and extracted the whole sordid story. Her friend had been arrested for tagging, an American term that fit appropriately. It was in all the papers that her world-famous parents—both classical artists—had an unruly daughter, a *street* artist, no less. They couldn't bear the stain on their good name. Not only that, at a very young age, those horrible people had told Saskia she was an accident, that they'd never wanted children. They'd expected her to be grateful that they'd let her be born. Like they owned her talent because they hadn't aborted her.

They told her to mend her ways, give up her street art. Or get out.

Saskia had taken to the streets rather than turn her talent over to them and lose herself to satisfy their demands. Adrian had done what she could for her friend, with lunches and dinners Saskia couldn't afford. She found Saskia a few patrons. It had never been enough to get her friend out of that dingy garret. She'd even offered to bring Saskia home, with her own room, but Saskia was proud. She wanted to make it on her own.

All these years later, she had. In such an incredible way.

Even before San Holo had come into existence, she'd made it. Her art was already becoming huge in England. But then Saskia met Hugo Lewis. Things might have been different if Adrian hadn't taken her eye off the ball while she attended uni for her law degree. She could have warned Saskia, maybe even saved her. Hugo had not only stolen Saskia's heart and innocence, he'd stolen her name, too, claiming her work as his own. That had finally broken Saskia. Just when she'd begun to regain her self-confidence after what her parents had taken from her, Hugo had stolen her belief in people all over again.

Back then, just as she did now with San Holo, Saskia had used a pseudonym. Lynx. No one had actually known who she was. Maybe part of that was fear of her parents finding out. She'd let Hugo act as her so-called manager, having him negotiate contracts, handling the money, the sales of her work. Hugo claimed it was so that Saskia could concentrate on her art. Adrian was sure he'd embezzled funds. Then bam, five years ago, without a single warning, he'd come out to the art world, saying that *he* was Lynx. At the time, Hugo's name had been bigger than hers, but he was savvy enough to know she would soon surpass him.

Saskia had no proof that he was lying. She'd let him handle everything. She'd believed in him. Maybe that was even worse than loving him.

What Saskia had gone through still made Adrian cringe. Though by then she was a lawyer, there was nothing to be done. Now Adrian was scrupulous about documenting everything, copyrighting each work, trademarking the pseudonym, so that no one could ever steal anything from San Holo. It was because of what happened to Saskia that Adrian had become an agent. With her law degree, she could negotiate and write contracts that were in her clients' best interests. So that no one, not even Adrian, could claim their work. She dealt with a lot of street artists, and most never used their own name.

After Hugo, Adrian thought a change would be good for Saskia. And for herself as well. Adrian's mother was American, hailing from San Francisco. Why not visit her aunt in the States? Adrian and Saskia had never left. It had been a great decision—a clean break for Saskia, a new beginning for them both. Adrian had fulfilled all the requirements and passed the California bar exam. Saskia had let Lynx go and become San Holo, bigger and better than ever.

Adrian had to admit that she'd done very well by Saskia's and her other clients' work too. Legally. Without embezzling. Making sure contracts were solid, getting their work out there with gallery showings, commissions, publicity. In fact, Adrian had been able to buy a flat on Nob Hill. Whereas

Saskia had never lived large despite her wealth. Though she had a beautiful Victorian in Haight-Ashbury, she still shopped at thrift stores. Mind you, she found some exceptionally cute clothing that suited her perfectly. Saskia also gave a lot of money to nonprofits, especially those related to artists.

It had been a long road for Saskia to get where she was. Adrian didn't want to see her screw it up with Clay Harrington either. But that glow on Saskia's face when she talked about the man said maybe it wouldn't be a bad thing. Adrian didn't think he was the ogre Saskia was afraid of. Her friend didn't trust anyone who could potentially abuse artists —she barely trusted anyone anymore.

Adrian would watch out for Saskia. The first inkling of something going sideways, and she'd pull the plug. But she didn't think it would go sideways at all.

For Saskia's sake, she hoped it was full steam ahead.

CHAPTER EIGHT

*S*ince she'd gone straight to Adrian's office after leaving Clay, Saskia had to go home to shower and change. She didn't dress to wow, but she loved the flowery tunic sweater she'd chosen over her favorite pair of comfy leggings. Gosh, she loved thrift stores. She'd found the sweater in a tiny shop in the Haight. She could afford to buy designer clothing, but she didn't care about that. The thousand dollars she'd pay for anything by a designer would help a lot of starving artists like she'd once been.

She arrived a few minutes early at Clay Harrington's warehouse. That was how she needed to think of him—as Clay Harrington. Not Clay, who'd done all those incredible things to her body last night.

She had to keep a cool head around him. He was just too good-looking, and even the thought of him—and last night— made her shivery.

She wanted to do everything all over again. And more.

But she had to act professionally and maintain control. Because he would push her relentlessly to find out who San

Holo was. If all that sensuality took over, she might let something slip. She might actually *tell* him.

The warehouse in the Mission District took up an entire city block, with two stories and lots of windows. All that natural light was perfect for artists. Though she mostly worked at night with the stars and the moon to light her way.

She patrolled the entire perimeter. By the time she made it back to the front, her heart was racing. It was totally doable. In the wider spaces between some of the windows, she could do something grander, but she imagined filling up even the narrow borders between each window set like the spines of books. It would be fabulous. She'd never done an entire building before. This chance had dropped in her lap like a gift.

She surveyed the front entrance, where a massive latticed window had been installed above the double doors. It struck her that she could paint on the glass, something she'd never done before. She'd have to research the right paint to use and how to treat the glass so the paint neither faded nor chipped. The challenge beat deep inside her.

She'd come here wanting to learn more about Clay's artists' platform, Art Space, wanting to prove whether he was on the up-and-up, as Adrian believed. The way her heart wanted to believe. If he was as caring with his artists and their work as he'd been with her body last night, then she wanted this commission. Her heart *begged* for this commission.

She threw open the front door, and the sun through all those windows lit up the lobby like a spotlight on a magnificent sculpture that took center stage. She could only stare and marvel.

A small bronze plaque at the bottom named the piece and identified the artist as Charlie Ballard. She was familiar with Charlie Ballard's metalwork. The woman was a genius.

Saskia had gone to Sebastian Montgomery's corporate head-quarters just to see *The Chariot Race*. The stunning piece dominated his lobby, different facets showing up as the sun moved across it. Saskia had stayed over an hour to watch it. But *this* was beyond anything. It shot straight through to her artist's heart.

Charlie had welded together *The Discus Thrower* out of gears, sprockets, springs, bits of pipe, and more, while shaping the face in bronze. But the discus itself was the crowning jewel. Shaping it like a palette, Charlie had filled it with a mosaic of all the colors a painter could possibly want. As the sun struck the disc, the mosaic seemed to glow. Perhaps Charlie had placed it just so, much as she had with *The Chariot Race*, making the sun part of the art.

She walked slowly around it, taking in its grandeur from every angle, then once again coming to a stop beneath the palette.

It was only then that she saw Clay. She had no idea how long he'd stood there while she'd been engrossed in Charlie's work, but he did nothing more than stare at her. Even as their eyes met, he still said nothing.

He must be wondering how the woman from last night had ended up here at the exact time San Holo's assistant was due to arrive.

She had to take control. Now.

Stepping forward, she held out her hand to introduce herself as if they hadn't just spent the most miraculous night together. "Hi. I'm Saskia Oliver, San Holo's assistant." She gave a nod toward *The Discus Thrower*. "Charlie Ballard is an amazing sculptor." He didn't take her hand, and she let it drop, rushing on before he could answer. If he even intended to. "It's a truly magnificent work."

As the silence went on, her heart beat harder, faster, and her blood roared in her ears.

Would he let her in? Or throw her out?

IT TOOK a lot to throw Clay off. But Saskia Oliver had managed to shock him.

How the hell could his dream woman of last night be standing here in his warehouse? Sure, he'd been determined to find her again. But *she* had found *him*.

Was it destiny?

His heart pounded hard, his breath stuck in his throat, and even his vision blurred around the edges as he looked at her. Christ, she was beautiful, all that gleaming dark hair falling over her shoulders, those deep cocoa-colored eyes, and the long, flowered sweater draping her beautiful body. Even the combat boots woke primal urges inside him.

Damn her for doing this to him.

But he refused to show any sign of weakness. Hands on his hips, he stared her down. Maybe he should have taken her hand, shaking it as he would that of an acquaintance. But they were so far from that. Exactly what, he didn't know. But *acquaintances*? Not.

Then he let almost every thought in his head fall out of his mouth. "I had no idea when we slept together last night." He felt the hardness in his voice deep down in his chest. "When you said it was just a one-night thing and it was over." This morning, he hadn't wanted it to be over. But what did he want now? "It never occurred to me you'd be part of San Holo's world." He shrugged as if it didn't matter. "But I'm good at compartmentalizing. While I'm shocked to see you here—" He didn't mind admitting it. "—I'll put that aside and grill the hell out of you about your boss." He hadn't forgotten his mission, and he made sure she didn't forget it either. "Because I am going to find out who he is."

She stood there, absorbing his tirade, if it could be called that, her face growing paler by the moment. He didn't sense fear or see a stalked-deer look in her eyes. But when she let out a breath, he heard the jitter in it. Nervous, then.

He tightened his lips to a thin line. "You knew who I was last night, didn't you?"

"Yes," she admitted. "Like you said, I'm in the art world."

"You searched me out after I made that offer to San Holo's agent?"

It wasn't possible. He'd only just left Adrian Fielding's office when he'd seen Saskia Oliver bopping down the street like she hadn't a care in the world. She hadn't seen him, just like she hadn't seen the robotaxi. But he wanted to hear her deny it.

"I recognized you after the car almost hit me." She nodded her head in punctuation. "But I didn't know about the commission for San Holo. Not until this morning, after —" After that freaking fabulous night they'd spent together. Then she added, "I didn't sleep with you because you're Clay Harrington or because you want something from San Holo." She blinked, her gaze cleared, and the jitters seemed to fall away. "I slept with you because I wanted to."

His heart went into overdrive as she said the only thing his body wanted to hear. He was a businessman, and astute, he liked to think. He'd have noticed if she'd had ulterior motives.

Then she smiled and damn near knocked him sideways. Christ, that smile. It made him think of the moment before she took him in her mouth. The moment before she took him inside her body. The moment before she drove him absolutely insane.

"So," she said. "Now that's out of the way, shall we get down to business? Here's how San Holo works."

Just standing next to her, scenting her as if she were his

83

mate, the memories of last night assaulting his system, he realized she'd blown every brain cell in his head. He'd intended to go on about meeting San Holo before he agreed to anything. He'd intended to grill her. But instead, he found himself simply looking at her beautiful face, that seductive body beneath the sweater, listening to the voice that stroked his every nerve ending.

"Adrian says you want a mural around the entire warehouse."

Entranced and speechless again—holy hell, he hadn't even invited her past the lobby yet—he could only nod.

"Here's what you do. Give us a basic idea of what you'd like." She shrugged. "Say you want dinosaurs. But you don't want mermaids or unicorns."

He found his voice. "No dinosaurs, mermaids, or unicorns, thank you very much."

She blinded him with her smile. "After that, San Holo runs with it. You get what you get. Which is San Holo's vision of what you asked for." She knocked him dead with an even more brilliant smile. "But I guarantee it will blow your mind."

Oh yeah, his mind was blown, all right.

She crossed her arms over her delectable chest. "Tell me how you're going to guarantee San Holo's anonymity while working on a mural that stretches all around this building. Which is massive, by the way. This project could take months." She stepped even closer to him, fogging his mind with the scent of fruity shampoo and mango lotion, and poked him in the chest. "That means maintaining anonymity from you too."

He'd let Saskia have the floor long enough. "I told Adrian Fielding that part of *my* deal was having San Holo meet my protégé. Dylan is a foster kid. Your artist is his hero."

Something he couldn't read flickered in her eyes, then she

gave a slight shake of her head. "Not going to happen. No matter how much you push, I'm not divulging anything about my boss. If you were to find out San's real identity, I have no idea what you'd do with that information. I am my artist's shield. No one gets through. If you can't guarantee that you won't peek while San is working, then this commission won't happen."

Her voice had turned almost hostile, and he cocked his head as though he might see her differently from another angle. "You're suspicious of me and my motives, aren't you?" He paused a beat. "Even after last night?"

She didn't wait even a beat. "I totally am." She gave a hard emphasis to her words. "*Especially* after last night."

He had to concede the point. Sex definitely complicated things. "Fair enough. In the art world, we all know tons of people have cheated and lied and stolen."

The hard light in her eyes said she knew that from personal experience. "Exactly."

Christ, how he wanted to plumb her depths and figure her out. She'd talked about trust issues, and here was further evidence of them. But he changed his tack for the moment. "Okay, so let me tell you about the warehouses."

He had a plan: introduce her to Dylan and all the other artists with studios here, and maybe the great artist would change his mind after she told him what Clay was actually doing.

SHE HADN'T IMAGINED he'd be angry she'd ghosted him this morning after a night of great sex. But he was a man, and the way she'd walked out had pricked his ego. Yet, after getting out his feelings—if a man ever truly got out his feelings—he was completely businesslike, as if he really could compartmentalize his emotions. That was the word he used. She wondered if she could compartmentalize as easily.

Nor had he given up on discovering San Holo's true identity. Maybe he'd try another frontal attack, or maybe he would skillfully glean information from whatever she said. But figure out who San Holo truly was? Like hell he would.

This could very well turn out to be a battle royal. She intended to win.

He drew her farther into the building. "This warehouse was my first, and it's really a prototype. Over the last five years, I've opened another four in major US cities. Our goal is to subsidize and support artists and help promote their work. We're also expanding globally." He flourished a hand. "Let me show you around."

"Sure," she said. "Show me around." This guy was slick and sly—so unlike the man she'd gone to bed with last night —and he had to have an agenda. Anybody this good-looking and this rich had to have another side to him even if she hadn't seen it.

But last night had been *sooo* good. She wanted it again. Even if it might be very bad for her.

It was like her brain was screaming no, but her body was one hundred percent in. Her heart—well, that was a whole different matter. After Hugo, her heart was immune. But Clay's scent reminded her of the spice of last night. Of the feel of his hair beneath her fingers, the touch of his lips on hers, the taste of him in her mouth.

If she went on like this, she'd never make it through the interview.

He was saying, "Each twenty-by-twenty cubicle has been turned into an individual artist's studio." He took a flight of stairs leading to a second-floor landing that overlooked the partitions.

The sight stole her breath. "There must be a hundred artists down there."

He smiled when she looked up at him, as he stood like a giant of men. "More than a hundred. Because we have collaboration—some artists working together." He leaned forward, hands on the railing, surveying the sea of generous workspaces. "We give each artist a stipend and pay for their studio setup. After that, they buy their own materials." He glanced down at her. "But if anyone's ever a little short, I don't make them stop working until they find the money for more supplies." A smile flirted with his lips. "They help each other too. They're all very supportive. It's not a horse race, where someone will win and everyone else loses."

Despite her suspicions and her resistance to anything being this good, it struck her that what he'd created was pretty amazing. "I read somewhere that you also sell the work for them."

He shook his head. "I don't sell it *for* them. The work sells itself. Because they're good. And getting better all the time." A note of fervor entered his voice, as if he were a minister preaching a sermon. "But I help them find gallery space and mount shows. I've also started a video platform where they can show their work in virtual galleries. They can also create videos to talk about their process, how they create, why they create, why they chose their art form, where they get their inspiration. That helps sell their work too. People love knowing how a particular piece came into being."

If she'd had a place like this when she was sixteen, what could she have accomplished so much earlier?

If he was on the up-and-up.

He jogged back down the steps, turning to her as she followed more slowly. "Let me introduce you around."

The artists here were of all ages, all ethnicities, all

genders. She'd probably find they came from all walks of life if she learned their history.

She especially enjoyed meeting Vic Carter, who made art out of reclaimed plastic, sculpting dolphins, whales, and other sea creatures endangered by all the garbage people threw in the oceans. His work was both brilliant and eco-conscious.

Artists worked in metal and clay and stained glass and paint. In these amazing studios, each artist had everything necessary to create their work.

Stopping at a studio shared by a man and a woman, Clay flourished a hand. "Bonnie Hale, this is Saskia Oliver."

In her late forties, her dark hair sprinkled with silver and cascading down her back, Bonnie wore overalls crusted with the materials of her work. She gave Saskia's hand a no-nonsense shake.

Clay turned to the man. "Otto Klein." His gray hair attested to his being somewhere in his fifties.

As she stepped farther into Bonnie and Otto's studio, she marveled at a partial mosaic on a lightbox. Pasted to the large shelf above it was a photograph of a bird of paradise, which they had emulated in glass pieces on the lightbox.

"This is amazing mosaic work," she enthused.

"Thank you," Bonnie said, Otto nodding his thanks. "We aren't illustrators, so we use photographs to guide our work."

Otto added in accented English, "We also use stained-glass patterns."

Pattern books lined the shelves beside cubbies for racks of glass. Remnants filled tubs arranged by color. Toolboxes contained everything from wheeled nippers to glass cutters to glass breakers, along with dental tools and tweezers. Below that were buckets of adhesive, and grout in various colors.

Bonnie followed Saskia's gaze. "Even though we use

patterns, the artistry comes out in our use of color and how we put the patterns together."

"It's beautiful and artistic work." She fluttered a hand from the photo to the glass bird of paradise on the lightbox. "You've taken a picture and turned it into a masterpiece."

Otto added gruffly, "We could never have stepped out of using other people's patterns and turning to photographs and other means of making our mosaics were it not for Clay."

Bonnie put a hand to her heart. "I worked on my kitchen table. Every day, I had to put it all away." She laughed. "I was always finding bits of glass on the floor. My husband left me when he found a glass sliver in the stew."

"I hope that story isn't true," Saskia said with a smile. "That could be dangerous."

Bonnie laughed. "Not far off. Let's just say he didn't care for my obsession with mosaics." Then she added, "Clay found us a place where we could spread out and set our creativity free."

"Clay is not an artist himself," Otto said, "but he gets us." He slapped a big hand to his chest.

"He speaks our language," Bonnie concurred.

Had Clay done a really good snow job on all these people? Because everyone she'd met spoke of him as if he were their selfless miracle worker.

Or maybe they were all doing a snow job on *her*.

But she shoved her reservations aside. San Holo wanted this fabulous commission. And the woman who had touched Clay last night was desperate to touch him again.

Their conversation ended abruptly when a young man, a teenager, flung himself into the studio, stopping his forward trajectory only by grabbing the edges of the two partition walls acting as a doorway.

All he said was, "Clay," his voice almost strident.

His dark blond hair fell just past the neck of his paint-splattered shirt. Tall and angular, his hands big, his feet encased in oversized tennis shoes, he was almost like a puppy who hadn't yet grown into his huge paws. His hazel eyes bored into Saskia for a long moment.

Though no one said a word, Saskia knew this had to be Dylan, the foster kid Clay had told Adrian about.

And she was dying to meet him.

CHAPTER NINE

$\mathcal{C}$lay was nonplussed for a moment, as though his shock at finding out Saskia had been his lover of last night would somehow communicate itself to Dylan. Nothing flummoxed him. He was always in command. Yet Saskia stole all his sense of control. Mostly because he wanted her. In his bed. Over and over again.

He pulled himself together. "Dylan Beck." He wagged a hand at his protégé. "This is Saskia Oliver."

Not wanting to get Dylan's hopes up, he didn't introduce her as San Holo's assistant. He also didn't want Dylan to do all the dirty work of trying to get her to give up the artist's identity. That was his job, not Dylan's.

He saw his mistake when Dylan raised one dark blond eyebrow, speculating on just who she was to Clay. "Nice to meet you."

"Clay tells me you're a street artist. In fact—" Saskia shot a glance at Clay. "—he says you're quite brilliant."

So Adrian Fielding had told her about Dylan. That was good. Maybe it would help his case in getting her to reveal who San Holo was.

Saskia had no compunction about revealing her own identity. "I'm San Holo's assistant. Clay is interested in having a mural painted on the outside of the warehouse."

Dylan said, "OMG," so dramatically that his chin almost hit his chest. He let go of the partition walls and stepped closer, as if he could scent something of San Holo on her person. "San Holo is my idol," he said in breathless tones. "I want to be just like him." He whipped his phone out of his back pocket and took only a couple of seconds to scroll, holding up the picture of the street art San Holo had produced the other night. "Clay and me, we found this. We were the first ones to see it." His voice rose with exhilaration at being this close to someone who actually knew his idol.

Clay had to clarify. "Dylan found it. He found the fleur-de-lis too." He turned to Bonnie and Otto. "We'll let you get back to work."

As he stepped out of the studio, Dylan and Saskia followed automatically. After a few strides along the aisle, Saskia said, as if it had just dawned on her, "Oh gosh, you're the one who put the art on social media."

Sensing no censure, Dylan stood even taller. "I knew right away it was his. Even before we found the fleur-de-lis in the alien's eyeball."

Saskia's smile threatened to bowl over not only Dylan but Clay as well. "San will want to thank you. Because that attention just made the canvas and prints of the street art much more valuable." She glanced at Clay. "Don't you agree?"

It was as though she was asking him to pump up Dylan's ego. He did it gladly. "Absolutely. If no one knows about it, nothing has value."

As they strolled along the row of studios, Dylan walked backward, his steps almost a bounce. "You can tell me who he is, since you're his assistant." He lowered his voice, trying to remain confidential. "I won't tell anyone."

Saskia laughed. It was such a beautiful sound, and so genuine that Clay could only like her more. There was something wonderfully carefree about her. He hadn't felt carefree for a while now, if ever.

With Dylan on tenterhooks, she said, "Okay," in the same conspiratorial whisper. "I'll spill the beans." She beamed a smile at him. "But only because I like you."

Clay held his breath. Dylan did too.

Until she laughed and shook her head. "Did you both really think I was going to reveal San Holo's identity?" Her grin took the sting out of her words. "I mean, Dylan, you're super likable, and I can't wait to see your art, but some secrets will always be secrets."

She was laughing again, finding the joke so hilarious that even Dylan laughed, obviously appreciating her honesty. Clay wasn't quite there with the kid, who was clearly falling for Saskia—who wouldn't?—and wouldn't give up on unmasking San Holo. Yet the sneaky way she'd messed with both their heads only made her smarter and sexier in his eyes. Last night, she'd intrigued him, seduced him. But here was another side of her, one he appreciated just as much. No wonder San Holo trusted her to keep his anonymity. She didn't even mind joking about it.

But Dylan eyed her. "I'll keep working on you. Someday you'll tell me."

Saskia wagged her finger at him without saying a word.

Then the boy burst out, "You have to see my studio. I never had a studio before Clay gave me one."

Instead of saying she was too busy, Saskia gave the kid a toe-curling smile. "I'd love to see it. And your artwork."

She enthused over every piece, bringing a shine to Dylan's eyes. Then she turned to the easel, which Dylan had covered with a drop cloth. He never showed his work until it was finished.

But when Saskia said, "Is this your current piece? I'd love to see it," Dylan whipped the covering away.

Clay gaped. "It's a butterfly." Which was not Dylan's usual style.

Saskia stroked her chin with thumb and forefinger. "It's a dragonfly." She looked at Clay, killing him with her beautiful smile. "But let's call it a butterfly-dragonfly."

Dylan merely stared at them both and said in the driest tone, "It's a cockroach. They can fly, you know."

Saskia put a hand over her mouth, laughing, not *at* Dylan but *with* him. "That's the beauty of your art. It's whatever is in the eye of the beholder."

The perfect thing to say, and the kid beamed his happiness.

Clay couldn't help nudging Dylan. "I think you're ready to put your work out there." He'd been subtly encouraging Dylan to step out, but though he took his paint cans on nighttime sojourns, spraying walls—in acceptable places, of course—with his elegant graffiti, Dylan was still reluctant to put his real work out there. Even after their walk around the Mission District yesterday, when the kid had found San Holo's new piece. "Take on a wall, Dylan. You're more than ready."

Dylan scoffed. "I tag walls all the time."

Clay gestured to the artwork in the studio. "But you don't put stuff like this on any of them. Not your true stuff that shows your real self."

When Saskia said, "Your stuff is really good. It deserves to be out there," Dylan turned a full circle, moving slowly, his gaze drifting over each piece of his artwork.

"Yeah, okay," he said, still tentative but a little more open. "Let me figure out what."

Saskia pointed at the easel. "What about the cockroach? What's beautiful about it is that people will see what they want to see. A butterfly. A dragonfly. Or maybe your cockroach is actually going to turn into that butterfly."

Clay liked her insight and the way she encouraged Dylan. Maybe that was an insight into the kid. He saw himself as a cockroach who wanted to fly. Now he'd see that not only could he fly, he could also turn into a butterfly.

Clay could have kissed Saskia then and there.

***

SHE WAS STILL ENCOURAGING DYLAN, just the way Clay had, when a tall, middle-aged man poked his head into the studio. Pushing his glasses up his nose, he said softly to Clay, "Can we talk a minute?"

Clay looked at her, bowed slightly, and said, "I'll be right back."

Saskia liked that he hadn't told the guy to bug off because he was too busy. He'd delighted in introducing her to so many of the artists working here today. And he obviously encouraged Dylan.

There was a lot to appreciate about Clay Harrington.

As the two men disappeared around the wall, Dylan grabbed her arm. "Clay is great, don't you think." It wasn't a question. "He's helped so many of us. I'd probably be in jail if I hadn't found Clay and Gideon."

Though she knew a bit of the story, she asked, "Gideon?"

"You haven't heard about Gideon?" Dylan rushed on. "He has this foundation, and he helps foster kids like me. Because his sister was a foster kid when Gideon was overseas in the Army and he lost touch with her. But he found her again. And now he helps us all out. He helps veterans too. He's amazing."

She'd heard of Gideon's foundation, Lean on Us. But the

way Dylan told the story made what Gideon Jones did even more impressive.

"That's how you met Clay?" she asked. "Through Gideon?"

Dylan nodded expansively, his hair flying. "Clay gave me this studio and helped me get all my tools and supplies. I mean, he is the absolute best."

The man was totally amazing.

She'd judged Clay negatively merely from reading articles about him and watching podcasts. But now, after what Dylan had to say, after she'd seen how Clay encouraged the young man and truly seemed to believe in him, she had to throw out all those uncharitable thoughts. He'd been nothing but a stand-up guy since they'd met. Sure, he was hungry for the kill, wanting her to reveal San Holo. But he still managed to be a good guy, one of a kind. The people here in his warehouse had only incredible things to say about him.

He couldn't do a snow job on *everyone*.

Honestly, she couldn't think of him as a bad guy anymore. Yeah, there were a lot of people in the art world who sucked. But maybe Clay wasn't one of them. She'd known him only twenty-four hours, and a final decision about him, good or bad, would take longer. But for now, Clay was getting a hall pass.

She couldn't help saying to Dylan, "When I was your age and just starting out, I wish I'd had a studio space like this for my art." Instead of the dirty garret she'd lived in with way too many artists.

Clay's voice came from right behind her. "You're an artist?"

Damn. She hadn't heard him move up on her. Turning to him, her voice breezy, she said, "I used to be, but I wasn't any good. I still do some of my own stuff." She shrugged to add emphasis. "But I'm a better assistant than I am an artist."

But Clay had latched on. "I'd love to see your work."

She stepped back, waving him off. "Oh, it's bad. Really. I'm a *much* better assistant."

How could she have slipped up like that? It could literally ruin her life. Had she forgotten her experience with Hugo? While she'd just decided that Clay was actually a good guy, she absolutely could not tell him. Mentally, she zipped her lips. *Don't do that again.*

Even if she was becoming totally enamored with Dylan. And with Clay.

Dylan finally saved her. Grabbing her arm, almost dragging her out of the studio as he said, "Oh my *gawd*," with such exaggeration. "There are so many amazing artists here. I have to introduce you to *everyone*."

She heard more glowing accounts of Clay in all the different voices.

"You know what? Honestly, I was living on the street."

"I was doing the art, and Clay came and said, 'I got a place for you to stay and a studio to work in.'"

"I was super suspicious at first, but he's the real deal."

Her head was spinning by the time Dylan had taken her the full length of the warehouse.

And she was ninety-nine percent sure Clay was the real deal.

CLAY WAS ALMOST jealous that he didn't have Saskia to himself. Yet he loved watching Dylan's hero worship just because the woman actually worked for San Holo.

It was, however, time to get down to business. "Maybe we should go to my office now to talk about the commission. I'm eager to hear what you think San Holo will say."

With a smile in her eyes, she said without embarrassment,

"Sure. But first, can I use that restroom I saw back there?" It wasn't a question, since she was already heading down the aisle.

The moment she was gone, like any seventeen-year-old, Dylan spoke without thinking. "Man, she's hot. And she knows San Holo." He put a hand to his chest as if he'd entered a state of bliss. "I think I'm in *looove*."

Dylan looked at him, one eyebrow raised as if he had some sort of sixth sense and could feel the connection between Clay and Saskia.

Clay found himself oddly defensive, barely keeping himself from snarking, *She's mine, punk*. Of course he didn't say it. That would be a dick move to a kid who was enamored.

Besides, Saskia *wasn't* his.

At least not yet.

WHEN SASKIA RETURNED, she pointed at Dylan. "You—" She gave him a sparkling look. "—need to get back to work on your masterpiece." She held up a palm. "Get ready to put it out there. The art world will go crazy for it."

Blushing to the roots of his hair, Dylan slapped his palm against Saskia's in a high five. Then he grabbed his paintbrush.

As they turned toward the stairs leading to his apartment on the second floor, Clay had to say, "You're really good with Dylan. I've been encouraging him. So has Gideon Jones."

Before he could explain who Gideon was, she said, "Dylan told me all about Gideon's foundation. You've both done wonders for him."

"But hearing praise from you, someone he doesn't know

well, really builds his confidence. I believe he'll put his work out there now."

Her smile radiated down on him. Before he lost total control and kissed her in full view of everyone, he flourished a hand for her to climb the stairs ahead of him.

When she walked through the door he opened for her, she gasped. "*This* is your office?"

"My office and my living quarters." He closed the metal door, cutting off the hubbub from below, the thick walls giving him privacy while allowing the artists to work at all hours without worrying they'd disturb him.

She gaped at the space he'd created for himself. Skylights took advantage of the afternoon sun, sparkling on the polished concrete floor that wasn't covered by area rugs. He'd designed an open plan, one grouping of sofa and chairs centered around his massive flat-screen TV, another around a fire pit he'd installed with an exhaust above for the smoke. Off to the right, a full kitchen contained all the amenities, as well as a breakfast bar and a dining table that seated twelve when extended. The only places partitioned off were his bedroom and the two bathrooms, one for him, one for guests. His workspace, desk, cabinets, files, and computers were all open to the rest of the flat. Two large monitors on the desk allowed him to track his investments, do research, and conduct business.

She put a hand on her hip. "Aren't you a billionaire or something? Yet you live in your warehouse?"

He laughed. "It works for me. When clients visit, we have comfortable sofas to sit on and technology at my fingertips." Then he said seriously, "I like to be close to the artists."

She eyed him. "That means if…" She stared him down. "And I do mean *if* San decides to take the commission, you'll be here all the time. How can we expect you to keep San a secret?"

"When your boss and I come to an agreement, I have no intention of spying on him." Then he smiled. Many had called it a shark's smile. Maybe it was, but for San Holo, not her. "I'm still hoping to change his mind about meeting Dylan."

The reminder was a dig at her, because he'd seen how much she liked Dylan. How much she wanted to help him. Maybe she could persuade San Holo to do the right thing.

But that was all for a later discussion. With a hand on her elbow, he guided her to the sofa. "Take a seat. Would you like some water? A soda? Some wine?"

"Tap water is fine," she said. "No ice."

He poured two glasses, utilizing a filtration system that made his tap water as pure as anything out of a bottle, then carried both to the sofa.

She'd boxed herself into the sofa's corner, and instead of pushing himself on her, he sat on the opposite end.

She was so beautiful with the sunlight streaming down on her. Sexy. Desirable. Fascinating. His heart and his body wanted to jump her right now, stake his claim, kiss her senseless. But his brain had to remain in control.

She took over the conversation. "You've been going on about Dylan meeting San Holo." There might be a bit of snark in her tone. "But if you want San to work with you, we need to know your basic idea for the mural." She spoke as if she and San were a team. She relayed what the client wanted, and San Holo executed. "Before you tell me, let me explain how San works." She pointed at him. "You say what you want." She swirled a hand in the air, encompassing the building. "Say, a mural having something to do with artists. Just basic stuff. No 'it *has* to be this or that.' But you also get to say what you'd absolutely hate to see. San's not going to add something that makes you want to throw up. Once that's all nailed down—" She arched a brow. "—you have to let it go."

He opened his mouth to speak, but she cut him off. "You get the version that comes out of the artist's heart and soul. Can you accept giving up control like that?"

"Quite honestly," he said, "I want what San Holo thinks will represent my artists. I want it to be inclusive. Here, we have all genders, all orientations, all ethnicities, all manner of artistic endeavors. Not just physical art, but the work of writers, poets, dancers, comedians, actors. Any artistic endeavor. I want people to see the mural outside and understand the spirit of what we're doing on the inside."

For a moment, she said nothing. Perhaps he'd blown her away. Until finally, she said, "I believe San has waited a long time to do something like this."

Maybe *she* wanted San Holo to do this.

And Clay wanted *her*.

CHAPTER TEN

*C*lay hadn't forgotten his original mission. "I need to meet the man first. How can I trust that I'll get what I want if I don't meet him?"

Saskia shook her head, her lips beckoning him. It took all his concentration to stay focused on her words. "Total anonymity," she said. "Take it or leave it."

Her chocolate eyes were even darker now, the color of rich earth.

He didn't back down. "What if I hate it?"

The smile seemed to grow across her face, first her lips, then her cheeks, then crinkles at the corners of her eyes. "Then you don't have to pay." Finally, the smile surfaced in her gaze. "But you won't hate it."

"You must have worked with San Holo for a long time to be able to say that." He liked her confidence. Even if it was confidence in her boss. Still, he kept pushing. Next to getting her into his bed again, his major goal was to fulfill his promise to Dylan. "San would really give up a lucrative commission—" He raised an eyebrow. "—and I will make it worth his while—because he refuses to meet with me?"

She shrugged. The answer was obvious. Yes, San Holo would walk away.

They were at an impasse when Saskia's stomach rumbled. He realized the sun had fallen behind a building. Rather than pointing out the sound, he said, "I'm hungry. Shall we eat while we're negotiating? What would you like?"

She put a hand to her stomach, acknowledging the growl. "I'm starving. Whatever you want. This is your area. You know all the best restaurants."

He tapped in an order for the best Japanese restaurant he knew, and since he was a frequent patron, their order arrived before they could truly get back into their negotiations. He locked the door behind the delivery person so they wouldn't be disturbed while they were eating.

Saskia followed him to the kitchen counter, taking a seat at the breakfast bar. "Wow, that smells good." Closing her eyes, she breathed in, and he had the urge to kiss her right then.

But they were still negotiating. Kissing would come later.

Popping the caps on two bottles, he poured the beer into clear mugs and slid one to her. With the first sip, she moaned, the sound sexy enough to break his concentration on everything but getting her into his bed.

Eyes closed as if it helped her savor the drink, she said, "That's the best beer I've ever tasted."

"It's Japanese. It suits the meal." The blissful look on her face suited her. He'd experienced her bliss last night, and he wanted it again. When his lips were on her.

They dug into the meal with chopsticks, dining on sushi, shrimp tempura, sukiyaki, and yakitori, skewered chicken. She moaned over every bite as if she hadn't eaten since that hamburger they'd shared last night.

Did she have any idea what she was doing to him?

Maybe she *wanted* to drive him crazy.

Once they were done, they closed up the leftovers and put them in the fridge, working together companionably. Then Clay led her back to the sofa, where this time he made sure they sat a little closer.

They didn't talk about the mural or San Holo. Instead, she got him to talk about himself, the warehouses, Art Space. Which meant he didn't stop talking. He loved bringing artists into the fold, actively searching them out. He encouraged, supported, showed their art, helped them make a name for themselves. They could put their art on his platform and be assured no one would harangue them. That was his specialty —making sure artists had a safe place for their endeavors.

But enough about him. He wanted to know everything about her. "What you do when you're not working for San Holo or dodging robotaxis?"

She laughed at the reminder. "There's not much to tell. The most interesting thing that ever happened to me was when a kind gentleman rescued me from certain death by a driverless taxi, shared a couple of drinks with me, and then..." She winked at him.

It was the *and then* that got him. He had to suppress a quake of desire. But she hadn't told him a thing about herself, except yesterday in the bar when she'd talked about trust. Clearly, she didn't want to reveal anything.

Still, he had to ask, "Why are you so wary of me? I mean, you haven't even told me where you live."

"I'm not hiding anything. I live in the Haight." She licked her lips as if suddenly nervous. "I've had some bad interactions with male artists and agents and buyers. They've colored my view of everyone in the art world." She smiled. "Adrian has proven herself to me one hundred percent." Then she added, "So has San Holo."

"Come on," he cajoled. "You get that I'm a good guy, right?"

Her mouth quirked in an almost smile. "While there are definitely things you're very good at—" She raised an eyebrow indicating exactly what those things were. "—the jury is still out on the rest."

Oh baby, he thought, *I'm going to show you just how good I can be everywhere—in bed, as well as out of it.*

———

CLAY HARRINGTON WAS TOO INTUITIVE. He'd immediately caught on to how suspicious she was of him. Coupled with the fact that he both lived and worked in the warehouse, how on earth would she keep her identity secret from him? But there was something about him that rang true. She was close to believing he wouldn't unmask San Holo unless she wanted him to. So many people had said so many amazing things about him. He couldn't pull the wool over their eyes all at once, and certainly not Dylan's. Being a foster kid, he would see through any façade people threw up around him.

The truth was, she *wanted* to believe.

Clay's home was amazing, minimalist and luxurious at the same time. It felt like the man himself, with everything out in the open for all to see. Except the hidden corner of his bedroom.

Was there a hidden corner of the man as well?

He leaned forward, catching her gaze, his eyes penetrating. "Tell me about your art."

Maybe the way to discover his hidden depths was to offer a bit of herself. Even if it was a mistake, she revealed something no one but Adrian knew. "My parents are painters." She didn't say they were both famous British classical artists revered all over the world. If she told him their names, he'd recognize them immediately. "They never felt I measured up."

"Consequently, *you* felt you never measured up?" Oh yes, he was intuitive, drilling down into her words.

"They set the bar high," she admitted, "making it difficult for me to ever climb over it." She put out a hand, not quite touching him. "But I don't want you to think I gave up art because of them. I can honestly judge my art very well for myself."

She could judge her own art. She knew when she'd painted crap. And she painted over it immediately. But she also knew when she'd created something incredible. Her parents had been wrong about her.

Clay didn't push for more, saying instead, "I have a friend whose parents didn't appreciate his art either." He paused long enough for her to recognize the pain in his words even before he added, "It didn't end well."

This time, she touched him, just her fingers on his forearm. "I'm sorry for your friend. It's really hard."

"I actually thought he might—" He didn't finish, and his anguish for his friend threaded through his voice. This wasn't an act. This was the real Clay.

She knew then, with absolute certainty, that she'd misjudged him. He was like Adrian, empathetic, even if he stood on the sidelines of other people's artistic endeavors. She felt a great appreciation for the man guiding Dylan Beck, the man guiding all the artists in this warehouse and on his platform.

If she didn't have so many secrets to keep, could they...? But she couldn't go there.

Clay took away her chance to say anything when he added, "My friend was the one who got me interested in art. Growing up, I never paid much attention to it. But Gareth opened my eyes. Now I can't stop seeing the beauty in what others create." Then he admitted, "As well as the commercial potential."

"There's nothing wrong with commercial potential." She smiled her understanding. "No one wants to be a starving artist. Someone willing to pay huge sums for your art shows great appreciation. It certainly makes San Holo feel good."

Clay scoffed. "Even as big as he is?"

She snorted. "San didn't become big by always giving away his art for free. He started with street art, sure, but when people liked it and wanted more, they paid."

"What about the pop-up art he paints on walls in the middle of the night?"

That was easy. "He gets paid afterward when he sells prints and the actual canvases he worked on while fleshing out the idea."

After a sip of beer, Clay set the glass on the coffee table. "If he loves people appreciating his art, why is he so adamant about anonymity? You'd think he'd want to be out there for everyone to shower him with praise."

She didn't have a ready answer and remained evasive. "Everyone has their reasons for doing something, and they don't always share them."

Clay cocked his head like a wolf assessing his prey. "So you don't know why?"

Again, she hedged. "It's not my place to ask. I'm just doing my job."

Hooking his ankle over his knee, he gave her a long look. "How did you meet the great man?"

She smiled widely. "You're trying to get me to say something that will help you zero in on who San Holo is. But I'm not saying another thing." Leaning close, she zipped her lips.

Something blazed in his eyes, a fire in their depths. Hands on her shoulders, he hauled her in, kissing her as if he would die without the touch of her lips on his.

She might die without his touch too. His mouth on hers stole any resistance she might have had. Without meaning to move, she found herself straddling his lap, her sweater riding up her thighs as she pressed against him, wanting him.

When his hand dropped to her breast, he pulled back long enough to say, "You said only one night."

Her breath burst out of her. "Okay. Two nights." Then she laughed. "Or maybe three."

In the next moment, his tongue delved deep, his hands everywhere, her fingers in the waistband of his jeans, feeling warm, bare flesh. Wanting him, needing him.

CLAY TASTED HER LIPS, the sweetness of her mouth, drank in the fruity scent of her hair, reveled in her supple body above him. He no longer cared about street art or commissions or San Holo. There was only her.

Saskia moaned as he plumped her breast in his palm, and he thought he might lose himself completely. Arching into him, she melded with the hardness of his body. He growled his need into her mouth.

He rubbed against her intimate parts, and she moved with him, mimicking the act of love. He felt like a teenage boy, ready to let loose right now. Her nipple pebbled beneath his palm, and she hiked her sweater higher, pulled him closer, as if she were riding the ridge of him.

No woman had ever stolen his breath like this, commanded him the way she did.

When she started to tremble, he knew that was exactly what she was doing—riding him—and he surged against her, caressing her through the fabric between them, pushing her to the edge. Her breath came in sweet puffs into his mouth. Christ, she was so close.

She pulled back then, eyes closed, mouth open in a delicious cry that shimmied straight through his body.

It was only with a mastery of will that he didn't come with her when she burst wide open. He had just enough control to keep up that hard ride against her. She leaned back, braced her hands on his knees, and pushed down on him, her thighs clamped along his.

There had been never been anything like this. Never anyone like her.

Finally, her shudders ended, and she collapsed against him, her head on his shoulder. A free, flirty smile on her lips, her eyes still closed, she murmured, "Oh my God." Her breath came out in a long sigh. "That was amazing." Laughter threaded through her voice.

Then she looked at him, her chocolate eyes dark as night, pulling him in. "Now let's see about getting these clothes off."

THOUGH HER BODY was deliciously sated, Saskia wanted more. She popped his shirt buttons free one by one until he took over and ripped the whole thing off, buttons flying across the polished concrete. He wore no undershirt, his chest sculpted and begging for her fingers to play in the soft whorls of hair.

When she tweaked his nipples, he groaned. "Do that again and I'll lose it right now. You had me so close to the edge, I almost came in my pants."

She reached between his legs, cupped his hardness. "We wouldn't want to waste this until you're inside." She squeezed him, loving the growl that slipped from his lips. Loving that she could do this to him.

She didn't wait for him to undress her, shimmying away and yanking the sweater over her head, baring her breasts in the see-through lace bra. For the first time ever, she wished she was bigger, yet the way he looked at her, his eyes hungry, made her feel she was perfect for him.

Then a memory of Hugo assaulted her. When she'd started to bring in money, he'd encouraged her to get a boob job. She should have known then she'd never be good enough for him.

Damn Hugo for getting in the way. She tossed him out of her mind like an overused paper bag she'd crumpled in her fist. *Take that, Hugo.*

Clay reached out as if she were a goddess he would never cease worshipping. Taking her breast in his hand, he flicked his thumb over the tight bead, and Saskia groaned.

She needed him so badly. Now. Scrambling away, she toed off her boots, and eyes on him, she snapped the front clasp of her bra, throwing it aside, then shimmied her leggings down, her panties going with them.

Naked before him, she drank in the fire in his eyes as it turned into a conflagration. He swung to his feet, kicked off his shoes, shoved his pants down his legs. Until he, too, was gloriously naked.

He was all sinewy muscle, sculpted chest, and hard male. Her mouth watered to taste him. Her body wept to have him inside her. "Sofa, floor, or bed?"

He rushed her then, grabbed her up in his muscled arms, and strode toward the bedroom. "Everywhere. Over and over. But first the bed."

She locked her ankles behind his back, his hardness riding her core. Then he fell with her onto the bed, not even throwing the covers aside.

"I need to taste you," he whispered and kissed his way down, down, down, until he was kneeling on the floor, his head between her legs, his tongue playing over her most sensitive parts.

She arched into him, and he added his fingers, gliding in,

out, over that sweet spot. Her tremors came all over again, fast, hard. Fisting her hands in the comforter, she exploded wildly against him, rocking, rolling, taking everything she could from him.

Sensation shot her to the stratosphere where nothing existed but his mouth on her, his fingers inside her, and the climax roaring through her.

When she subsided on the bed, lifting only her head to look at him, his hot blue eyes and his luscious dark hair were the only things she could see. He laughed gently and caressed her with his tongue once more, the aftershocks still shooting through her body. Until finally he sat back and licked his lips, tasting her.

Nothing had ever been more seductive.

She lay on the bed, unable to move. He rose, walked backward to the side table, and pulled out a pack of condoms.

"I don't want you to think I keep an endless supply here." A sheepish grin creased his mouth. "But after last night, I knew I had to find you. I bought them so I wouldn't be caught flat-footed again."

She laughed, sweetness bubbling up inside her. "If you hadn't done that, I would have sent you to the living room for my bag to get the packet I bought today."

They smiled together, the unspoken knowledge between them that they would come together again. It was inevitable. Even predestined.

She rolled and crawled across the bed, throwing aside the extra pillows and pulling the covers to the bottom. "Do you want to ride?" she whispered seductively. "Or shall I?"

CHAPTER ELEVEN

*H*is mind reeled at the knowledge she wasn't afraid to say anything to him. He loved that she gave him choices.

Then he climbed between her legs, pulling her thighs over his, as he sat back on his haunches. "First, I'll ride."

"I like that." Her eyes glittered, and he wanted to fall into her seductive smile.

Rolling on the condom, he sat for a moment, hard and high between her legs, his heart beating fast at the gorgeous sight.

Then he entered her. Slowly. She closed her eyes, groaned, and he loved the look of pure satisfaction on her face. He didn't thrust deep, but rocked gently, playing that hot button between her legs as he moved. Grabbing the brass rails of the headboard, she arched and wrapped her legs around him, trying to take him deeper. He resisted, sliding over her G-spot, relishing the tight grip of her body.

She moaned, opened her eyes to look at him. "Oh God, Clay. Please. More."

He shook his head. "I want you to be coming hard when I drive deep inside you."

She threw her head back, and her muscles clamped down on him. He growled, groaned, barely held off—but he needed her to be coming when he filled her.

Her legs began to shake, tremors shuddering through her body. She was close, and he circled faster around that hot little bead of pleasure between her legs. Then he felt the sharp, tight spasm around him, and she cried out.

He thrust into her in that perfect moment, ground against her. She gripped his butt, pulled him deeper and deeper still. He rode out her climax, taking her hard and fast, relishing every exquisite contraction of her body. Until a pulse rose from deep within him, and with her next spasm, he shot like a rocket inside her, losing his mind with the sensation of her body clutching him and her nails digging into his bare butt.

He lost himself completely inside her.

CLAY WOKE TO FULL DARK, a warm bed, and her mouth on him.

Christ, the feel of her lips, her tongue, her skin against his. This must be what heaven was like. His body rocked to her rhythm as he pushed himself deeper, the action involuntary.

He whispered, "You're driving me crazy." He was so damn thankful no one had climbed the stairs all evening to interrupt them.

She laughed, the sound vibrating through him, ratcheting his need one rung higher on the ladder of desire.

Squeezing his shaft in her hand, she rose to suckle on the tip. Not only was his mind blown, but everything else was too. He gasped out the words a moment before he lost it. "Don't make me come now. I want to come inside you."

She raised her head to look at him, her hand working him, keeping him just short of the edge. "Then you'd better get busy. Because I am so ready for you." Her voice dropped to a husky drawl that strummed every nerve ending in his body. Then she handed him a condom. "This time," she added, "I want to ride."

In a swift, graceful move, she climbed over him. He was so hard that sliding the condom on was easy, her touch turning him to steel. On her knees, she straddled him, her womanhood on display, droplets of her desire shining.

He wet his lips, but he didn't beg. Her hand wrapped around him once more, she whispered, "Are you ready?"

His words came out in a feral curse. "I'm so freaking ready that I might just come before you even get me inside you."

She laughed. "No, you won't."

Then she lowered onto him, so maddeningly slowly that his eyes damn near rolled back in his head. She allowed him to penetrate her inch by slow inch until his erection was buried deep inside her. Then she clenched around him.

He growled. "You're not just driving me crazy. I'm already there. I'll never get my sanity back."

He savored the laughter falling from her lips. "You're not crazy yet. But I'm working on it."

Leaning forward, she braced her hands by his shoulders, moving in that crazy-making rhythm. The quiver of her sex around him told him how good it was for her too. She liked it slow over her G-spot, and he put his finger on her, rubbing that sweet button between her legs.

She gasped, closed her eyes, relishing the sensation the way he relished the feel of her clutching him. They played the game, him trying to push her over into climax, her trying to keep that slow, steady rhythm even as her body began to quake. Her arms shook on the bed, and he knew she had to be close.

But he let her keep taking him at that slow, agonizing pace.

Her skin grew hot against his, and her moans grew louder, cascading from her lips. Then he felt that suddenly tight grip as she convulsed around him. Hands on her hips, he drove up into her, going deep, their bodies pounding. It should have been agony, but nothing had ever felt so good. They worked each other, with cries and unintelligible words, their bodies slick, melded together.

Until he felt that orgasmic pulse inside, and a deep throb shot up his shaft. He growled, he groaned, then he pulled her down one last time, holding her still, grinding against her, giving them both one last glorious blast of pleasure.

Then she collapsed on him.

He held her tight, their hearts pounding against each other, and wondered if he could ever let her go.

———

SHE WANTED to tell herself it was only this good because she'd gone so long without sex. Because nothing could be this good. Better than anything she'd ever known. Better even than the high she got as she stepped back from a piece of her art and knew it was remarkable.

Nothing could feel like the pulse of him inside her. Nothing like his arms enveloping her. Nothing like the musky scent of him, of her, of their sex.

She didn't want to move, didn't want to free him from her tight grip.

Of course, by morning, she'd see it for what it was. Good sex. Nothing wrong with good sex or coming back for more good sex. But in the morning, she would see it was nothing miraculous.

Yet she let the miracle of it wash over her now. Especially when he whispered against her hair, "That was so freaking good." His guttural tone set her cells vibrating.

"We've got the whole night," she murmured. Morning was hours away.

Beneath her, he laughed, and she felt it purr through her.

"We can do it all night long," he agreed. "But we need sustenance first."

When she sat up on him, the night air cooled the perspiration on her skin, and she ran her hand over his chest, feeling that same delicious sweat. There was a part of her that didn't want to let him go.

But she couldn't admit that. "There's all that leftover Japanese food." Climbing off the bed, she strolled naked out of his bedroom, feeling his eyes on her the entire way.

In the living area, she grabbed his shirt off the floor and tugged it on. There was still one button left. Then she pulled everything out of the refrigerator. She already had the microwave whirring when he came in, wearing a pair of sweats.

Standing behind her, he blanketed her back with his bare chest as he enfolded her in his arms. When the microwave beeped, they ate while standing at the counter, feeding each other, stealing kisses between bites and sips of beer.

He made love to her twice more in the night.

In the morning, she would call it *good sex*. But for now, she'd never known lovemaking like this in her life.

SASKIA LAY SLEEPING in his bed, the morning rays bathing her body in jewel tones. Clay jogged out for croissants from the corner bakery, returning to hear the shower running. More than anything—certainly more than was good for him—he wanted to step under the spray with her and make love to her again, with his hands, his tongue, his lips, his body.

But maybe she needed a rest. He brewed coffee, using perfectly roasted beans imported from Kenya by Will Franconi, Maverick importer extraordinaire.

He smelled her then, scented with his manly shampoo.

It wasn't the rich coffee aroma or the croissants that made him salivate. It was her.

He turned to find her dressed in the same outfit she'd worn yesterday, though he wished she were still wearing his shirt, as if she'd claimed it and him. With a quick glance at the sofa, he saw his clothes were now neatly folded.

"Thank you," she said with an exaggerated groan. "Coffee. Just what I need."

He poured her a mug, pushing it toward her along with the cream.

She poured liberally while he took his black.

She didn't meet his eyes, which was unusual for her. When discussing her boss and his artwork, even when talking to all the artists downstairs, she'd watched with rapt attention, listening to every word.

"I don't normally do this," she said. "Keep jumping into the bed of a man I barely know." Just as he thought, she felt a little awkward with him. "Not even once, let alone twice." Her lips curved with the slightest hint of the beautiful smile that always did him in.

She gestured to the coffee and breakfast before them. "But you do, don't you?"

Busted. He was the furthest thing from a monk. Although he didn't jump into *every* bed. Nor did he flit from woman to woman, one right after the other. That would be just plain rude.

He didn't want to lie. "Yes," he admitted. "I've done this a few times. But—"

She held up her hand. "You don't need to explain. Straight-up sex without emotional ties is clearly working for us." She fluttered a hand between them. "So far, at least." A beat of silence fell before she said, "What if we agree that when one of us wants out of whatever it is we're doing, we just say so and it's done? We won't let it affect our working relationship."

Last night, she'd said *two or three times*. His heart bloomed with the idea that she was offering more. Except that he didn't want straight-up, unemotional sex. Not with her. It was insta-lust, of course, because they'd known each other only two days.

But his gut, maybe even his heart, was telling him it could be so much more.

If only she gave it a chance.

***

EVEN AFTER ALL HER emotions of last night, when morning came, Saskia knew it had to be just sex and nothing else. It was the only way she could work. Yet a tiny part of her heart lurched. Especially since she was lying to him about who she was.

The thought wrapped her insides up in a neat, guilty bow. How could she keep on lying to him? But how could she tell him the truth? She'd just offered him a casual relationship. It was that word. *Relationship*. It didn't imply straight-up sex with no emotional entanglements.

The worst was that she actually *liked* him.

A part of her—tiny but growing—felt she needed to tell him the truth.

But the bigger part shouted that the only way to keep a

secret was by telling no one. If she even hinted to Clay that she was San Holo, she'd have to explain why she worked this way. She'd have to tell him about her parents, about the intervening years, about Hugo and how much trust she'd put in a man who hadn't deserved it.

She just couldn't admit it all and see the regard Clay had for her drain from his gaze.

Wrapping her hands around the coffee mug, she sipped gratefully, then took a croissant.

When she bit into it, it felt almost as though she were biting into Eve's apple.

CHAPTER TWELVE

Camille and Dane were out and about in San Francisco for the morning, though Fernsby suspected that, as soon as he left the flat, they'd sneak back into bed. Young love. Those two had googly eyes for each other, even if Dane was now just shy of forty.

But it was the perfect opportunity for Fernsby to visit Clay Harrington's warehouse. He had yet to see Charlene Ballard's latest sculpture, and Lord Rexford needed a long walk on this beautiful Friday morning in spring. As did Fernsby. It was how he kept fit. How he kept the mini dachshund fit, too, with all the treats Dane sneaked to the dog behind his back.

He'd stopped at the bookstore along the way—another reason for the excursion.

As he entered Clay's warehouse of artists' studios, he was elated to find the statue gleaming in the morning sunlight that fell through the skylight above.

Charlene Ballard was indeed a magnificent metal artist. He read the piece's title plaque—*The Discus Thrower*—then took his time surveying the sculpture from all angles.

As he made the full circuit, he became aware of Clay watching him. Beside him stood the most beautiful of ladies, with flawless skin, silky dark hair, a delightful flowery tunic sweater, and black leggings showcasing toned calves as if she, like he, walked or hiked. Even the combat boots she wore, Doc Martens or some such thing, somehow suited her despite her delicate frame.

He perused the couple even as he appeared to peruse the statue. Clay stood a smidge too close to the woman who, Fernsby concluded, was somewhere in her early thirties, despite a costume that might be worn by someone ten years younger. A sensual aura surrounded them, like a bubble that would burst if he poked it.

Well, well, well. Had the dear fellow been caught at last?

He'd known Clay Harrington for sixteen years, since he'd first come to work for Dane as his most excellent butler. He'd seen Clay grow from a high school boy to a green university student receiving his inestimable education at Harvard to the impressive man who stood before him now. In all that time—Fernsby knew the ins and outs of the entire family—he had never seen that enchanted yet somewhat mystified look on the young man's face. As though he'd stumbled onto something he hadn't expected, hadn't wanted, and suddenly found he couldn't live without.

Fernsby wanted to applaud. Or perhaps dance a jig around Charlene Ballard's amazing sculpture. But being Fernsby, he merely said, "I hope I'm not disturbing you," waiting a beat before adding, "Sir," and letting his gaze settle upon the young woman.

Instead of introducing him, which Clay should have done as propriety dictated, the young man asked, "What are you reading?" He pointed at the book under Fernsby's arm.

Fernsby held it up. "It's the latest Mathilda Sullivan mystery. I've read all her books." He did not extol the virtues of Mathilda Sullivan's writing nor admit the books were marvelous. He had the entire series in hardback and had read each more than once.

Someday, perhaps, if the deity willed it, he might have them autographed.

Then he announced, "Lord Rexford and I—" He never called the long-haired dachshund T. Rex, the way everyone else did. "—were out for a stroll and decided to stop by to see Charlene Ballard's latest creation." He looked down his nose at Clay. "It would be mere politeness to introduce me to your lovely friend." Again, after a pause, he added, "Sir."

"Of course," Clay said, as if he were so enamored that he thought Fernsby would naturally extract her name from his very thoughts. "This is Saskia Oliver. I'm negotiating a commission with San Holo, the famous street artist, and Saskia is his assistant."

"And I am Fernsby." No further explanation was necessary. He raised a brow, looked at the young woman, liked her without knowing another thing about her, and held out his hand. "So nice to meet you, Saskia."

She shook with a good grip. He liked a woman who had a good grip.

He perambulated around the sculpture once more, stopping at a point where he could see the two of them standing close together. "Ms. Ballard's latest work is once again amazing."

Charlene Ballard patrolled junkyards and garage sales for bits and pieces she melded into the most intricate artwork. She was also engaged to Maverick media mogul Sebastian Montgomery.

When on earth would the two get married? Perhaps he needed to work his magic with them, as he had with Dane and Camille, and with Ransom and Ava, Clay's older sister.

So many unmarried couples. So many unattached Harringtons.

His work was cut out for him.

But now he needed to give his unbiased analysis of the sculpture. He stroked his chin thoughtfully. "It feels as though the subject is angry. Throwing away his work because he thinks it doesn't measure up." He glanced at Clay. "Is that the message you hope to give the artists here?"

He gazed at the artist's palette in *The Discus Thrower*'s hand. He couldn't imagine that had been Charlene's intention.

But instead of Clay defending his choice, the young woman stepped forward. Saskia. Such a lovely name. Hopefully she didn't shorten it to something appalling like Sas.

"Look at the young man's face." She pointed to *The Discus Thrower*, his face in bronze while the rest of his body was metal gears and other odds and ends welded together. "He's glowing. Look at the palette. It's the only color in the entire statue. All the colors he could want to use. He's not throwing *away* his art. He's throwing everything *into* his art—all his energy, all his creativity. That's what it represents to me."

This incredible insight from an assistant? She was absolutely right. She had read its true meaning. While Fernsby, on purpose, because he'd wanted to gauge their reactions, had expressed the opposite view.

She was like Clay. He wasn't an artist, but he lived in the art world, and he understood both artists and their work. Though she might be an assistant, this young woman knew the artistic temperament.

Fernsby gladly admitted his error. "Sometimes you believe art says one thing. But when you look closely, you find it says exactly the opposite. Thank you for pointing this out to me, young lady."

She smiled, a radiant smile, which she then turned on Clay.

Shooting stars exploded between them. They'd spent the night together. Fernsby was absolutely sure. Because Clay Harrington had never looked at a woman like that.

This young woman was real. She had depth.

She was perfect for him.

SASKIA MET Adrian for lunch on Saturday at a trendy restaurant on Market Street, elegant with white tablecloths, crystal wineglasses, and busboys carrying little scrapers to scoop away breadcrumbs. The tables were separated by planters, giving the patrons a sense of privacy.

Adrian had chosen a window table, because she enjoyed watching the passersby. "This place is owned by Ransom Yates."

Saskia gave her a gentle, "Mmm," not terribly interested in who owned the restaurant.

Adrian raised one eyebrow. "Ransom Yates is now dating Ava Harrington." She paused, waiting for Saskia's reaction.

Saskia didn't feel like giving one. She studied the menu instead.

"She's Clay Harrington's older sister." Adrian sat back, giving Saskia a self-satisfied smile.

"Are you trying to worm information out of me about what I've been doing with Clay over the last couple of days?"

Adrian gave a dramatic eye roll. "I can't believe I actually have to drag the details out of you." She ended on a note of exasperation.

Adrian had waited two days before she'd forced a meeting with Saskia—which for Adrian was being quite patient. Normally, she'd have called right after that first meeting.

Saskia had let things slide because the commission was with Clay. And because she'd slept with him.

It wasn't just one night. It wasn't just two nights. She had no intention of stopping. Still scrutinizing the menu, she admitted, "I slept with him again. In fact, I've been at his place every night."

Adrian clapped once, not enough to draw attention. "I knew you wouldn't be able to stay away from him. Out of his bed, I mean." A gleeful sparkle lit her eyes.

Saskia set down her menu, leaned her elbows on the table, laced her fingers, and rested her chin on them as she looked at her friend. "Here's the problem."

Adrian choked out a laugh. "How can there be a problem when you're sleeping with a disgustingly sexy billionaire who wants to give you a commission where you command the price?"

Saskia pursed her lips.

Adrian rushed on, "Don't tell me it's because he's Clay Harrington."

"I'm over that problem," Saskia said. "Now I feel bad that I'm not being truthful with him."

Adrian stared at her long enough for their waiter to step up to the table. Dressed in a white shirt and black pants, he was far above casual. All he needed was a tie and a suit jacket and he could have been in a boardroom. "What can I get you ladies? We have an amazing peach mimosa."

Adrian jumped on the offer immediately. "We'll both have one."

"Could we also have water, please?" Saskia added.

"Of course," the waiter said effusively.

Before he could leave to get their drinks, Adrian said, "We're ready to order as well." She raised an eyebrow at Saskia, who simply nodded. "I'll have the sand dabs."

"Excellent choice." He scribbled on his pad and turned to Saskia.

Still undecided, she said the first thing that popped into her mind. "Shrimp Louis, please."

The man beamed. "Also excellent. I'll be back with your drinks."

"They're very attentive here." Adrian turned to Saskia when he was gone. "You probably thought I'd forget about what you just said." She leaned forward, mirroring Saskia's elbows on the table. "You've never had a problem playing the assistant before. What makes Clay different?"

Saskia heaved out a breath. "Because I'm sleeping with him."

Adrian gave a jerky shake of her head. "You slept with him on Wednesday night and had no compunction about pretending to be San Holo's assistant on Thursday. What's changed?"

"He's just..." She didn't know how to describe Clay or her feelings about him. "He just seems like a nice guy."

Adrian looked her over with a penetrating gaze. "You've avoided men like him for years. Even though he *seems to be a nice guy*—" She added finger quotes. "—he's still a billionaire. I don't imagine you get to that place without a few black marks on your soul."

"That's just it," Saskia said with an urgent hiss. "I don't think he has any black marks."

Adrian stared at her. Finally, as if she were getting over her shock, she said, "Everyone has black marks on their soul."

Saskia snorted a humorless laugh. "I thought that was only billionaires."

Adrian growled. She was pretty when she growled like that. Men must love it. "I can't believe what's gotten into you. First, you sleep with a man for the first time in five years. Which I think is absolutely marvelous. But then, instead of shutting down this commission immediately, you want to investigate. And now you feel guilty about keeping secrets from the client? You have me worried, girlfriend."

Saskia said in her own defense, "I've never had a problem keeping my secret before because I wasn't sleeping with the client. This is completely different."

The waiter brought their drinks at just that moment. How much had he overheard? Then again, who cared? Smiling, he set the glasses on the table. "Enjoy, ladies." And whisked away.

Adrian picked up her glass, tilting it toward Saskia's, and they clinked. The peach mimosa was delicious, sliding down Saskia's throat, the bubbles making her giddy. But maybe that was Clay and last night. All the nights.

The interruption had given Adrian time to think. "He's gotten to you in a way no one else has." She stared Saskia down.

In little more than a whisper, Saskia said, "Yeah. He has."

Adrian enjoyed another sip. "Which brings me to the real reason I asked you out to lunch. I gave you two days to think about the commission. I didn't even call. Aren't you proud of me?"

Saskia said dryly, "You already said you waited because I slept with the client."

Adrian held up a silencing finger. "But I'm still proud of you." She just had to push. "Have you made up your mind?"

Saskia needed another gulp of mimosa. "I want to do it. It's a huge challenge. I can't turn that down. It's not just the money." Finally, she sighed. "I just don't know how I'll keep my secret from him the entire time. He actually lives at the warehouse. He's got his own apartment above all the artists' studios." Which was a major complication.

That didn't seem to faze Adrian, who said softly, "Maybe you don't need to keep it from him."

Saskia thought about that. If she asked Clay not to tell anyone, he wouldn't. But he would be so disappointed if she didn't tell Dylan. Though Dylan was a great kid, she feared that in his excitement, the secret would get out. Even if he never meant to give it away.

"I just don't know." Then she added, "But I'm going to take the commission anyway."

Adrian didn't jump with glee, though Saskia suspected she wanted to. "I'll get to work on the contract, then."

"Wait until I tell him first, okay?"

The waiter arrived with their sand dabs and Shrimp Louis. When he was gone, Adrian heaved a great sigh. "I hate to do this, but I've got some rather unpleasant news." She let the word hang while Saskia's stomach dropped. "I heard from one of my other clients that Hugo is in town."

Saskia's heart jumped into her throat, strangling her.

Adrian gave her a moment to digest the bad news without having to answer. "She even had the gall to say I should snap him up if he's looking for a new agent."

Saskia let out a disgusted, "Oh my God."

But Adrian said smugly, as if she were buffing her nails against her stylish jacket, "I told her I'd rather handle a rattlesnake than Hugo Lewis."

"You don't think he's looking for me?" Saskia actually trembled.

Adrian let out a snort, not caring what anyone around them might think. "God, no. He can't have a clue you're in San Francisco." Then she shrugged. "But just in case, be on the lookout and keep on the down low."

Wasn't this the perfect moment for Hugo to show up? When she'd finally taken another man into her bed.

Hugo had always had impeccable timing.

SASKIA REFUSED a latte and rushed out of the restaurant while Adrian stayed to sip her espresso.

Adrian badly wanted Saskia to find someone who would heal her heart after what that ass Hugo had done to her. Damn the man for showing up now. Maybe she shouldn't have told Saskia. But better hearing it from a friend than having a chance meeting on the street.

Saskia badly needed a new man. Five years had been far too long. She had such a giving heart, but she'd buried it deep. There was another problem besides Hugo, and that was Clay Harrington. Adrian feared he wasn't the right man to heal Saskia's heart. If only he wasn't in the art world. If only he wouldn't care that Saskia was actually San Holo.

But Saskia had been with him three nights in a row.

While part of Adrian had to admit she was a little jealous, she also felt that Saskia was getting in too deep too fast.

Then again, who was she to talk?

Maybe *she* needed someone to heal her heart. Except that Adrian's heart had never been broken. Between going to uni, getting her law degree, moving to the States, and setting up her agency, she'd never given herself the chance to have her heart broken. She'd been too busy for anything long term and always kept everything short term. So far, that suited her fine.

But listening to Saskia gush about Clay, seeing that glow on her friend's face, Adrian was beginning to think that maybe it was time to find a long-term someone.

She just had to figure out how to meet that perfect man.

CHAPTER THIRTEEN

Over the weekend, Clay had taken her out to dinner, and Saskia couldn't help keeping an eye out for Hugo. The exclusive, expensive restaurant was just the kind of place where he'd want to be seen by all the right people. He would throw himself at everyone who was anyone, in case he could somehow use them later.

Those two or three nights she'd planned to sleep with Clay had turned into five. By Monday morning, Saskia knew in her petrified little heart that she couldn't stop.

He'd said he wanted a mural relating to art, in whatever way San Holo wished to portray it. How could she resist? But despite telling Adrian she'd take the commission, she had yet to tell Clay about San's decision.

She claimed she was still scoping everything out for San, taking pictures so she could tell him what the space was like. With a new client, she usually made up her mind right away. She could tell whether she'd be able to work with the person. And she'd never once considered telling them who she was.

After five nights with Clay, the fact that she wasn't being truthful weighed heavily on her. This thing with Clay was so different from any other client she'd ever had. But then, she'd never wanted to sleep with any of them.

On Sunday, Adrian texted her a few times.

Have you told him yet?

Are you stalling?

Have you changed your mind?

Adrian didn't call her, but the texts were pressure enough.

After another night with him blowing her mind, then this morning's elaborate breakfast of bacon, eggs, fried potatoes, and fried tomatoes that reminded her of a full English back home, she didn't know how she could say no. She didn't *want* to say no.

But she wasn't sure how she could say yes, with all her lies choking her.

———

WHEN THE DOOR of Clay's apartment opened and an unfamiliar man walked into the loft, Saskia jumped like a frightened rabbit and almost knocked over her juice glass on the breakfast bar.

"Sorry," Clay said. "I should have warned you. I saw him coming on the monitor and opened the door for him." It had been automatic to push the button on the end of the bar to unlock the door. "Saskia Oliver, this is Gareth Tate." He clapped his best friend on the back.

Her shock clearly fading, Saskia bounded from the barstool and stuck out her hand. Before Clay could say that Gareth was just dropping off some contracts for him to sign, she jumped in. "You must be one of Clay's artists. What's your medium?"

Clay tensed. He'd told her only part of the story the other night—that his friend's parents hadn't appreciated his art. She obviously didn't realize Gareth was that friend. Or that his art was a closed subject. Back in university, Gareth had been a prolific painter. Clay had even helped him mount a show for his work. It hadn't gone well. No, that was too mild. Gareth's work had been trashed. The light-hearted, artistic Gareth had disappeared after that, turning into this buttoned-up, executive-style man before them. Even his rich, coffee-colored eyes had become a simple brown.

But Saskia was already going through a litany of artistic endeavors. "Sculptor, metal artist, potter, painter?"

Clay thanked heaven that Gareth didn't freak out. Instead, he flapped a hand as if he were trying to ward off everything she said. "Oh no, I don't paint anymore. I'm Clay's lawyer."

She looked first to Clay, then back to Gareth. "Oh," she said with obvious disappointment. "So you used to paint, but don't anymore?" When Gareth didn't answer, she asked, "Why did you stop?"

Clay cringed, having no idea how to avert this disaster. He wasn't a helpless man, but he felt helpless now.

Gareth shrugged his wide shoulders beneath the tailored suit jacket. "Long story. The art world just wasn't for me."

She tucked her chin, gazing at Gareth as if she were a cat trying to figure out why he didn't immediately bend down to scratch her ears. "Really?" Then she puffed out just a sound. "Hmm." She looked him up and down, from his short lawyerly auburn hair to that buttoned suit jacket to his shiny loafers. "Because you've definitely got that artist vibe about you."

Having seen her take in his appearance, Gareth admitted, "I dabbled in college."

She touched him, just a sweep of her fingers across his forearm. No one had seen Gareth's artwork since their university days. He'd hidden it all away, taken back everything he'd given Clay to put in the show. Clay was pretty sure he'd destroyed it all.

But Saskia was so enchanting. Whatever Gareth felt in that touch made his tension melt away. She cocked her head again, as if the careful animal in her scented that Gareth wasn't a threat and that maybe he was about to give her a treat.

She asked softly, "Do you display it in your house just for you to see?"

Clay felt jittery, his gaze flashing between the two of them. Gareth would walk out now.

Instead, his friend smiled. A real smile. Not a trapped smile. A smile that reminded Clay of the Gareth of ten years ago. When he'd been a happy artist instead of a staid lawyer. Then his friend shocked the hell out of him by saying, "No. It's all in a storage unit."

Clay barely stopped his jaw from hitting the floor. How had he simply assumed Gareth had gotten rid of it all, even as he mourned its loss?

But Saskia, that amazing woman, had drawn it out of him. She was incredible. A miracle worker.

She blew Clay away yet again by saying, "I'd love to see it sometime."

Then Gareth did the most staggering thing. He pulled out his phone, scrolled through the contents, and finally said, "I have pictures."

Saskia stepped inside his personal space to look at his phone. Clay couldn't move. He wasn't merely astounded—he was completely dumbstruck. Not just by Saskia and how she'd gotten Gareth to open up in less than ten minutes, but by Gareth himself. Clay wanted to horn in on their moment, to gaze at the photos. But he stood back watching, when normally he would never have allowed himself to be a mere observer.

All the time, he'd honestly believed Gareth had burned all his paintings. But Clay saw the truth. Gareth couldn't bear to destroy his work. His heart and soul lived in those paintings. He was finally seeing the true Gareth again after so long. The one whose art still inhabited him.

Saskia said on barely a breath, "This is amazing." She knew art. She worked for San Holo.

Clay couldn't stop himself. He had to see the painting Gareth had shown her.

He barely swallowed a gasp.

It was the self-portrait. But a completely disjointed self-portrait—the nose in the wrong place, the eyes too far to the left, everything off-kilter. It was this painting the critics had trashed.

Clay could still remember the comments.

Do you think you're van Gogh or Picasso?

This is just mimicry.

The artist is merely blending other people's styles. He has no style of his own, and I doubt he ever will.

But Saskia knew none of that. "Wow, this is a self-portrait, isn't it?" She looked at Gareth as if she saw him in a way Clay hadn't for years. "Looks like you felt all twisted up about which direction your life should take—law or art?"

She was spot-on.

It was how Gareth had sometimes felt back then, beneath the happy-go-lucky façade, forced into law school by his parents but wanting only to paint. With Clay pulling him in the other direction, wanting him to put his art out there.

Saskia saw it all in only one self-portrait.

Stepping back, she surveyed Gareth, her face glowing. "This is brilliant. Why aren't you doing this?"

Gareth shrugged again. "Because I'm a lawyer."

She laughed that beautiful laugh. "Well, you need to dump the day job and get into one of Clay's studios." She turned to

Clay, her smile as brilliant as Gareth's self-portrait. "And you need to find a new lawyer."

He expected Gareth to fob her off, but his incredible artist friend said, "You know, you make me think maybe it's time to try again."

Clay wanted to hug her, kiss her, grab her up in his arms and whirl around the room with her.

Here was a woman he could be with for more than a few weeks, a few months, or even a year.

Here was a woman he could fall for.

CLAY TURNED to her the moment the door closed behind Gareth and the contracts. "You're amazing."

His statement stunned Saskia. "What do you mean?"

"I mean that Gareth hasn't talked about his art in ten years. I didn't even know he'd kept all his canvases."

"I'm sorry," she said. "I didn't mean—"

"You just did an incredible thing." His voice dipped low, as if emotion had overtaken him. "He even said he'd think about painting again."

His big, warm hands cupped her face, his lips on hers. He kissed her with fervor and yet with reverence, then whispered against her mouth, "Thank you for doing that for him."

She had to back off a step. "I didn't do anything but look at his paintings."

Clay guided her to the couch, pulling her onto his lap, his arms wrapped around her. "Let me tell you what happened when we were at university. Then you'll understand what an extraordinary thing this is."

She heard the ache in his slow tones and saw it in his eyes, which had gone a paler shade of blue. "He was such a fantastic painter. That self-portrait was the tip of the iceberg.

He was happiest when he was working on a new painting. But his parents wanted him to be a lawyer."

She ran her hand through his hair. "He's the friend you mentioned the other night, the one whose parents didn't like his art?"

He nodded. "They said he'd never make a living as an artist. That he'd be, quote, a starving artist, unquote, and they wouldn't pay for a starving artist to go to university. That if he wanted a Harvard education, it was to be at Harvard Law, like his father."

Her heart went out to Gareth, and she thought of how her parents had said her art would never be good enough. But it just wasn't good enough for *them*. The rest of the world didn't agree.

"I'm so sorry for him," she said, her voice breathy with emotion.

"They never actually belittled his art. They never *said* it," he emphasized. "But it was there in the way they harped on him, comparing him to van Gogh, who died a pauper. Nothing about how great his art was, only that he'd starved for it. If only he could paint more like this artist or that artist. Gareth was too offbeat, too out of step." He leaned his head back against the sofa, sighing heavily.

She felt his heart break for his friend. Her heart broke, too, for Gareth, another soul whose parents just couldn't handle who their kid really was.

"I hear how much it hurt you to watch him with his parents," she murmured, her voice soothing.

He laughed, soft yet full of derision. "Maybe I encouraged him even more because of how much they discouraged him. I wanted him to sell and be a great success. I knew his art was worth that."

"You gave him what his parents couldn't."

He shook his head. "I pushed him too hard. I helped get

that show together for him." He scrubbed a hand down his face. "But the critics absolutely trashed him, said his work was just a copy of much better artists. That if he wanted to be like van Gogh, he should just cut off his ear and be done with it. It was excruciating."

She leaned into him, rubbed her cheek against his. "I'm so sorry. That must have been so horrible for him. And for you."

She felt him swallow, how hard it was going down, and his voice choked as he said, "I found him in his room with some pill bottles lined up. He hadn't taken anything. I just saw those bottles all in a row. I don't know where he got them or what the pills actually were."

"But he didn't take them. You stopped him."

Again, he shook his head. "Maybe he never intended to. But it hit me like a gut punch. I kept thinking how I'd pushed him to put his stuff out there. I allowed him to be subjected to what they threw at him."

She felt everything right along with him. She understood Gareth's despair, how badly it hurt when you weren't allowed to be what you needed to be. She'd gone the starving artist route, while Gareth had left his art behind. That must have ripped him in half. It had ripped Clay apart too.

Then she saw the truth. She pulled back enough for him to see her face as she spoke. "That's why you built your warehouses for artists. To give them space, to help them find their own place. Because of Gareth."

He let out a breath. "I saw him totally trashed, and his parents adding fuel to the fire, telling him that if he'd listened to them, he'd never have been so hurt." Something glimmered in his eyes—not tears, maybe just the pain he'd felt all those years ago. "If I could have given a spot to Gareth, I would have. But he never considered it. He threw out all his art supplies long ago. That's why I thought he'd destroyed all his paintings." He stroked her face. "I never would have known if you hadn't talked to him."

He'd begun the conversation by saying she was amazing. But in the circle of his arms, hearing his story, she knew he was the amazing one. He had loved his friend so much that he'd built warehouses all over the country for artists. He'd used the money he received for his nutrition app to start his platform for them. Even though he'd thought his friend would never use a studio, he'd built them anyway.

Her first impression of a man using artists for his own gain had been completely and totally wrong. He'd created all of this with the purest of hearts. Out of friendship. He wasn't a user. He was a giver.

Her mind raced. How could she incorporate that into the mural? How could she show this community of artists? It wasn't just the artists themselves, it was all the people who believed in them too. It was friends like Clay.

In that moment, she so badly wanted to reveal herself as San Holo. She'd hated lying to him when she was sleeping with him. She hated it even more after seeing the kind of man he truly was.

Yet she'd trapped herself in this web. Her anonymity was San Holo's trademark. It was the artist's mystique. It also protected her from men like Hugo Lewis. But Clay was nothing like Hugo. He wouldn't steal from her. But her secret had tied her up with no way out. She couldn't tell Clay without Clay telling Dylan. From there, it would grow, the way releasing that image of her latest work on social media had grown.

She wouldn't be able to control it.

And Clay would hate her for her lies.

Maybe he felt some of her inner turmoil, because he reached up to caress her cheek. "In some ways, you and

Gareth are alike. He didn't think his art was good enough. Neither do you."

She saw the similarities—their unacceptable art, parents who didn't believe in them. But there was a bigger difference. She *had* believed in her art. Her parents had disowned her for it. She wanted to laugh, an incredibly sad laugh. Not only had they disowned her, they'd never wanted her in the first place. She'd been an accident. They'd even thought about getting rid of her—then had the nerve to tell her how grateful she should be that they hadn't.

Clay's voice pulled her back. "You were so good at encouraging Gareth. Dylan too. Maybe you need some encouragement to try your art again."

It was almost like he was forcing another lie out of her. "No." She shook her head. "I don't think so."

But he wouldn't let it go. "I don't understand why San Holo doesn't encourage you." Then, on a lighter note, he added, "I really need to have a talk with San about how he should treat his employees. Maybe I'll look at your stuff and tell him he needs to find a new assistant."

She almost laughed. "Are you paying me back for saying you need a new lawyer?"

His smile warmed her, especially after the emotion they'd just gone through together. "Tell me who San Holo is so I can have that talk with him."

She wagged a finger in his face. "You're so tricky, but no, I'll never tell you." Then she had to say, "Really, my art is nothing like Gareth's. A person knows their own limits."

Though they were joking, the guilt stabbed her again. *I'll never tell you.* It sounded so final. How could she keep on sleeping with a man who didn't know who she really was? The thought was an ache in her soul.

For the first time in five years, since she'd become San Holo, she wanted to tell, wanted to take credit. She wanted Clay to look at her like she was a genius, wanted to feel his admiration. To know that *she* was San Holo—not some man, but *her*.

But wanting all those things from Clay was like walking on hot coals and expecting them not to burn her feet. She'd been alone a long time, and it had worked well for her. Even though Clay was nothing like Hugo, he was still a threat to the life she'd built for herself.

She put the final question to him. "If San Holo does agree to do your mural, are you going to turn the whole thing down because he won't meet with you?"

He didn't even hesitate. "I want the mural. But I also want Dylan to meet his hero." She actually winced as he went on, "I'm hoping that after he starts the mural, he'll change his mind." Then he smiled, the sexy, wicked smile that got her blood pumping. "And I'm going to work on you about taking up your art again."

He wasn't just dangerous; he was a triple threat.

But she knew what she had to do.

SASKIA COULDN'T EVEN REMEMBER the excuse she gave Clay for leaving his flat only an hour after Gareth. The moment she was out on the street, she called Adrian. "In thirty minutes," she said before Adrian could get out a word, "I want you to call Clay and tell him that San Holo will paint his mural."

She could almost hear Adrian fall out of her seat. Her friend laughed. Then they laughed together. Saskia added, feeling the smile shooting to Adrian all the way through the phone, "I've also found you a new client."

Gareth Tate really needed to give up his law career.

And San Holo needed to fill the walls of Clay's entire warehouse with all the images wanting to burst out of her.

CHAPTER FOURTEEN

*N*o boilerplate contract would do for this commission. Adrian and Saskia had gone over the details, and two days later, on Wednesday morning, they gathered in Adrian's office. Saskia, the supposed assistant, Clay, who was seated at the desk opposite Adrian, and Gareth Tate.

Adrian had sent a copy to both of them, and Clay and Gareth would have had a long conversation about the terms.

Sitting on the sofa, Saskia tried not to chew nervously on a thumbnail while she waited to hear what Clay had to say.

Adrian spoke formally. "We've detailed how your expectations will be handled."

Clay looked first at Adrian, then at Saskia, and he chuckled softly. "According to this, I'd better not have a lot of expectations."

Adrian raised an eyebrow. "I told you how San Holo works. So did Saskia. You agree to give him free rein within your guidelines."

Clay laughed again, the same good-natured laugh he used with Dylan or any number of artists in his warehouse. "It seems I'm allowed a few guidelines," he drawled, then looked directly at Saskia. "Saskia has practically guaranteed I won't be disappointed."

Before Saskia could say anything, Adrian shot back, "Very few of our clients have been. In fact, most were amazed that San Holo gave them what they were looking for, even if they didn't know exactly what that was."

Gareth stood against the wall next to the water cooler, arms folded, probably wondering what the hell Clay had gotten himself into. Adrian turned to him. "I'm sure you've looked for flaws in the contract. But you won't find them."

He smiled, saying in a deep but warm voice, "All I do is warn Clay. He signs what he wants."

That described Clay precisely. He would listen to his lawyer, but he would do what he wanted. Though she'd known him only a week, Saskia understood that about him.

"Of course," Adrian said, "the contract also stipulates that you will protect San Holo's identity with tents around the scaffolding and security keeping people away." She pointed at Clay. "No one gets past security. Not even you."

Clay closed his eyes, his lips stretched in a grin. Until, again, he glanced at Saskia. She'd been quiet during the meeting, afraid she'd beg him to sign the contract. He'd been elated when Adrian called to tell him San Holo had accepted the commission. The sum was extraordinary, more than she'd been paid for any mural to date. Then again, it was an entire building, not just one wall. Before she even started to paint, she'd have to make hundreds of sketches, testing ideas and throwing many out before she decided on the final.

But had she persuaded him to stop trying to uncover San Holo's identity?

Feeling his cheeky smile deep down inside her, igniting all her nerve endings the way his touch did, she knew he hadn't given up. He'd keep at her as long as she allowed him to. He wasn't above letting Dylan do his dirty work either, telling her how badly he wanted to meet his idol. What would he think if he knew his hero was actually a heroine?

"I'm ready to sign," Clay said. After a flourish of his pen, he rose and held out his hand to Saskia. "Why don't we get some lunch and let the two lawyers hammer out the rest of the details?"

Saskia had her lovely Victorian in the Haight for which she'd paid cash, and she did what she wanted, ate where she wanted, flew off for two- or three-day trips to foreign locales where she could do her street art, and booked a first-class ticket if she wanted.

But this commission? It put her on a whole different plane, no pun intended.

She stood and took his hand, the touch shooting heat through her. "That would be lovely." Then she added, "But I need to get together with San this afternoon and go over more details." She had to start working on her sketches.

That could become a future problem. Clay would wonder why she wasn't spending every night with him as she had over the past week. But nights were when she did her best work. And she certainly couldn't do that work in front of Clay.

She'd have to make excuses. Or change her habits and work during the day.

Nights making sketches? Or nights in Clay's bed?

There really wasn't a choice.

THE DOOR CLOSED behind Saskia and the client. The new boyfriend.

It was an exceptionally lucrative contract. Adrian hadn't tried to push Saskia into it. Her friend had to make up her own mind. But Adrian knew in her heart that this would be as much a game-changer as that very first mural bearing the fleur-de-lis had been.

She turned to Gareth as he said, "Since Clay has already signed, there's really no further details to work out."

She smiled at him. "I wasn't talking about those details."

He pulled out the chair Clay had been sitting in and faced her.

The man was definitely a good-looking bloke. Tall, oh yes, she'd seen that as he leaned against the wall. He had beautiful muscles, sculpted from hard workouts. She would love to give them a squeeze. He wore his auburn hair short, the way she liked it, and his jaw clean-shaven, also the way she liked it. Although a little scruff on his chin after five o'clock would be delightful. And those eyes, the color of her first cup of coffee in the morning and the piece of dark chocolate she allowed herself in the evening.

She held in a dreamy sigh. Because this man might become something more than just a handsome man whose muscles she'd like to squeeze.

"Saskia told me you're a painter. She was quite impressed with your art."

The fine lines of his face seemed to harden a moment, though she had no idea why. So she added, "I'd love to see your work."

"Saskia might've exaggerated," he drawled.

"Why don't you let me decide?"

He took out his mobile phone, scrolled, tapped, then handed it to her.

How she wished she had these up on her big monitor. The first was an amazing self-portrait, the one Saskia had told her about. It was all the Impressionists rolled into one, and yet, it was uniquely this man's. Even without seeing it in the flesh, so to speak, she felt the emotion brimming in every line, every swirl of paint, every blotch of color. It was brilliant. There was no other word for it.

She asked politely, "May I look at the rest?"

He gave her a simple, "Yes."

There were paintings of Harvard University, rowers on the river, one of Clay, seascapes, cityscapes. And people. He was exceptionally good with people's faces, showing their emotions with just a few strokes.

She couldn't help herself. "Why are you hiding all this on your mobile? You should be selling it."

He shrugged, the move so eloquent that it told her all the reasons why. "I realized back in university that I would make a better lawyer than an artist."

She snorted, not caring how inelegant it sounded. "Balderdash." An archaic word, but better than *bollocks*.

"There were several critics who disagreed with you."

His gaze fastened on her lips as she licked them. "So you did put your work out there. And what? Someone told you it was rubbish?" It was blunt, but she always spoke bluntly.

"I was royally trashed," he admitted.

She felt his pain. Being Clay's age, in his early thirties, whatever happened had gone down ten years ago. Wounds that immense took years to heal. Saskia still hadn't healed from hers.

"So you reinvented yourself as a lawyer," she said, rather than using the British term *solicitor*.

He merely nodded.

Leaning back in her chair, she toyed with a pen. "I had to reinvent myself too. I came to the States and decided to become an agent. I still use my law qualification, which helps me stand out from other agents."

Holding her gaze, he said, "You certainly stand out."

Adrian wasn't sure if that was a compliment, but she decided to take it as such. "Thank you."

Then he asked the inevitable question. "How long have you been representing San Holo?"

About to say, *We go back a long way*, she realized that would give him too much information. Yet that was how comfortable she felt with him. Comfortable enough to almost make a slip. "I'm afraid I can't address that. How long have you known Clay?"

"From our university days. Clay has been a great help to me."

She eyed him from beneath her lashes. "But you're a lawyer instead of an artist, so how exactly did he help you?"

He looked past her to the magnificent view of the bay. "Clay saved me from despair."

Her heart ached for him as it had for Saskia, but she pressed on. "Over your art?"

He nodded. "That's what Clay does for the people he brings into his warehouses. Many of them are hanging on by their fingernails." He didn't seem to mind the cliché. "He pulls us all out of the gutter."

She said softly, "But you weren't in the gutter if you were attending Harvard."

"Sometimes the gutter is metaphorical."

She heard in his tone that he loved Clay the way a man loved his best friend, the way two men bonded.

"Do you think you'd mind," she said, as if she were musing, "if I sold your work for you?"

"Don't you mean *try* to sell it?"

She caressed the photo on the mobile's screen. "Your work will sell itself. All I have to do is get it shown."

He barked a laugh. "That's not what people thought ten years ago."

"Obviously, none of them had a decent brain cell to work with." She stared him down for a long moment. The muscles of his face tensed as if he were grinding his teeth. "Please.

Allow me to represent you. I can make us both a lot of money."

"I make a lot already," he shot back.

She didn't give up. "But I can make you a lot more doing what you love."

He swallowed, and she watched his Adam's apple bob. There was something about his body's tension that said he wanted to jump out of his seat and punch the air. Maybe he'd been waiting ten years for someone to tell him this. Maybe he hadn't been able to listen to Clay because Clay was his best friend.

She was an agent. So he believed her.

"Shall I draw up a contract?" she asked. "Or will you?"

THE PAST WEEK of Clay's life had been incredible. Filled with seven days and eight nights of passionate lovemaking the likes of which he'd never known.

He was counting the days because he was afraid it would end. Even if he believed Saskia loved all they did together. He could make her come for a minute. And more than once. Over and over. He'd never been like this with any other woman, and he was afraid he never would be again.

This was special. *She* was special.

But they still lived their lives. Saskia did her thing during the day. In fact, yesterday, after signing the contract, she'd been off assistanting the entire afternoon, coming to his apartment only after eight that night. She'd looked drawn, as if she hadn't eaten all day, and he'd fed her immediately.

She'd been with San Holo, who'd probably grilled her for every detail. Clay had signed the contract, agreed to anonymity, but he would keep working on Saskia to get her to talk San Holo into meeting Dylan.

Now, as they ate a late breakfast in the kitchen, they discussed the practicalities of how he would guarantee San's anonymity, such as a movable tent that could be rolled around the building.

Before a bite of eggs, Clay said, "If you let me meet the man, there'd be no need for all this secrecy."

She laughed and poked him in the chest. "What about all the other people walking around San Francisco? We'd still need a tent to keep everyone out. And security."

He had yet to let Dylan know the commission was a reality. The kid hadn't even come to his studio yesterday. But Clay would still tell Dylan that somehow, some way, he would arrange a meet between the great man and the up-and-coming street artist. He'd never even considered that he'd have to back down.

Even as they ate scrambled eggs on toast—the way Saskia liked them and he was beginning to like them too—he had a brilliant idea. "I know how we can do it."

She waited for his brainchild.

"I don't have to meet the man. Because it's about Dylan. You can talk him into meeting with only Dylan. We'd find a completely private place where they can talk for hours. Then San Holo melts away again without Dylan ever knowing his real name."

She immediately shut him down. "No way. Even if I could get San to agree, there'd be a leak. Someone would find out."

He wanted to smack his fist into his palm. It *was* a brilliant idea. But he smiled instead. He'd keep working on her, and eventually Dylan would worm his way into her heart, and she'd get San Holo to agree.

A clamor started downstairs, the noise carrying through the thick walls of his apartment. They'd both risen to their feet when footsteps hammered on the stairs. His gut wrenched as he imagined vandalism or, worse, one of the artists needing an ambulance.

He opened the door just as Otto raised a fist to pound on it, barely missing Clay's face.

"You must get down there," Otto said in his accented English. "It is Dylan. The scum of the earth have spray-painted hateful things all over Dylan's wall, saying it is total crap. Things like, 'Who does this guy think he is? What the hell is this, we can't even tell.'"

The man's face crumpled in on itself with the pain of Dylan's trashing. Because every artist in his warehouse had been there. They all knew.

A tear opened up in Clay's heart.

He didn't even ask what wall. He knew. He'd encouraged Dylan to put his precious art out there, and Dylan had finally done it. Only to have it trashed.

It was the worst thing that could have happened.

It was like Gareth.

And Gareth had never painted again.

CHAPTER FIFTEEN

*C*lay almost elbowed Otto out of the way, taking the steps three at a time, Saskia close behind him. He skidded to a halt just outside Dylan's sacred studio.

A groan welled up from deep in his gut as he surveyed the devastation. Dylan came from a rough neighborhood—a criminal father, an addicted mother. He'd taken a knife to every single canvas in his studio, slashing them to ribbons that fell off their wooden frames.

Clay wanted to fall to his knees and weep. There was only one piece left intact. Dylan had purposely saved it for last. His dragonfly/butterfly/flying cockroach.

Heedless of any danger, Clay stepped into the fray, grabbing Dylan's arm. Saskia's gasp rang out behind him. But he had to think only of Dylan now, of what he could say to the boy.

While Dylan was a strong kid, Clay was stronger, and he held Dylan's arm as he murmured in his ear, "Don't worry, Dylan. Your work is brilliant. People often don't recognize that brilliance when they first see a new artist's work. But I'll take care of this. I promise."

Though Dylan's chest still heaved, the tension in his knife arm lessened, and his words came out in a harsh murmur. "You said I was ready. You said people would love it." He stared at the as-yet-untouched canvas. "I did it in the dead of night. Just like San Holo. I signed my name." Finally, he turned tear-filled eyes on Clay.

The sight of this amazing young man's stricken face cracked his heart wide open. All his blood seemed to drain out of the massive fracture he was sure would never be healed. *He* had done this to the kid. *He* had encouraged him.

Only he could fix it.

"They came to see San Holo's latest," Dylan got out. "And I —" His voice broke on a sob. "I did mine in the same alley. I wanted it to be a tribute. But people posted a photo of my goddamn stupid flying cockroach all over the internet. They said I'd never be like him. I was a wannabe, and I'd never be anything more. That I'd fade away like all the terrible street artists who thought they could be like Banksy or San Holo."

Tears leaked from his tormented eyes. With Dylan's arm slack and the knife falling to the floor, Clay wanted to take the boy into his arms. Yet he was terrified it wasn't what Dylan needed.

He turned to Saskia in the doorway. His ruptured heart reached out to her, and she understood his anguish, clearly felt the same herself. "Let me talk to him," she whispered.

It was the right thing. She was so good with Dylan. She would talk him down.

Because Clay didn't think he could live with himself if she didn't.

***

SASKIA SAT on the only stool in the studio. She half expected Dylan to pick up the knife and slash the last painting.

"Come here," she said, her tone gentle.

He grumbled back, "I'm not talking to anyone."

She had to be stern with him and used a rougher, louder voice. "By God, you will talk to me. Turn around."

He answered in a grumpy teenager's tone. "*Okaaay*, man."

She took his hands in hers. He was a tall young man, but she had a feeling he would grow even taller. He was thin, too, the bones of his wrists standing out. He wasn't yet eighteen, and he would grow into his body.

Just as he would grow into his talent.

When he didn't pull away, she said, "Your work is fantastic, no matter what anyone else says. They're jealous. They see genius, and they can't handle it. You're so young, and your work will get even better. You'll find your own style." She squeezed his fingers, and when he didn't squeeze back, she kept talking. "Sometimes what we make isn't perfect in other people's eyes. But if you want to be an artist, you need to have a thick skin. Like a cockroach's carapace."

Dylan glanced at the door, at Clay who still stood in her periphery, and said with the stubbornness of youth, "No, Clay said he would take care of me."

She shook her head. "Clay is a wonderful human being and an amazing mentor. He wasn't wrong in telling you to put your real, brilliant, heartfelt work out into the world." She paused to let that thought sink in. "But you're a little ahead of the curve. People didn't get that *they* had to see what was in your painting. That it could be a dragonfly or a butterfly or a flying cockroach. Or whatever *they* needed to see. Their minds were closed."

She thought of Gareth's self-portrait, knowing he'd been through the same thing. People hadn't understood. So he'd stopped painting. She wouldn't let Dylan do that.

"Until the rest of the world catches up with you, Dylan, it'll be a rough road." She had to be real with him, couldn't spoon-feed him tender words. If she did, he might never make it. "This is just how it is. You have to hear what they say and ignore it. You have to not care." Just like she hadn't cared what her parents said. "Not everybody will see your brilliance. Not everyone sees San Holo's brilliance either."

He snorted. Here was the moment when she wished she could tell him. She hated lying to Clay, but it broke her heart not to let San Holo speak to Dylan. The way he felt right now, she was afraid he wouldn't believe her any other way. But she had to test him. "Do you think you can hack it?"

He stared at the floor. Then his gaze flashed like fire over the ruins of his art.

She prompted him. "What's your answer?"

Finally, his shoes scuffing the floor, he mumbled, "I can hack it."

It was a start. He might hug himself when he fell asleep tonight, maybe even shed an ocean of tears when no one could see. But this was a start.

She didn't let go of his hand. "I know you can. I just wanted to hear you say it." She pointed at the destruction. "You can redo your work. Or you can paint new stuff that's even better. But trashing everything isn't how you want to handle this kind of thing in the future, right? Destroying what's good because you feel bad?"

Dylan took another long moment to answer. "Yeah. You're right." Finally—thank God—he gave a half-hearted smile. "Some of my stuff is actually kinda good, right?"

She held his hand tight. "Your art is amazing." She pointed at the one painting he hadn't destroyed. "Your cockroach really did fly, no matter what anyone else says."

She smiled, then glanced at Clay standing in the doorway, his face impassive, immovable, unreadable. He left Dylan's studio without another word.

CLAY BOUNDED up the stairs to his loft, his guts roiling.

How could Saskia think that Dylan had to put up with such cruel criticism from the jerks who'd trashed him? He didn't understand her.

In the flat, he threw himself into his computer chair, brought the monitors to life, called up the internet, and began searching all the online comments.

His guts ached for Dylan. Just as he'd been responsible for what happened to Gareth, he was responsible for Dylan. He would fix this, and his fingers flew over the keys as if they had minds of their own.

He scented her first, even before he heard her footsteps. Damn, the way she smelled. Her beautiful mango aroma made everything in him tighten.

Yet that sensual need didn't erase the ache in his belly.

He spoke without looking at her, because that might be his undoing. "Why would you tell Dylan that he should just take it?" He couldn't keep the hurt out of his voice. "He's been through the wringer, and we need to help him. I have bots that can get rid of all these nasty reviews."

The warmth of her hand on his shoulder seeped through him, and he saw the haloed reflection of her in the screen.

Then her soft, sweet, gentle voice washed over him. "You can't do that, Clay." She didn't pause long enough for him to speak. "Because the minute you're not in his life deleting bad reviews, he's going to be ill-equipped to handle any criticism." She stroked his nape, sifted her fingers through his hair, slayed him with her touch, and robbed him of words. "I get what you're doing, and your idealism is beautiful. But I've seen it all as San Holo's assistant. San would tell you himself that this is the reality Dylan has to face."

As much as he wanted to drink in the sight of her, the

scent of her, he stared at the screen instead, fighting for control.

Her soothing voice drifted over him again. "Even San has to face it. Honestly, a couple of times, clients hated his work so much they painted over it."

Clay couldn't resist the temptation to turn to her then. "Didn't that just kill him?" His voice sounded hollow.

She shrugged. "San has a thick skin. The artist in him knew the work was good. They were just people who didn't get it." She smiled. "Luckily, San always has the canvases on which the original idea grows before going on a wall."

But Clay wondered if San Holo's reaction was worse than Saskia knew. He couldn't imagine the great artist not throwing a fit when his work was painted over. Maybe the man showed only Saskia what he wanted her to see.

His voice came out low and hoarse. "No one would dare paint over San Holo's work now. It's too revered."

Once again, she shrugged. "In the beginning, the work was painted over. Because that's what happens with street art. But you're right," she admitted. "No other street artist paints over San's art now." She caressed him just above his collar. "But clients don't always feel the same. Even if he is an icon."

"But Dylan is just starting out," Clay protested, the ache rising up his throat. "My life's work has been about creating a space where no one gets to trash anyone else's work. It's okay for people to say whatever they want about San Holo, because there are so many people who know he's amazing. But that's not true for a fledgling artist like Dylan." When she opened her mouth, he rolled right over her words. "Look at Gareth. He never painted again. Not until you encouraged him the other day."

He turned back to his computer, and her hand fell away, trailing warmth down his arm. "I get how you feel," she said in the softest of voices. "Especially because of Gareth. But there's another side. Think about kids. They have to learn how to walk. They have to walk to school by themselves. They have to enter the real world and see how it feels. You have to let artists judge for themselves what people say and decide whether a comment can actually improve their work. Reviews and comments make artists think. You can't take that lesson away from them, even if it hurts them when it's happening."

She made him think of his brother and sister, Dane and Ava. That's how they'd been with him, with all of them really. They'd smoothed the way for their younger siblings. Today they'd call it lawnmower parenting. When their parents died in that avalanche during their ski trip twenty years ago, Dane and Ava, being the two eldest, had dropped out of school to take care of the rest of them. They'd all helped train Gabby in soccer so she made her high school team on the first tryout. They'd sent her to cooking school in Paris. Troy had wanted to become an Olympic diver, and they'd done everything in their power to get him there. They'd worked their asses off to get Clay into Harvard, and he'd wanted to make the big bucks to pay them back. By the time he graduated, though, both Ava and Dane had already made it big, Ava well on the way to creating her billion-dollar eldercare corporation, and Dane turning one resort into a worldwide empire. They'd enabled their siblings to do what they loved while creating empires of their own.

It was after the tragedy with Gareth that Clay had recognized another thing big bucks could do. "This is what I've worked for all these years. To help artists like Dylan. Like Gareth." His heart hammered with emotion. "That's why I created my nutrition and exercise app, so it would go viral, and I could sell it. I took the proceeds—five hundred million —and grew that money until it allowed me to build Art

Space and fund these warehouses. Because I wanted to protect them. So nothing like what happened to Gareth happened to anyone else."

"You are such a beautiful idealist," she said softly.

He wasn't sure it was a compliment.

BEING an idealist might be a beautiful thing, but sometimes it blinded you to reality. And Clay had blinders on. "How could you ever in this world create a space for artists where you can protect them from other people's opinions? Because once their art goes out into the world—" Saskia spread her hands to encompass the entire globe. "—someone will say, 'Your art is crap, and I don't like it.'"

He shook his head, his hair tangling in his vehemence. "I won't allow anyone to come on here and cancel people." He slashed his hand through the air. "No one can unload onto one person."

"I agree bullies can't be tolerated. But not every comment is made by a bully. Sometimes they're honest opinions, and they have to be allowed." She wanted to fold him into her arms, stroke his hair. But she had to get him to listen. "You want to save artists from pain, and that's a lofty goal. I get that you're passionate about this because of Gareth. But artists have to grow a thick skin. Because once they, in whatever medium, put their work out there, it isn't theirs anymore. Books, music, paintings, street art—it's all the same."

He stabbed a finger at his computer monitor. "If these negative comments make a person stop painting, then that's bullying."

She shook her head, even smiled softly. "Haven't you ever

left a book review and cited the reasons why you didn't like the book?"

Clay's jaw tensed. "I refuse to leave reviews."

"But sometimes those comments help a writer see they need to make a change."

"There are so many people who use the anonymity of the internet to be cruel."

"That's because all you remember are the mean comments. But I can pull up a book review and show you parts that are negative and yet are still useful." She could have proven it right then, but he wasn't ready to accept her philosophy. She tried another tack. "If it were possible to create that perfect world with no negative criticism, we wouldn't have the diversity of art that we do. Sometimes a piece of art is made specifically as an *'eff you'* to the people who say, 'You're no good.'"

Clay sighed as if he were tired of the argument. "I agree that sometimes it can spur great works. But that's not what they've done to Dylan."

"But often great art is created under difficult circumstances. San Holo knows that from experience." When she was only sixteen and her parents refused to support her artwork, actually throwing her out, she'd reached for her goal of being a great street artist with everything in her. That didn't mean cruel remarks were okay, but artists could use some valid comments for the good of their work. "Art contains our hopes and dreams. But it also contains our pain. It's amazing that you've given people a place to create and the support they need. But one day, you have to let them fly and trust that you've done everything you can to make them strong in their belief in themselves and their art so they can take anything anyone dishes out. Just like San Holo can have someone paint over a piece of his art and come out of it stronger than before."

She so badly wanted to tell him who she was. But he was an idealist, and he would hate her for lying to him, for sleeping in his bed, for making love to him, and never offering him her soul.

The guilt tied her insides into knots until she thought she might be sick. But she kept that stiff upper lip she'd learned from her parents.

After a deep breath, he looked at her, his eyes pools of misery. "I hear what you're saying. But I'm still gut-punched by Dylan's pain."

"Dylan will be stronger, I promise you that. We'll both help him through this terrible time."

There was nothing left to say. Only something left to do. Saskia bent to kiss him softly, without desire—though that would come later—and with reverence for the man he was and the things he tried to do for the people he cared for.

CHAPTER SIXTEEN

*A*fter his talk with Saskia, Clay spoke with Dylan again. The kid was already cleaning up his studio, figuring out what he could salvage. He would be okay, and Clay began to see that Saskia had a point. Then he turned inward, as he often did when he needed to think things through.

But he couldn't forget Gareth's reaction, and his fear for artists like his best friend. The real world would crush some of them. He couldn't allow any lingering consequences for Dylan.

Saskia had left, off to confer with San Holo about the mural, Clay assumed. Hopefully, she would talk with the artist about Dylan, especially because he'd painted in the same alley that San had a week ago. He could only hope the great man would impart some wisdom that Saskia could relay to Dylan, something strictly artist to artist. Maybe Gareth could help, too, and lend advice from someone who'd been through the same thing.

Then Clay did the only other thing he could. He called for

an emergency family mastermind. Everyone was in, and they could all make it by late afternoon.

A few months ago, his sister Ava had started the mastermind as a space for everyone to air their issues and solicit advice. His brothers and sisters were his best friends, always there for each other, even in the middle of the night.

Not quite the cocktail hour yet and a Thursday to boot, the elegant Asian fusion restaurant in San Francisco's Chinatown was far from full. Clay had nevertheless reserved the large round table in the middle. His family were all there for him when he entered. Even Fernsby, who'd been with Dane —and the whole family, truth be told—for over fifteen years. He was tall, thin, and ageless—no one knew exactly how old. Fifty, sixty, or, good Lord, even eighty. There was just no way to know. But Fernsby dispensed advice like an ancient oracle.

Fernsby, always a miracle worker, had managed to get the restaurant owner to allow him to bring in Dane and Cammie's mini dachshund, T. Rex. That man could talk anyone into anything.

Clay gave his sister Gabby a hug and whispered in her ear, "Thanks for coming."

Ava had somehow inherited the red hair of some distant, even far-flung relative, but his younger sister was blond like their mother. Gabby had driven up from Carmel with Fernsby, Dane, and Cammie. She owned a bakery on Ocean Avenue, the main drag of Carmel-by-the-Sea. She'd also franchised her vegan cafés in cities all over the country, where they all used her recipes. She had no ego, and if one of her franchisees came up with something extraordinary, she incorporated it into the menu, giving full credit.

He moved on, kissing Cammie's cheek. Then he said to all of them, "Thanks for coming on the spur of the moment."

Dane clapped him on the back. "We're family." Which said it all.

Cammie and Dane had been an item for a year, though Cammie had been his personal assistant for more than ten. Now his project manager, she oversaw the logistics for Dane's new resort for kids and adults with special needs. She was also the love of his life, though it had taken too damned long for Dane to realize that. Or, more aptly, until he would admit it.

Ava, statuesque and only a few inches shorter than Clay, threw her arms around him, then backed off, holding him by the shoulders. "Of course we're here, little brother." She waved a hand over the group, including Ransom Yates seated next to her. "You were all here for me last year when I had that catastrophe with the caterer."

After firing her caterer, Ava had been frantic to find a replacement for her five Bay Area eldercare homes. Though she had facilities all over the country, and internationally, she used regional caterers for each. Clay was pretty sure he'd been the one to suggest she try Ransom Yates, a celebrity chef who also catered large events.

Did that mean Clay was also responsible for their love story? Shaking Ransom's hand, he didn't miss the gleam in the man's eyes as he turned his gaze back to Ava.

That was definitely love. Same for Cammie and Dane.

Then it hit him in the chest. Could this be what he felt for Saskia? He hadn't known her long, but his feelings were different than they'd been with anyone who'd come before. Perhaps even cataclysmic.

As he took a seat next to Ransom at the round table, he asked, "Where's Troy?" just in time for his brother to breeze in. Troy was a couple of years older than Clay. In fact, all his siblings were two years apart. The timing was so exact, he had to think his parents planned his mother's pregnancies around their worldwide ski adventures.

Troy threw himself into his chair, out of breath as if he'd been running. "Sorry I'm late. I had a meeting with a new vendor that took longer than expected."

Troy had gone from gold-medal Olympic diver to spokesman for several sports manufacturers, and now he'd built his own sporting goods line into a conglomerate with stores worldwide. But he still found time to deliver inspirational speeches to youth groups.

Clay clapped him on the back. "I just appreciate that you made it."

Troy acknowledged that with a smile. "So what's the fire burning under your butt?"

Clay took the mic, so to speak. "Dylan put out his first real piece of street art." His family knew about Clay's mentorship. "This isn't like the tagging he does, but something he's been working on in his studio."

Gabby put her hand over her mouth before he'd finished, obviously anticipating what was to come.

Clay gave the bad news. "He got trashed. Badly. He was so upset he slashed all but one painting in his studio, and only because we stopped him before he got to it."

A collective gasp filled the restaurant. They knew the kid, and they felt his pain.

Sitting back, Dane folded his arms. "What can we do to help?"

"Actually, I think he's taking it fairly well now," Clay admitted. "Saskia had a talk with him." At Dane's raised eyebrow, he explained, "Remember the mural I wanted to have done on the warehouse? I've commissioned San Holo. Saskia is his assistant."

Ransom added, "He's an amazing street artist, probably rivaled only by Banksy."

"Saskia?" That could have been a twinkle in Fernsby's eyes. "You mean the woman with whom you're having intimate relations?"

Heat rose to Clay's cheeks as if he'd been caught out in something. He was years past blushing, if he'd ever blushed at all. Until now.

"I can't believe you just said that, Fernsby." Gabby shot him a glare.

Fernsby merely arched a brow.

Then all his siblings got in on the act, hooting, hollering, clapping him on the back, filling the near empty restaurant with their clamor.

He raised his palms, sending them all back into their seats. "Saskia Oliver is her name, and she's actually my problem." He wagged a finger. "Not for the reasons you're implying."

He narrowed his eyes on Fernsby, but the man remained impassive. He didn't even smile. Though generally short on smiles, since Fernsby had brought Dane and Cammie together, then Ransom and Ava, a smile or two sneaked in more often.

Troy jiggled his finger in his ear as if he hadn't heard correctly. "I thought Dylan was the problem."

"Saskia had a talk with Dylan," Clay explained. "Even before I left, he was deciding what he could keep and what he had to throw away."

Troy winked. "Then it's woman troubles?"

He wasn't going to talk about intimate details in a restaurant, even an uncrowded one. "The problem is what Saskia said to him. More importantly, what she said about Art Space." Naturally, his family knew all about his video platform for artists.

Gabby looked at him with empathetic eyes. "What did she say?"

"She basically told him he had to suck it up and accept criticism if he wanted to be a great artist."

"That's blunt." Ava's voice was harsh.

Clay shook his head. "She said it in the nicest way possible. She actually got through to him, too, which is why he cleaned up his studio instead of going off on another tear."

"But he's good now," Troy said. "I don't understand the problem."

"I'm getting there. Saskia came upstairs while I was online taking down Dylan's horrible reviews so he wouldn't have to look at them ever again."

They were all silent. So silent Clay could hear T. Rex's soft snoring as he lay in Fernsby's lap.

He was forced to continue. "Saskia said my doing that wouldn't help Dylan grow the thick skin that all artists need. That he has to learn to accept criticism." He once again felt the guilt over what he'd done to both Dylan and Gareth, pushing them to put their art out there before they'd grown the thick skin Saskia talked about. "You know Gareth hasn't painted again after he was trashed."

"We know," Troy said, his voice gentle with empathy. "That's why you built your warehouses and started Art Space."

Clay's throat closed up, and all he could do was nod.

"Ever since," Fernsby said, "you've been busily purging any negative reviews for your artists."

Clay didn't even nod at that. They all knew he had.

"And dear Saskia told you to stop." Fernsby leaned forward. In fact, everyone did, turning the spotlight on Clay as Fernsby asked, "You want to discuss who is right in this matter."

Clay pointed a finger. "Bingo."

Dane was the first to wade in. "I read every bad review

about my resorts. Many of them have good points. I'm able to fix things because of them."

"I've dropped baked goods," Gabby said, "when reviews said they were dry or tasteless or just plain gross."

Ava leaned her chin on her fist. "I've added new services to my eldercare homes because reviews have told me something was lacking."

They sided with Saskia. And they were probably right. But he still couldn't get that row of pill bottles in Gareth's room out of his mind, even if his friend had never actually gone through with it. Nor could he stop seeing Dylan's ruined artwork.

Troy rocked back in his chair. "Both good and bad reviews give you direction."

"But that's business." Clay heard the agony in his own voice. "It's not like having your creativity crushed right out of you."

Fernsby spoke then, his voice dipping into a deep intonation. "May I tell you the story of the first time I baked mille-feuille?"

"Mille-feuille is difficult to make." Gabby looked straight at Fernsby. "Especially when it's vegan."

The man snorted loudly, the sound startling the dog before he turned a circle on Fernsby's lap and settled again. "How many times, my dear, must I inform you that butter and eggs are the staff of life?" The baking rivalry between Fernsby and Gabby was legendary, and he looked down his long nose at her. "May I continue, Gabrielle?"

Fernsby never shortened anyone's name. Thank goodness Clay was just Clay. Gabby smiled sweetly, almost baring her teeth at him.

"As I was saying before I was so rudely interrupted, my first thousand mille-feuilles were rubbish. Every single person I tried them on gagged or spat them out. My reviews were terrible because my mille-feuilles were not fit for consumption. Luckily…" He raised his finger. "I tried them only on friends."

Fernsby had a thousand friends? Clay had never seen the man with another soul. He'd never even taken a day off. Or a night.

"Had I not listened to every single review," Fernsby intoned, "I would never have discovered what I was doing wrong, or perfected the flaky pastry with butter cream or had so many discerning critics say *my*—" He splayed his hand against his chest. "—mille-feuilles were to die for."

He stared at Dane for confirmation.

Clay's brother had to say, "They are pretty damn good."

Fernsby snorted. "They are *perfection*."

Even Clay had to admit they were.

"It's commendable, my dear man, that you are a supportive force in your artists' lives, that you have the money to help them, to show their work, to make sales for them. But the delightful Saskia does indeed have a point. Even on *Britain's Greatest Bakers*—" Fernsby had won the top award on last year's show and made sure no one ever forgot it. "—I didn't always like the criticism I received, but—" He held up a finger to make his point. "—I learned from it."

This from a man who professed he had nothing more to learn.

But Fernsby wasn't finished. "As long as it's honest criticism, one can always glean a helpful tidbit. I'm not saying you should accept maltreatment on your amazing platform. That is unconscionable. But criticism can be useful."

Clay eyed him. "*You* learned from criticism? But I thought you already knew everything."

The man almost seemed to preen, growing taller in his chair. "Everyone has something to learn. Right now, sir, you need to learn from the lovely Saskia."

Dane grimaced. "I actually have to agree with Fernsby."

Troy pointed out, "Look what happened after your friend Saskia told Dylan he had to suck it up if he wanted to be a great artist. He turned around and cleaned up the mess he'd made. Now his work will be even better."

Clay saw it all then, as he looked from one mastermind to the next. Then finally to Fernsby.

He couldn't baby the artists in his warehouses. Not anymore.

"Maybe my job is to provide ways for my people to deal with the harsh realities out there. Counseling. Classes. Lectures."

"Let's brainstorm it," Dane said.

Clay had come to the right place. To his family. To the ones who always found answers for each other.

FERNSBY WATCHED the young man master the char siu, mapo tofu, scallion pancakes, and sticky rice, expertly using his chopsticks. He was a goner, as young people were wont to say, hooked on the girl right and proper. Snared. Smitten. Head over heels. There were so many clichés, Fernsby couldn't think of them all. And look at how quickly the couple had become close. This was probably their first argument. If it could even be called an argument. Rather, this was a difference in viewpoint.

The boy had blinders on where she was concerned. He saw what he wanted to see—a beautiful, wonderful, amazing, selfless woman.

But Fernsby recalled what she'd said about *The Discus Thrower*, that he wasn't throwing *away* his art, he was throwing all his energy and creativity *into* it.

Then there was her advice to young Dylan Beck, that

artists needed to grow a thick skin and *use* criticism rather than become a slave to it. If it were taken in the right way, it could work wonders for creativity.

That girl didn't think like anyone's assistant. She thought like an artist.

He said to Clay, "Sir, tell us more about the lovely Saskia Oliver."

The young man seemed suddenly to shine like a ray straight from the sun. He told them everything he knew. Except the prurient details, of which Fernsby was sure there were many.

But what Clay knew wasn't all there was to the girl. Certainly not.

How much more was there? And just what would the young man do when he finally discovered what that "more" truly was?

CHAPTER SEVENTEEN

*I*t was late, darkness had already fallen, and Saskia wasn't back.

But Clay had so much research to do to find the right people to help his artists.

She arrived quietly, so as not to disturb him perhaps, that he didn't realize she was there. Not until her sensual scent wafted over him, and she whispered against his ear, "What are you doing?"

How she'd managed to walk so softly in her heavy Doc Martens, he didn't know.

He held up a finger until he'd hit Send on another email. Then he turned to her.

God, how she affected him every moment he was with her. So beautiful, this time in a long hoodie that reached her thighs and black leggings that hugged her calves. He wanted to tear off the hoodie and bury his face between her breasts.

He explained his plan. "I've approached several therapists in order to add counseling as needed for the artists. I'm also looking at guest lecturers who are brilliant in their fields. Harvard." He flapped a hand one way. "Stanford." He flourished the other. "Oxford. I want them to give video talks about the philosophy of art and the headspace artists have to live in. About the challenges of the artistic life. The talks will be recorded live so people can ask questions, then they'll be available in the archives." He swirled his hand around his head, trying to encompass all the ideas. "I've also ordered copies of Elizabeth Gilbert's book *Big Magic*. Enough stock for all my warehouses and all the artists."

She clapped her hand over her mouth and stared at him. Then said in a breathless voice, "That book is all about how once you're done creating a work of art, and you put it out there, it's no longer yours, and you have to let it go."

He'd read the book long ago and didn't know why it hadn't struck home at the time. "She's saying that everyone will have their own take on your piece of art based on who *they* are. You can't control what they'll think or say about it."

This was what Saskia had been trying to tell him. He'd been so devastated by what Dylan had to face that he hadn't thought of the book until this evening. He hadn't thought of anything but getting rid of the bad reviews.

She trailed her fingers from his nape to his shoulder. "You get it."

"I do," he said. "It'll really help people."

He wanted to pull her onto his lap, kiss her until they were both breathless. But he had to tell her all his thoughts first. "No one has ever gotten through to me in the way you have. I wish I'd told you that earlier." He closed his eyes briefly, then reached for her hand, stroked her knuckles with his thumb. "I called an emergency mastermind session with the family." When she made a little *hmm* of a question, he explained, "We get together once a month to go over any issues each of us may have. Just talking with them—" He let out a laugh. "—especially Fernsby, helped me see how right you were."

"I met Fernsby the other day, right? When he came in to see Charlie Ballard's sculpture?"

He nodded. "That's Fernsby. He's Dane's butler, but honestly, he's way more than that. Don't ever tell him I said this—"

She scoffed. "I'll probably never see him again."

He wanted to tell her that he hoped she'd see Fernsby over and over. But that would be pushy. "That man always knows the right thing to say at exactly the right moment. He made me see—in fact, all of them made me see—that I've been creating a fake Disneyland at Art Space where never a harsh word is spoken."

She smiled at him, and he thought there might be tears in her eyes. "You really do get it."

He held her hand to his cheek. "You made me see that people can learn from the harsh words if they're open to hearing what's behind them."

Those tears blurred her eyes. "That's right. Because you won't always be there to fix things."

"It's my job to provide ways for all my artists to handle the bad times without going off the deep end."

He realized now what his brothers and sisters had been trying to tell him all along. He remembered words like, *It's a lofty goal, and it's amazing you want to do this. But are you really sure you can pull it off?*

He'd always been so sure he could. He owned galleries, sold the artists' work, provided virtual galleries, and made sure everyone got a showing. He acted as their agent, taking a small percentage because that agent's fee made them feel like real artists. He'd thought it was working, but Saskia had shown him something was missing.

He reeled her in, set his arms around her waist. "I have all these warehouses full of artists creating amazing art, and I never weigh in on it because even though I'm not artistic myself, I understand that the artist has to create their own vision." He looked at her for a long moment. "It was like you with Dylan. You understood where the artist in him was coming from, maybe from your experience with San Holo."

She ran her fingers through his hair. "I've had a lot of experience in the art world. But you understand artists too. Now you've learned something as well. Your heart wanted to fix things. But you see that, ultimately, they have to fix it for themselves."

He closed his eyes, relishing the feel of her fingers on his scalp. "You have such wisdom about the artistic tempera-ment." Then he looked at her. "I'm really surprised you didn't continue with your own art, with all your insight."

She said with a shrug, "Given the artist I work with, I've learned so much over the years."

He could resist no longer and pulled her onto his lap, right where he'd wanted her from the moment she walked into the apartment. He held her tightly with all the feeling he had, all the gratitude for how she'd made him see when he'd wanted to shut his eyes. Then he kissed her with all the passion filling his soul.

CLAY KISSED her until she couldn't breathe, until they were so close it was as if they were one being.

But she had to push back because she had so much more to say. "What you're doing is amazing. TED Talks for artists. You could have a therapist talk about how to deal with unsympathetic or unsupportive parents."

"Like Gareth."

And like her. "Experts who can talk about ways to live on a small budget." She gasped. "These lectures could be for every artist, not just the ones in your studios."

He tightened his grip on her. "We need Dylan on this." A hint of pain still clouded his eyes, but there was excitement too. Almost a frenzied look. "We need to ask what Dylan needs right now, after what happened to him. Did you see him downstairs?"

He almost dumped her off his lap as he leaped up in his enthusiasm. She savored his fervor as much as she savored his kisses, his touches, the feel of him inside her. "He was already working on a new piece."

He held her shoulders, looked into her eyes, and whispered, "You did that for him. Now it's my job to do that for everyone else. I need his help to do it."

She was already backing away. "I'll get him for you."

She felt as if she'd witnessed an amazing metamorphosis —Clay coming to life with all his brilliant ideas. She dashed back with Dylan in minutes, her heart racing, her skin flushed with exertion, but also from Clay's breath-stealing kisses and all the ideas spilling out of him.

Dylan threw himself onto the sofa, leaning back, resting one booted foot on his knee. "What?"

The young man wanted to sound tough, but she could see him still bubbling and roiling inside, despite the new piece he'd started after cleaning up his studio.

Instead of standing over him, Clay sat on the opposite end of the sofa, and Saskia took the armchair. "After what happened to you, Saskia has made me realize I need to provide counseling to help artists through that kind of thing. How to prepare before it even happens. I'd like you to help me see what's needed."

Dylan abandoned his sullen posture, sitting up, looking at Clay. "You want *my* opinion?" He pressed his hand to his chest as if he couldn't believe it.

Clay snorted. "I absolutely want to hear from a brilliant artist who's just had critics jump all over him. I can't fix that for you, but I can help you find ways to fix it for yourself."

Dylan's shoulders grew straighter, and the lines of his face appeared stronger. He seemed to mature right in front of her. As though Clay asking for his opinion was more important than what people thought of his artwork.

They bandied ideas back and forth, not like a successful man in his thirties and a teenager, but like equals. Though she added a few comments, she wanted this to be between them.

Something transformed inside her as she saw Clay in this new light. She adored his idealism, but she loved how good he was with Dylan, listening intently, jumping up to add things to the file he'd created.

He'd actually listened to her and acted on what she said. Clay was a doer. The moment he realized she had a point, he'd acted, making plans even while she'd been at home working on ideas for the mural.

She ordered takeout, and they talked while they ate. Watching them, her heart felt so full.

Finally, Dylan rose. "Holy heck, man, I'm drained." He mock-glared at Clay. "You took every idea right out of my head and there's nothing left."

Clay clapped his shoulder. "Get some rest."

Then, before she registered that he was moving, Dylan hugged her. "Thanks."

She cupped his face. "You did really good today."

He laughed. Here was the Dylan of yesterday instead of the Dylan of this morning who'd blown through his studio, tearing up all his hard work.

He stepped back. "Are you coming to the birthday party on Sunday?"

"Is it your birthday?" She'd thought that was three months away.

Dylan shook his head, his hair flying.

"It's a Maverick party for all the kids," Clay explained. "Paige and Evan's twins are a year old, and Jorge and Noah are turning eight. We're holding a party at Dane's Napa resort." A smile, as beautiful as the sun shining down on a new day, spread across his face. "The entire Maverick family, including all the Harringtons, will be there." He smacked his forehead. "Why didn't I think of that? Of course you're invited."

Her heart seemed to seize in her chest. This wasn't a business meeting or takeout dinners over talks about San Holo's work. This wasn't even them in bed.

This was her meeting his *family*.

"You gotta come." Then Dylan slapped Clay's back. "Okay, I gotta crash." He stomped across the loft floor and slammed the door behind him.

In the sudden quiet, Clay said, "Please. Come with us."

Oh no. She was falling for him. She loved what he'd done with Dylan. She admired his idealism and how he took care of his artists and his friends. She felt more for him than she would for a man she'd simply fallen into bed with.

Yet she'd been lying her butt off to him the entire time.

She couldn't have a real relationship with Clay because it would mean telling him she was San Holo. He'd never forgive her for holding back the truth. In fact, she'd never have a real relationship with anyone if the only person she trusted with the truth was Adrian.

She was lying to a man she was falling for. Lying to Dylan, who badly wanted to meet her alter ego.

Guilt welled up from the pit of her stomach and swallowed her entire soul.

Clay was still waiting for an answer about the party. "Everyone would love to meet you. I told them at the family mastermind that you're the one who got me to see the truth."

He laughed. As if he didn't have a care in the world. "They want to meet the woman who actually made me change my mind about something."

Her thoughts whirring, she said numbly, "Sure. That would be great." She had three days to think of an excuse.

Even as he reached for her, she circled around the coffee table until she was backing toward the door. "I had a really draining day with San." And with her guilt. "Would you mind terribly if I went back to my place? I just need to crash." She used Dylan's words.

Confusion washed over Clay's face, his brows knitting in a frown. "But—"

She held out her hand in a plea. "I'll see you tomorrow. I promise."

As she fled, she asked herself how she could make any promises to him at all. Because she'd built a web of lies she didn't know how to tear down.

SAN HOLO PAINTED in near darkness, only one small lamp lit in the studio. But Saskia couldn't bear to look at herself in the long cheval mirror she used for self-portraits. Not that anyone would have recognized her from any of those paintings.

The lies ate her up from the inside out. She'd seen the hurt in Clay's eyes when she'd left. Clearly, she'd blindsided him.

But if she'd stayed, they would have made love. She simply couldn't stomach being intimate with him again while she fed him lies. Not when it felt like so much more than *just* sex. She craved his touch, but her lies and her guilt would crush her right there in his bed.

She wanted to tell him. She would never feel clean on the

inside if she didn't. She couldn't make love with him because he'd want to know why tears came to her eyes afterward. But how could she tell him, knowing he'd never forgive her?

She studied her work, all blacks and browns and streaks of gray. Dark and ugly, reflecting the dark of her soul, the guilt of her lies. She grabbed a can of black spray paint, obliterating the entire canvas.

Pacing back and forth, she wore down the studio's hardwood floor. Then she threw herself into a chair, stared out the window at a streetlight. Repeated the actions—pacing, staring, flinging herself into that chair.

Fog rolled in, muting the streetlight. Muting her whole being.

She wasn't sure she could even paint again. All her lies would steal her talent. Steal San Holo from her.

The only person she'd ever trusted with her secret was Adrian. But then, she'd known Adrian since she was sixteen. Adrian had seen her grow from a nameless street artist to Lynx to San Holo. Saskia had known Clay only a week— eight days, to be exact. She'd even thought he could be a dirty rotten scoundrel like Hugo.

But that week had shown her how different he was from her first impression. Her gut and her heart believed every word his artists told her. She believed in what Dylan said. She believed in what Clay had done tonight, researching all the resources he could offer them. Even asking Dylan for his opinion.

She believed in *Clay*.

But if she believed in him, didn't that mean she had to trust him one thousand percent? The way she trusted Adrian?

The thought was like a sledgehammer to her stomach.

She *did* trust Clay. The way all his artists did. The way Gareth did. The way Dylan did.

One thousand percent.

She had to tell him. No matter what his reaction was, he deserved the truth. So did Dylan. She wouldn't even run it by Adrian. For the first time in five years, she would put her heart before her art.

Even if Clay hated her once he knew.

CLAY PACED his loft from one end to the other.

She'd left. Had he done something wrong, pushed her too hard about San Holo's identity? Did work always have to come before everything else? Or could he lead with his heart and give up the hunt for once in his life?

Yes, he'd promised Dylan. But he was coming to realize that finding out who San Holo was had been all about his desire to win. Maybe winning wasn't everything.

Unless it was winning Saskia's heart.

He almost texted her. Almost called her. Almost raced to her.

But he didn't even know where she lived, except that her home was somewhere in the Haight. He blamed himself for that too. Everything had been about him—his warehouses, his artists, his promise to uncover San Holo. He'd never asked anything about her life outside of her job. Because that was all that mattered to him. That and getting her into his bed.

No wonder she needed a break. He'd driven her away.

He sent her only one text then, because she'd been clear about needing space tonight.

Whenever you're ready, let's talk. He didn't even beg for an answer.

When she was ready, he vowed, he'd tell her she'd become more important to him than anyone or anything else.

CHAPTER EIGHTEEN

*R*ather than make the long drive to Pebble Beach after last night's family mastermind, then all the way back again for the Maverick birthday party on Sunday, Dane and Camille stayed at the Nob Hill flat. As did Gabrielle.

Fernsby's thoughts had buzzed all night.

Clay was immersed in his relationship with the lovely Saskia. Of which Fernsby wholeheartedly approved.

But the larger question was, who exactly was Saskia Oliver?

The precise answer came to Fernsby in the sleepless hours just before dawn.

He'd gone immediately to the warehouse. After he'd served breakfast, of course. He had standards and would never leave his employer in the lurch even if he had a mission.

When he arrived, however, Saskia Oliver wasn't there, and Clay had rushed off to some important meeting.

Bollocks.

But he knew, because he was Fernsby and knew everything, that the woman would show up sooner or later. He waited on the corner for his first sight of her, wanting to speak to her before Clay did.

There she was, almost running, head down. She would have barreled right into him if he hadn't been so quick on his feet.

Fernsby steadied her with his hands on her shoulders. "Dear Miss Oliver. The very woman I wish to speak with."

She tried to wrench out of his grasp, saying in a near frenzied voice, "I have to talk to Clay."

He held tight and said to her, when she finally looked him in the eye, "I know who you are. And it's not San Holo's assistant."

Her lovely mocha-with-a-hint-of-cinnamon eyes went wide, and he saw clearly what he hadn't realized the other day. She had artist's eyes, taking in every detail of his worn and craggy face.

He said what had to be said. "You're San Holo."

She didn't gasp. She didn't faint. But with his hands on her shoulders, he was sure he felt the flutter of her heart. "Wow," she said. "You're good."

He dropped a hand to her elbow and started walking, guiding her. "Shall we have coffee and a biscuit and talk?" He smiled down at her. "Before Clay returns."

They said nothing until they were seated inside the coffee shop, their cups on the table between them. He'd passed on the biscuits, however. They didn't look up to snuff. Even Gabrielle's vegan biscuits would be preferable.

The steam vented on the espresso machine, the barista yelled out names, and people talked, laughed, even shouted to be heard over everyone else.

Without even a fidget, she said, "What was my tell?"

"My dear, Clay obviously hasn't told you that I—" He

placed the tips of his fingers to his chest. "—am Fernsby. I know everything."

Her lips twitched, not quite a smile as she waited for his answer.

"It was how you spoke of *The Discus Thrower*. That he glowed because he was throwing everything he was into his art. Only a true artist would have seen that." He tapped his temple. "Though I'll admit it took me a few days to truly comprehend. But when I coupled that with what you told Clay about what artists really need, it was obvious." Then, because he had to give credit where credit was due, he added, "Which was all very true, my dear."

She sipped her latte, but he knew her mind was humming, perhaps pondering how to get out of this conversation.

He couldn't let her, so he said what he had walked all the way across town to say. "You must tell Clay."

She dropped her head to the table with a thump, their cups bouncing. She breathed so fast he was afraid she might hyperventilate. Until she sat up again. "That's why I came to the warehouse this morning. From the beginning, Clay has wanted to know who San Holo is. For Dylan. Because San Holo is Dylan's idol. I decided last night that I have to tell him the truth, even if he hates me."

"Maybe he will. Maybe he won't. That doesn't matter. You must tell him anyway." Then he offered her a bit of himself. "For almost sixteen years, I have considered him one of my sons. Trust me when I say he's a bigger man than you think."

Then she couldn't stop talking, throwing words at him as if they were missiles. "I'll admit that I had major reservations about him at first, but one by one, they've been blown apart. He's a better man than almost anyone else I've ever known." She sighed, a painful, guttural sound. "I just don't want him to hate me. I don't want to see that look in his eyes when he realizes I've been lying to him from the start."

Fernsby laid his hand over hers. He'd never been touchy-feely, but this young woman needed soothing. "Maybe some of what you told him has been lies, Saskia." He used her name now, offering it as another touch of comfort. "But I don't believe it has *all* been a lie." He gave her a soft smile. He actually could smile when it was necessary. "Is it a lie when you kiss him?"

She shook her head, her silky hair falling across her shoulders. "No."

"As I thought. But back to your main concern—will he be hurt that you have lied to him?" When she winced, he added, "I understand why you did it—I know all too well that it's a rough world out there. Tougher on some than others."

She shot him a look of astonishment, as if he'd seen right into her soul. Which he had. Because he was Fernsby.

"But is he worth going through the pain of telling the truth?" he queried.

"Yes," she said softly, as if fear constricted her throat. Then, in a stronger voice, she said again, "Yes, he is."

Saskia threw herself across the table into his open arms. As though he were the wise grandfather she'd never had. With his arms around the young woman, and excessively pleased with his results, he allowed himself a grin.

His work here was done.

AFTER LEAVING FERNSBY, Saskia raced to Clay's warehouse.

Her heart pounded with the hope Fernsby had given her. Clay was a good man. The best man. He might be upset. But he would forgive her.

Inside, Dylan shrugged. "He got a phone call. Then he took off in a rush."

There was no way she could tell Dylan before she told Clay, so she stepped back into the lobby beside *The Discus Thrower*. And her call went directly to voicemail.

She wanted to jump up and down in frustration like a child. But this couldn't be said in a voicemail. Her message was as brief as his text had been last night. "You told me to call when I'm ready to talk. I'm ready."

There was nothing to do but return home. But once there, she couldn't go into the studio, couldn't look at the black canvas.

She could do nothing but wait.

CLAY RUSHED home like Hermes with wings on his heels.

Saskia had left him a voicemail. She wanted to talk, and he'd been stuck in all those freaking meetings.

It had been one of those days where everything was an emergency. Dressed in sweats and sneakers, he'd been about to go for a run to burn off some of the tension when one of his investment guys—he had several, including the Maverick ventures—had called to say a deal was going south. Without bothering to change, Clay had jumped on it, even though all he'd wanted to do was ignore his work and go get the girl of his dreams.

He couldn't get to his loft fast enough. If she wanted to talk, she'd be waiting for him there.

But as he passed Dylan's studio, the young man stepped out. Clay had the awful desire to swat him aside as if he were a fly. But of course he wouldn't do that to Dylan or any of the artists.

Dylan didn't give him a chance to get a word in. "Have you seen this?" He held up his phone.

"Seen what?" Clay didn't care. He only wanted Saskia.

But Dylan got right in Clay's space and punched Play on the video he'd queued up.

Before he even registered the words, Clay recognized the man.

In the video, his face bloated and florid, the man spoke in the rough voice of a two-packs-a-day smoker. "You all know me. Hugo Lewis. I'm also the famous street artist Lynx."

Though Lynx was a famous street artist, his work had gone downhill over the last five years.

Lewis continued in that smoke-laden voice with a definite Cockney edge. "I'm holding this press conference out of the goodness of my heart." He held his hand over his heart for emphasis.

"I know everyone in the world—" He spread his arms to encompass the globe. "—wants to know the real person behind the artist San Holo."

Clay sucked in his breath, held it, until he saw spots before his eyes. But it didn't stop Hugo Lewis's words.

"Until now," Lewis said, "only her agent has known San Holo's identity."

Clay dimly registered the pronoun. *Her*. Not *him*.

Lewis once more reached out to the world. "I have recently learned that her agent is right here in San Francisco. Adrian Fielding. She's been keeping San Holo's secret for five years. I believe the public deserves to know. I believe that keeping her identity a secret is a marketing ploy to raise the value of her paintings."

Her, her, her. Why did Lewis keep saying that?

But Clay's stomach was in free fall. He imagined he heard it splatter on the concrete floor at his feet.

"That is why I, myself—" Once again his hand went to his heart. "—revealed my identity five years ago to be Lynx. Because it wasn't fair to keep you all in the dark. It wasn't fair to make the value of my paintings rise simply because I didn't tell any of you who I was. Even Banksy speaks to his public. He might gray out his features, but he talks to us. But not San Holo." He wagged his finger in front of the microphone, accidentally touching it and setting off ear-splitting feedback. "So I made it my mission to find out who this mysterious San Holo is. For you. The public. The art world. For all the people who deserve to know."

Clay didn't think he could breathe, and yet, he sucked in a gulp of air that almost choked him.

Just as he choked on everything Hugo Lewis said.

"I brought you the world-famous street artist Lynx." Lewis's voice rose with his momentum. "Now I'm bringing you San Holo. Because that is what the art world and the world at large deserve." He was making out that he was so altruistic. *Dammit, get to the point.*

His sales were plummeting. Lewis wanted San Holo's fame to plummet too.

The journalists crowded around Lewis raised their voices to a cacophony. The man patted the air, bringing the noise level down, letting the crowd know he wouldn't reveal anything until they hushed. Until he had his moment in the limelight.

Then he leaned in, his lips almost kissing the microphone, and said very softly, "San Holo is Saskia Oliver, who's been pretending to be San Holo's assistant. But she's not. *She* is the artist. She's been lying to you all along. To every person who has ever purchased a piece of her artwork. I can't let that go on. That's why I'm bringing her name to you. Saskia Oliver," he repeated.

The crowd fired questions at Lewis, but Clay had heard

enough. So had Dylan, who punched Pause when the man's mouth was wide open, his yellowed teeth front and center.

Pain slid under Clay's sternum as if it were a knife.

Dylan turned to him. "Did you know all along?" He rushed on before Clay could answer, his voice excited, exhilarated. "Like, that's so cool. You said you'd find her, and you did. When were you going to tell me?"

Dylan didn't feel gutted. He didn't even sound angry. To him, it was super cool that Saskia turned out to be San Holo.

Clay wanted to pound his head against the wall. He should have known. Yet he still fought it. "This can't be true. She would have told me."

Dylan stared at him, his mouth agape. "Like, you mean, you didn't know either?"

Then he whooped and hollered, bouncing around the hallway outside his studio until everyone close by stepped out of theirs. "I was the first one to find San Holo's new street art. Now I'm the first one to know who she actually is. Our very own Saskia." He punched the air, then came back down to earth. "Okay, so this Hugo Lewis knew first." That didn't faze him. "But I was the one to tell *you* first." He pointed at himself, then Clay.

Clay managed to say, "Yeah, that's great. You got the jump on me, buddy." Then he pulled out his phone, looked at it as if there was actually something to see. "I just got a text. Important stuff. Gotta go."

He damn near ran out of the warehouse, leaving behind a dumbfounded Dylan.

Saskia had yanked his feet—and most especially his heart —right out from under him.

And she'd done it with a lie.

SASKIA HAD WAITED to hear from Clay. And waited. Until she couldn't stand one more minute.

Adrian had called and texted multiple times, but Saskia ignored each one. She couldn't tell Adrian that she had to let Clay know the truth, afraid her friend—and agent—would try to talk her out of it.

But the longer it took Clay to call her back—or even text—the more it made her crazy.

She raced the couple of miles from her Victorian sanctuary in the Haight to Clay's warehouse in the Mission District. To his home.

When she ran up the stairs, he wasn't there. None of the artists knew where he was or when he'd be back. Even Dylan wasn't around.

She'd have to hang out until he returned. She *had* to talk to him. Because if Fernsby had figured it out, then Clay would too.

She closed her eyes, standing in that long hallway, the sound of music and voices and grinders and potters' wheels burrowing inside her, making her want to explode. Until finally Dylan walked in, a bag of takeout food in his hand.

He stopped short a dozen feet away, staring at her like she was the bug-eyed alien in her last work.

His feet planted wide, his boots slapping the concrete, he pointed at her with his free hand. "You are way more sneaky than I ever gave you credit for."

His words made no sense. "What do you mean?"

He laughed, a chortle rather than a loud sound that would fill the entire warehouse. He closed the distance between them until he was two feet away, a cheeky grin filling his face. "I always figured you were a woman," he said. "Your art has such sensitivity."

Her stomach hit rock bottom, her heart raced, and blood

pounded in her ears. Her voice seemed so small when she asked, "What are you talking about?"

This time, he laughed outright. "That video. Hugo Lewis." Then he looked at her, really looked, something indefinable in his expression. "You know about Hugo Lewis's video outing you as San Holo, right?"

Her blood curdled into cottage cheese.

The young man went on relentlessly. "He did some YouTube press conference." He shot her again with that cheeky grin. "But I knew it all along. Not that it was you, exactly. But that San Holo had to be a woman."

Over the rapid beating of her heart, she knew he'd never had a clue. But now he'd convinced himself he did. "Let me see," she snapped.

Pulling his phone from his pocket, he held it in the same hand as his cooling food, while his fingers raced over the screen.

There was Hugo spilling her secret, claiming he was doing it for the good of the art world. She hated him all over again.

She had to get to Clay before he saw this.

"I showed it to Clay." Dylan laughed as if he hadn't just blown up her world. "I can't believe I got the scoop on him *again*. He didn't even know, and he never would've guessed."

He was so excited, he didn't pick up on her emotions or notice how pale she'd gone as all the blood drained out of her head.

"That's just so cool," he went on. "You're San Holo. And you love my stuff."

"Yeah," she whispered. "I love your stuff."

Dylan beamed, then said almost sheepishly, "Can we talk later?"

"Absolutely. Later." She couldn't deny him.

Now she knew what Adrian's calls and texts had been about. Everything had gone south. Sideways. Pear-shaped.

"Do you know where Clay is?" She could barely hear her own words above the roaring in her ears.

He shook his head, his hair wisping about his face. "No. He got another text and took off. I haven't seen him since. That was like…" He gave a full-body shrug. "I dunno, a couple hours ago?"

She felt herself dying inside. Shriveling. Turning into a desiccated mummy without any wrappings.

Outside, darkness was falling. Already dressed in black from her sweater to her leggings to her boots, she grabbed one of the baseball caps in Dylan's studio and clapped it on her head. "I gotta go," she mumbled. "Work to do."

As she fled, hopefully disguised beneath Dylan's baseball cap, he threw out, "To your studio to paint canvases for the mural?"

She couldn't get out a sound, just gave him a half-hearted flutter of her hand. Outside, she stood on the corner to wait for Clay where no one inside could see her. She could only hope he'd come back.

And that he would listen to her.

CHAPTER NINETEEN

*C*lay ran.

He ran along the San Francisco streets, pulling down five-minute miles on the flats, seven on the hills. But the punishing pace didn't work. He was only more worked up, especially when he passed a building covered with street art, even if it wasn't San Holo's.

How had he missed it? Her identity was so obvious now. But everyone—all those intelligent people—thought San Holo was a man, that he was British.

The ache filling his body wasn't the grueling run or his stupidity at not figuring it out. It was the realization that he'd made love to her without even knowing her. The thought hurt so badly his legs might have crumpled beneath him if he hadn't already been running on muscle memory.

She'd never cared for him at all. Because you couldn't lie to someone you cared about.

He thought of his parents. They had been everything to each other, to the exclusion of everyone else in their lives, even their kids. They told each other everything. They were devoted. They did everything together.

They even died together.

That was what love meant to him. Total immersion in each other. Total transparency.

But Saskia had excluded him from the most important aspects of her life.

It meant she wasn't in love with him. Maybe it meant she could never love him.

The thought crippled him, and he stumbled, catching himself on a light post before he could fall. Then he went on running. Barely able to breathe, he rounded the corner on which his warehouse sat.

There she stood. Alone, lit only by a flickering streetlight.

Dressed in all black, she was like a wraith in the night. A ghost. A phantom. Wearing a baseball cap pulled low. He couldn't truly see her face, but he knew it was her by the lines of her body.

But he didn't know *her*. He never had.

He watched her for a moment as she paced back and forth. A pulse of love beat through his chest, rising up his throat to strangle him. But he shoved it back down. She'd lied to him. Over and over.

How could he ever trust her? She could lie again, and he would never know.

This morning, everything had seemed within his grasp. True love. Though he'd always shied away from the intense love his parents had, he'd wanted it. With Saskia.

But there was no coming back from this.

Then she saw him.

SASKIA PACED THE CORNER. He'd have to return eventually. It was late now, and she felt like San Holo, dressed all in black, baseball cap masking her features as if she were sneaking into an alley to paint.

The comparison chilled her. She wanted to come off as open to Clay, but instead she just looked disguised.

She hadn't called Adrian or dealt with Hugo. She needed to talk to Clay first before anyone else. He was more important than all the secrecy. More important than any other person.

She'd totally screwed up. Her body felt like a mass of tensed muscles, the sensation so painful she wanted to cry. She'd only just admitted that she wanted some kind of relationship with him, and for a little while, she'd hoped the truth would set her free.

But now that seemed completely out of reach. If she'd told him the truth yesterday, it might have been repairable. But learning it from a stranger on social media? No, he wouldn't forgive that.

After all the glorious nights they'd spent together, after working on his plans for classes and lectures to help his artists through the emotional baggage that came with being a creative? After keeping her history secret from him—about her parents, about Hugo, even when he'd told her about Gareth and how that affected him? No, he wouldn't forgive any of that.

Then she saw him.

Running down the hill, hell-bent on getting to the warehouse, maybe even to seclude himself in his loft, he stopped, he came to an abrupt stop so violent it must have hurt his knees.

He just looked at her.

Everything she might have dreamed of having with him ended there.

The seconds ticked by.

Clay's entire body ached from the demanding run. He wasn't ready to confront her. But she was here. She'd seen him. He couldn't get away. They had to talk sometime.

He walked to her side, trying not to stalk her like a raging bull, trying to keep his emotions bottled up.

His insides were knotted, his heart and lungs in a bind that made it hard to breathe, hard to pump the blood through his veins. Yet he stood before her, and in the nicest way possible, without a single betraying inflection in his voice, he asked, "Why didn't you tell me that you're San Holo?"

Her mouth opened, but nothing came out.

He wanted to punch his fist into the wall. Because she had no justification for not being honest with him. Because she didn't even have an explanation.

Even as he tried to remain calm, harshness crept into his voice. "You've been dishing it out, but you can't take it? Why are you anonymous if the reality of art is that once you've put it out there, it's no longer yours? Why are you telling Dylan he needs to take the criticism when you don't take yours?"

Pain reverberated through his fist and body as if he *had* actually hit the wall.

Finally, her voice washed over him. "San Holo's name is attached to everything I do. I see the reviews. I get the criticism. Just because it's a pseudonym doesn't mean I don't know what people say."

Leaning close, he breathed in her sensual scent, remembered the taste of her lips, the sweetness of her skin. "Then why weren't you honest with me?" Then, because the hurt was a living, breathing part of him, he said, "You led me on. Nothing we did meant anything to you."

She reached out, and he automatically backed away, one

step, two. Under the lamplight, even with the brim of her baseball cap, he saw the leap of anguish in her eyes.

He steeled himself against it. "After everything we've been to each other, why didn't you tell me?"

She looked down at the sidewalk, shuffled her Doc Martens on the concrete, then met his gaze. "Hugo Lewis is my ex-boyfriend. He stole my art, and I couldn't get it back. My parents burned me. My ex-boyfriend burned me. I have to admit to being a little gun-shy." As she spoke, her voice got stronger. She grew taller, no longer the slumped figure he'd first seen huddled beneath the streetlight.

He felt for her. He remembered Gareth's torment when he'd been trashed. He'd seen Dylan destroy his own work. To know that someone had stolen her art from her, her very soul from her, hell, yes, he felt for her.

But he wasn't Hugo Lewis. "I hear all those reasons. I totally understand them." He spread his hands as if he were giving her the world. "But I've been falling in love with you."

She hugged herself, her shoulders rolling together as she curled in on herself again. But he couldn't stop the flow of his feelings. "Every time I made love to you, I didn't even know you. Now you're implying I'm just like your ex-boyfriend, that I might *harm* you."

Crazy that it didn't even hurt to say he'd been falling in love with her. He'd never said that to any woman, ever. But he'd wanted to tell her, wanted her to know how special she was.

Yet her words had been like a knife, a betrayal of everything they'd done together. "You should know me better than that by now. I would never steal your art. Or hurt you in any way. Even if it's only been little more than a week, you should know that."

Maybe he should have grilled her for every single detail

about Hugo Lewis. About her parents. Made her explain it all.

But he didn't have another piece of his soul to give her.

His pain was written in his eyes, on his face, in the tense lines of his body.

His words gutted her in return.

I've been falling in love with you.

Now, when it mattered, she'd lost him. She wanted to fly into the night like a bat, to some dark place where she could wrap her arms around herself and hide. Her voice barely above a whisper, all she could say was, "I thought about telling you so many times."

His eyes bored holes straight through her body.

More words rushed out of her. "I swear I was going to tell you today. Didn't Dylan tell you I was looking for you? Didn't you listen to my voicemail?"

He planted his feet firmly on the concrete. "Really?" The disdain in that word spiked through her. "Today? You were going to tell me today?"

She cringed, wanted to run, but she held her ground.

"Why were you going to tell me today?" he asked. "Because you got wind that your dick of an ex was going to out you?"

His words were an assault even worse than Hugo's, because she deserved Clay's anger. But she couldn't let him think she'd planned any of this. "I had no idea Hugo would do that." Her hands, her arms, her whole body wanted to reach out to him. "Fernsby already guessed. But I was going to tell you even before he talked to me."

He barked a humorless laugh. "Oh, so *Fernsby* told you to come clean."

197

She shook her head, her hair flying as the ball cap fell to the ground. "I promise I was coming here to tell you, but Fernsby found me before I found you."

He stood as still as a tree trunk. The moment seemed to go on and on, his gaze like a laser beam scanning her. Finally, in a voice so soft she almost couldn't hear it, he said, "I don't know what to believe anymore."

Then he turned and walked away.

And took the broken pieces of her heart with him.

CLAY SAT ALONE in an all-night fifties diner filled with tourists, couples out for a late meal, and teenagers laughing and screeching at videos on their phones. He'd ordered a hamburger because he felt guilty taking up space and drinking only coffee. But he'd been unable to touch more than a bite of one French fry.

Before he could talk himself out of it, he dialed Adrian Fielding's cell number.

Without allowing her even a hello, he spewed the words at her. "The deal is off. I don't need Saskia—if that's even her real name—to paint even one damned wall for me."

Adrian didn't react. "You saw the press conference. Did you talk to Saskia? Is she okay?" Her voice rose slightly on the question.

"I sure as hell did talk to her. She actually claims she was going to tell me." He was as angry as he could ever remember being, not only with Saskia but also with Adrian, who'd helped perpetuate the lie, and with himself for believing it. "The two of you are running the biggest racket in the business. How can you live with yourselves?"

Still, Adrian remained calm. "I protect my clients and friends. Any answers you want, you'll have to get from Saskia

—if she's willing to give them to you. Believe me, she has her reasons. Good ones. You've heard from her ex, so now you've seen what a jerk he is."

He wanted to smack his fist on the table. "You both lied to me before Hugo Lewis ever came on the scene. In fact, you've been lying to all your clients for years. You want to protect your artists. Great. But what about protecting your clients?"

"None of our clients has ever been harmed by Saskia's anonymity. In fact, they like it."

"I didn't." He was revealing far too much, but he couldn't stop. "There's no excuse."

He could almost see Adrian shaking her head. "Hugo did this because he's jealous that she's so big, and she did it without him. Once he claimed he was Lynx and put new art out there, it lost all its value. He's trying to do the same to her by stripping away her anonymity." She took a breath, and he could have jumped in, but he let her finish. "She trusted him, and he abused that trust. You have to see why trusting anyone else—even though you've become closer over the past week than I've seen her with anyone since Hugo—is nearly impossible for her."

He remembered what Saskia had said that night at the bar, that she wished she could trust more and fear less. It seemed so long ago. Yet it was little over a week.

He didn't want to come off like some bad guy who couldn't forgive her for being afraid to open her heart again. He should have remembered what she'd said that first night. He should have tied it all together with what Hugo Lewis had done, what her parents had done. Because she'd revealed enough for him to get it. But he hadn't given her a chance to tell him all the details.

He wasn't sure he could now.

He pointed a finger as if Adrian could see him. "I can

forgive a lot of sins. But not straight up being lied to from the start."

Then he punched the End button before Adrian could say another word.

And before he could forgive Saskia right there on the phone.

SHE WENT OUT with her spray cans in the middle of the night. Tagging had always been how she dealt with fear and anger. Only this time it wasn't working.

Her mind spiraled from hurt to shame and guilt to anger to hating how unfair love truly was. She'd always had these spirals, but never before had she added love into the mix.

But she had to face it. She loved Clay. Even if falling in love in little more than a week seemed straight out of a romance novel.

Everything she painted looked like Clay's face. Even when she tried painting only letters, his face worked itself into the art. Along with hearts.

Disgust for herself filled her. She loved him, dammit, but she'd messed it all up. Why should he forgive her? She'd done nothing to earn his trust. Since Hugo, it had always been about people earning *her* trust. She'd never even tried to earn Clay's.

She sprayed black over everything she'd painted, as black as her soul felt.

Then she stood in front of all that unrelenting black. If she'd told him everything right there under the streetlight, no sketchy thumbnails, just the entire story—about her parents throwing her out when she was sixteen, about Hugo not only claiming her art, but stealing Lynx? If she'd totally revealed herself, maybe Clay would have understood.

Instead, she'd done what she always did—doubled down, told him the bare minimum, expecting him to figure out the rest.

She hadn't told him her truth. Maybe she'd been afraid even that wouldn't change his mind.

Leaving the alley, she sat in the glow of a streetlight halfway between Clay's place and Haight-Ashbury. Busy throwing the blackness of her soul against a wall, she hadn't picked up any of Adrian's calls. Now she looked at the latest text.

Clay called me. Where are you? Are you okay?

I was out doing art. Hopefully Adrian would think that meant she was okay. Her stomach knotted. *It's over between us, isn't it?*

Adrian texted back immediately, as if she'd been waiting. *Maybe. It all depends on what you want.*

Saskia didn't hesitate. *I want him. I love him.*

It hit her again like the impact of a comet. She loved the man he was—the tender lover, the caring patron, the intelligent businessman, the amazing friend.

Adrian's text pinged. *Then do whatever it takes.*

Even as she typed them, her words sounded whiny. *What if he doesn't love me back?*

He'd said he'd been falling in love with her. *Falling* in love. Not *in* love.

But Adrian's texts were relentless. *He does love you. I know it. You know it. Remember when I talked about a man like him, a billionaire, that he must have black marks on his soul?*

Saskia nodded as she typed back. *I remember.* But Clay didn't have any black marks.

Adrian's next text echoed her thoughts. *I was wrong. He's one of the good ones. So clean up this mess. Talk to him. Refuse to back down, even if he tries to push you away.*

Her thoughts telegraphed themselves right onto her phone screen. *That's exactly what he'll do.*

Adrian's words flowed. *But isn't true love worth everything?*

Saskia didn't hesitate even a second. *Yes, dammit. Why couldn't I see it sooner? None of this would have come crashing down around me.*

Adrian's next words soothed her. *You had your reasons. But now you have a better one. If I were a betting woman—which I am —I bet the two of you make it to the other side of this, even if it's ugly for a while.*

Saskia held her phone in her hand, read the words again, mulled them over. Then finally, she typed, *Bet it all.*

It was obvious those two needed a little help.

Saskia had already said she loved the guy. But Adrian knew that if she didn't do something, they'd never have the talk they needed. Saskia might kill her for what she was about to do, but she was convinced it was the right thing.

Sitting in her snug flannel pajamas on the sofa in her elegant Nob Hill flat, she sent Saskia's address to Clay. Her friend had never told him exactly where she lived—just in case Clay decided to pay her a visit. And saw her studio.

She waited for a return text. It didn't come.

Nevertheless, Adrian went to bed knowing she'd done all she could.

For now.

CHAPTER TWENTY

*C*lay had caught the proverbial forty winks, but that was about it. He could think of nothing but Saskia— her touch, her luscious kiss, her sweet scent, her beautiful eyes, her luxurious hair he loved to run his fingers through.

But then he'd think of her lies. She hadn't told him who she was, the first lie. When he'd outright asked her more than once if she was an artist, she'd lied again. She could have helped Dylan immensely if he'd known who she was. His mind brushed over how much she'd helped Dylan even wearing her Saskia persona.

More than just think it through, Clay needed to talk it through.

It was early. But Fernsby was an early riser even on a Saturday.

The moment the man answered, Clay unloaded on him. "Where are you? I need to talk."

In his cultured British drawl, Fernsby said, "I'm wherever you need me to be, sir, as always." Then he added, "I'm walking Lord Rexford by the marina."

Clay got there pronto. Despite the early hour—just past

eight—the path along the bay was filled with joggers, bikers, and dog walkers. Ducks paddled in the pond, bobbing for their morning meal.

Clay got right to it the moment he reached Fernsby's side. "She said you already guessed who she was, even before Hugo Lewis's press conference." He'd sent the link to Dane, which meant, naturally, that Fernsby would have seen it too.

The dog stretched his flexible lead to its max, running here, sniffing there, piddling his scent in different spots. But as soon as Fernsby clucked his tongue and said in a stern voice, "Lord Rexford," the dog was back at his heel. Fernsby had a way with animals and people.

Then he answered Clay's implied question. "It was in the way she described Charlene Ballard's sculpture. It's what an artist would say. When the two of you had your tiff over how to handle criticism of an artist's work, again, the things she said didn't come from an assistant but an artist."

Clay smacked his forehead and muttered under his breath, "I should've seen it. I'm an idiot."

"You were falling in love, sir. Lovers see only what they want to see."

Maybe he should have argued, insisted he wasn't falling in love. But why bother? It was the truth. "But she lied to me." He couldn't help feeling the betrayal yet again.

Fernsby sidestepped a bicycle ridden by an older lady. "I'm sure that's the way you—and even the lovely Saskia—see it. But I believe it's more of a gray area. She *omitted*."

Clay dug in. "She *lied* when she said she wasn't an artist. That her art wasn't good enough. That she gave it up to be an assistant."

"That's because Saskia Oliver doesn't paint. Only San Holo paints. San Holo is the artist, not Saskia."

"It's not like she has a split personality," Clay scoffed.

Fernsby turned the tables. "Have you shared absolutely

everything with her?" Fernsby paused only a beat, not giving Clay a chance to say that of course he had. Especially when he hadn't. "Have you told her about your parents? Have you told her *they* are why you've never had a long-term love affair? Why you date only arm candy? Because your parents' exclusive kind of love was too much for you to handle?"

Clay stopped in the middle of the path, a bike's bell clanging as the rider veered around him. He could only stare wide-eyed at Fernsby. "How do you know that?"

Fernsby flapped an airy hand. "I am Fernsby. I know everything."

Of course he did. That's why Clay had called him.

"Allow me to tell you a story, sir."

"Is this anything like the mille-feuille story?"

"No," he said. "This is a love story."

A love story? Fernsby? Impossible. Then again, Fernsby did love his mille-feuille.

"I once knew a woman when I was a very young man."

Clay tried not to gape. Fernsby had never been young. He'd hatched just as he was.

"She didn't lie to me." The staid man walked on as he spoke. "But she held back an important bit of information. When I learned of this *omission*—" He used the word purposefully. "—I couldn't forgive her. Like you, I was young, and I thought it was a lie. That omission broke me."

Clay recognized the pain in the man's voice, even after thirty or forty or fifty years.

"At the time, I believed I would never forgive her. It was only later, after many, many years to ponder, that I forgave her in my heart. I finally accepted why she hadn't told me." He put a hand to his heart. "I hold no animosity. If she were here today, I would tell her that." He paused for another long moment. "If she were here today…" He trailed off.

Clay heard the unspoken words. If this mystery woman

were here today, Fernsby would have been on her like San Holo's paint on an empty wall. "You're saying I shouldn't waste years? I should forgive Saskia now?"

Fernsby's touch of melancholy fluttered off into the breezy day. "Exactly, sir. Get over yourself and don't waste precious time."

Clay knew what he had to do. Right now. Without wasting another minute.

As SHE TURNED onto her block, Saskia saw Clay pacing outside her cute Victorian in Haight-Ashbury. She didn't even question how he'd discovered where she lived.

After her night out, spray paint covered her clothes. All she wanted to do was run into his arms, not caring whether anything got on him.

But her feet seemed planted in concrete, her Doc Martens nailed to the ground. All she could say was, "You're here."

That gave her such hope.

Until he said, "I canceled the mural."

Everything in her—the guilt, the fear, the love, the hope— all fell to the sidewalk, smashing to pieces as though they were made of glass.

"Of course you did." A shudder ran through her entire body. "I've already thought over my list of good—" She air-quoted. "—reasons for what I did. But there's another thing I should have said."

A pair of lovers skirted around them, releasing their hands only to entwine them again once they'd passed. Clay stared at her, waited.

That made it all the harder. But she had to tell him. "I love you." Her heart crumpled like a piece of paper balled in her fist when he remained silent. But she went on. "Not just a little. All the love there is in the world—that's what I feel for you."

Was that the slightest uptick of his lips? Or her imagination? "True love?" he murmured. "Is that what you're talking about?"

Everything inside her came back to life because he hadn't walked away. He'd come looking for her.

Now, as he looked at her, waiting, she felt they might fall into place, despite all the things that were still a mess. "The truest love there is," she whispered.

Suddenly, though it seemed as if neither of them had moved, they were in each other's arms, kissing with lips and tongues and their whole bodies. It was unlike any kiss that had ever come before. Because this one was honest and pure and sexy all at the same time.

She heard clapping and stepped back to see the lovers applauding and smiling for them. Then the two men wrapped their arms around each other's shoulders and strolled off down the road, renewed by that brief display of love.

CLAY DREW her to the front stoop of her Victorian and pulled her down beside him. She smelled so damn good. She tasted even better. Better than his memories of everything they'd done together. "I came down on you for what you didn't tell me, but I played just as big a part in nearly destroying everything between us."

"No, you didn't," she said immediately, taking the blame when Clay knew it lay equally with him.

He squeezed her hand. "You told me all along you wouldn't reveal San Holo's identity. I just wouldn't accept it. But what I'm talking about goes back to my family. I never told you about my parents." He'd told her Gareth's history, Dylan's history, but he'd never talked about his own. "They died when I was a freshman in high school. They were trapped in an avalanche while skiing."

She stroked his arm. "I'm so sorry."

He kissed her knuckles in gratitude. "They left behind a lot of debt, and Dane and Ava had to take care of the rest of us." He smiled, thinking of all they'd done. "But in a way, my brother and sister were like helicopter parents, sacrificing themselves to do everything for us. They did all they could to help us reach our goals. If we hurt, they wanted to fix it. Ultimately, I did the same thing with my artists, needing to fix everything for them. Not that what Dane and Ava did was bad. They were the best, and I'll always be grateful to them. But I wanted to emulate them. Until you showed me how wrong that was, that I had to let people grow. Ava and Dane, even though they looked out for us, they still let us grow."

Saskia gazed up at him with all her love in her eyes. "You did the very best for your artists. You weren't bad for them. You provided workspace, materials, sales support."

He shook his head gently. "I don't think what I did was bad. But you taught me a better way, and I'm grateful for that. But let me get back to my parents. Dane and Ava made sure we had everything we needed because our parents never did." His chest felt suddenly constricted. "Their love was so exclusive that it could contain no one else, not even us. I thought that's what love was supposed to be like. Exclusive. Consuming. And totally transparent about everything. That's why I've always avoided it. I had so many goals that I couldn't let love get in the way. Then I met you."

She looked at him with tears brimming in her eyes. "And I met you."

"You changed everything," he whispered and caressed away the single tear that slid down her cheek. "I believed you were supposed to love the way my parents did, giving everything to that other person, holding nothing back. That's why I was so angry when you didn't share who you were and everything else about yourself. Because it meant you couldn't possibly love me."

She gripped his hand. "But really, that was all about me. Not you."

Three guys trooped down the street, probably to get breakfast, and she whispered, "We're making a spectacle out here."

"We're not," he said. "But I wouldn't care if we were." Then he told her more. "I was wrong for revering the way they loved. I can see now how unrealistic my parents' love really was. I actually think it was obsession, and that's not good. Love needs to be inclusive rather than exclusive. You have to let your family in, especially your kids. You have to let your friends in. You can't be *everything* for that other person. It's impossible."

Another tear trickled down her cheek. He kissed it away as she whispered, "But I wasn't inclusive with you at all."

He clucked his tongue. "What should I have expected? I didn't tell you about myself either. I would have, but we haven't even known each other that long."

She smiled gently. "Long enough to fall in love."

He cupped her face. "Yes, long enough to fall in love. But not long enough for us to learn everything about each other. I didn't give you time to do that. I pushed and pushed to find out who San Holo was. That made you nervous. I made it all about what I wanted instead of what you needed."

She put her fingers to his lips. "I should have trusted you before I slept with you. I did it all backward. But truly, I was going to tell you yesterday before Hugo had that press conference. I had no idea he'd ever do something like that. I'd only just learned he was in town."

"I believe you were going to tell me." Then he had to ask, "Why do you think he did it?"

She dropped her head into her hands for a moment before looking at him again. "I was twenty-two, and my art wasn't making huge waves, but I was getting some recognition. Then I met Hugo. I thought he was wonderful." She sniffled, and he heard the regret in her tone. "He was a fairly important artist then, and he felt like my mentor, praising my art, telling me how big I was going to be. I thought he loved me, that he meant every word. Maybe he did. We were together five years, and I was gaining greater fame as the artist Lynx."

He gaped, couldn't help it. *"You're* Lynx? Not Hugo Lewis?" She'd said Hugo had stolen her art. But what he'd actually stolen was her *name*?

"Yes. I was Lynx." Her jaw tensed, her teeth grinding with her feelings about Hugo Lewis. "He acted as my manager. I let him take care of everything so I could paint. Adrian didn't like it—" She gasped. "Oh, I didn't tell you that Adrian's been my best friend since we were sixteen."

"You *are* British." Clay allowed himself a chuckle. At least he'd been right about something. But there was so much they had to learn about each other. He would love every new discovery.

"Yes. Both of us came here five years ago, after Hugo." She'd obviously wanted to start her life over. "I practiced sounding like any other street artist in San Francisco. Very American," she said with a smile. "Anyway, Adrian never said what she truly thought of Hugo when I was with him. If she had, I probably wouldn't have listened. Lynx began earning big. Then suddenly, out of nowhere, Hugo told the press that *he* was Lynx."

"That ass," he said on a hiss.

"Believe me, I've called him worse." Her eyes were dark

with all the things she'd called him. "But I couldn't say anything. No one would've believed me. They all thought I was just a hanger-on of the great Hugo Lewis." She closed her eyes and hugged herself the way Clay wanted to hug her.

Her pain over what Lewis had done raked through him like hot coals. He burned with anger, with the need to hold her, to make everything better. But that's what he'd always done—tried to make everything better. What she needed right now was for him to listen.

"Hugo broke my heart," she said on a whisper of breath. "I didn't know how to fight him. I just wanted to run away. Adrian suggested we should get away from the Hugo Lewis show and visit her aunt in San Francisco. Then we decided to stay." She sighed. "Maybe I should've left London long before that. Gotten away from my parents."

"You said your parents didn't approve of your art." They'd talked about that when he'd told her about Gareth.

She sucked in a breath, held it a moment. "I didn't tell you any of this either."

They both had so much they hadn't said. "Tell me now."

"It wasn't just my art. They didn't approve of *me*. They always told me I was an accident, that they hadn't meant to have me. They acted like I was the luckiest girl in the world that they'd decided to keep me." She raised her hands and gave a half-hearted, "Woo-hoo." Her pain lanced through him. "You see, they were both famous artists when I came along. They expected me to do exactly what they told me to. But I just *couldn't*." She clamped her teeth and balled her fists. "I was arrested for tagging when I was sixteen, and they let me stew in custody for days. When their solicitor finally got me released, they told me I could never paint another wall." She closed her eyes as if the thought of never creating street art again killed her. "I couldn't stand it. I said no way, that I had to paint what I had to paint. Isn't that how artistic talent works?"

Christ. How awful to hear that your parents actually considered getting rid of you. His parents might have lived in a world where only they mattered to each other, but they'd at least paid for nannies to take care of them. But Saskia's parents had told her they'd never wanted her at all.

He stroked her knuckles with his thumb, tried to take her pain inside his own body so she wouldn't have to feel it anymore.

"When I refused to stop, they said I was an ungrateful wretch who wanted to deface property instead of making something of the talent *they* had given me, like they owned it. They told me that if I continued on my course, I couldn't live with them. I refused to beg. So I left."

He saw now exactly how her life had been. How she'd survived and made herself into a mega artist, how truly amazing she was. He had his whole family to surround him after their parents died. She'd had no one but Adrian, who'd been a kid herself.

He didn't know how her story could get worse, but it did, and all he could do was hold her.

"I lived in a tiny garret with six other artists," she told him. "We all had pallets on the floor, and I lived out of charity shops. There were never enough blankets. Adrian was always trying to give me more." She swiped at another tear. "But I survived."

"Oh, you are a survivor."

He remembered again what she'd told him that first night, before he'd even known her last name. *I'd like to learn to trust more and fear less.* She'd had so many reasons *not* to trust, especially him, a man who was part of the machine that had allowed Hugo Lewis to steal her name and her work.

"I understand why you didn't trust me in the beginning.

How could you trust anyone after what happened to you? All along, I expected too much from you." He raised her hand to his lips, kissing her gently.

"The worst of it," she said, "is that my parents actually did steal some of my belief in myself. Despite all my pep talks with Dylan and Gareth, I've never truly owned my art. I've been afraid to put myself totally out there and be ridiculed."

He realized how much it took for her to admit that. "Thank you for telling me." He trailed his fingers down her smooth cheek. "In some ways, our paths converged. I was almost sixteen when my parents died. We both had major upheavals in our lives that shaped us. We both had parents who never made their kids a priority."

"But that's no excuse," she protested. "I should have trusted you with my secrets. I should've told you about Hugo, about my parents."

A sledgehammer of realization hit him. "Christ, you're British." He hadn't realized exactly what that could mean. "Your parents are Patricia and Julian Oliver?"

She nodded.

The Olivers were famous British classical artists. He'd seen their paintings. They were masters. He'd never bought their art because the style didn't suit his taste. Now he was glad he hadn't. "I'm appalled they let their daughter live in an overcrowded garret without even adequate heating." He wanted to pummel them as badly as he wanted to beat up Hugo Lewis. "Clearly, they were threatened by your talent."

"Maybe." She shrugged. "But I swore I'd never let them hold me back. I believe that made me stronger."

He had to agree.

"And your parents—" She snorted as if they didn't deserve the title. "—were idiots to miss out on how amazing you and your siblings are. I'm not talking about the money you've all amassed, but about how caring you are."

He leaned in to kiss her. "I'm proud of you for how you moved on from what your parents did, from what Hugo Lewis did. And how much bigger you are than Lynx."

She gripped his hand tightly. "I've tried to act like I was fine, but Hugo's betrayal tore me apart." She bit her lip. "What my parents did hurt even worse. But I'm also thankful because I wouldn't have become San Holo if I hadn't been trying to prove to them that I could do it."

He understood the feeling. It was the same drive that had led all the Harrington siblings to excel in whatever they did.

Now he smiled. "All right, so tell me the real story about how you met Adrian."

She laughed, her face brightening for the first time. "I drew a caricature of her. I used to sit on street corners and try to sell my art to tourists. Adrian said she loved the drawing even though I don't think she actually did. She said she hated being curvy, and that's how I drew her. Still, she liked me, and I liked her, and she took me to lunch, and—" She shrugged. "—then we were best friends. She never gave me money, but she'd always buy me food because she said I was too skinny. And she gave me clothes and stuff she said she didn't want anymore. She took care of me, and I will always love her for being my friend in the darkest time of my life."

She stood then, held out her hand. "Will you come inside and see where I live?"

"I'd love to."

This was one of the biggest gifts she could give him. Her space. The place no one but her best friend had ever seen.

CHAPTER TWENTY-ONE

t was as though the boulder she'd been carrying since she was sixteen had finally rolled off her back. Saskia led Clay into her home, revealing herself to him.

"Your home is like your art."

With the sun streaming in, the bold colors stood out, the teal walls peppered with her designs in lighter colors and her signature fleur-de-lis. If he looked closely, he'd find Lynx too. The sofa was fuchsia, with lava lamps in bright colors, from oranges to greens to blues, scattered around the room. She'd scoured charity shops to find them. Even the rug burst with color in its geometric pattern.

"It's so you," he whispered.

She said just as softly, "I didn't think you knew the real me."

Clay reeled her in, wrapping his arms across the small of her back, holding her in a loose hug. "I was hurt. I didn't believe I knew you. But I *do* know you… in the ways that count."

She looped her arms around his neck. "And I know you."

She'd revealed all the worst parts of her life, and he'd

given his story to her too. They'd both led lives that were far from perfect, but they'd overcome.

"Welcome to my home." To her life, to her love.

"Thank you for letting me in."

With those words, she knew he understood that he was special. That she'd given very few people insight into who she really was. People thought they knew her through her art, but they couldn't know the hidden core inside, the fearful core, the distrusting core. But Clay had seen her from the beginning, even if he didn't know it. He'd recognized the artist in her, encouraged her as he did all his other artists. But she'd blown him off.

She never would again. "I love you, Clay Harrington."

His eyes were suddenly ablaze. "And I love you, Saskia Oliver slash San Holo slash Lynx. I love all of you."

She laughed. "You make it sound like I have multiple personalities."

His wicked grin heated her insides. "I love every one of them. Especially the succubus that comes out when we're in bed." He snugged her closer to him, letting her feel what the press of their bodies did to him.

How had she survived these last two nights without him? Suddenly, she wanted him with the intensity of a fever running through her veins. Trailing her hand down his arm, she wrapped her fingers around his. "Then we need to let my inner succubus loose again."

She led him up the narrow, carpeted stairs.

She'd treated the house like it was a piece of art that needed to be restored—cleaning and polishing wood floors, taking down faded wallpaper, painting walls, buffing hardwood paneling.

At the top, she turned, backing down the hallway, pulling him with her. "I'd show you my studio, but I'd rather show you the bedroom first."

He leaned in to kiss the tip of her nose. "That's a fantastic idea."

She'd painted her bedroom in the bold colors she loved—red wine walls, rugs to match, purple comforter, and dusky rose pillows. When she flipped on the lights, lace doilies over the lamps would dance color across the walls. But now the sun shone through the sheer curtains, bathing the bed in light and warmth.

"Just like you," he whispered. "Full of life and color."

Lying back on the purple comforter, she rested on her elbows and smiled at him. "I need you to make love to me right here until the sun goes down."

Make love. It had been so long since she'd said those words.

"I would love to." He crawled across the bed to her on all fours, like a stalking jaguar. Then he stopped. "Please tell me you have condoms in the house."

Her laugh was husky with desire. "I thought *you* were going to carry them in your wallet." Fist in his shirt, she pulled him down. "I don't want to use one. There's only been you. And I won't get pregnant. I'm on the pill." She felt the need to explain. "It helps with the cramps."

His lips a hairsbreadth away, he whispered, "You're safe with me, I promise."

"I've always felt safe with you."

Straddling her, he reached for the dark hoodie she wore, unzipping it, pushing the sleeves down her arms. Then he murmured in awe, "You are so damned beautiful."

Through his eyes, she felt beautiful. He tugged the tank top out of her leggings and pulled it over her head. She'd worn a jogging bra, far from sexy, yet he leaned down to kiss the spot between her breasts. "I love the feel of your skin." He licked her right there. "I love the way you taste."

With his words, his touch, his kiss, he made her feel beautiful and sexy. He tugged the bra over her head, tossed it aside, and then he bent to take the tight bead of one breast between his lips.

Saskia arched, moaned. "I love the way you make me feel."

He lifted his head long enough to say, "I love the way your scent goes to my head."

He licked, laved, sucked until her body arched up to grind into his. Then he trailed kisses down her body, backed off the bed, taking off her leggings and panties, holding them like they were war prizes. "I love how you look just like that," he murmured. "Naked, with the sun streaming across you."

"Take off your clothes," she said. "I want to memorize the sight of you."

Stripping off his shirt, he threw it on the floor, revealing rippling pectorals and washboard abs. "You don't have to memorize it. You'll be looking at it for the rest of your life."

The rest of her life. She craved that.

He stripped until he stood before her like a magnificent jungle beast. Finally, he crawled between her legs, gazing down at her. "My mouth is watering for a taste of you."

Then he teased that tight button with his fingers, his tongue, his lips, sending her flying into the sky. She moaned, then a deep groan rose up from her throat as sensation rocketed through her body. He fit two fingers inside her and worked her deliciously from the inside. She couldn't resist the heady combination as everything rushed down to her core and exploded outward. Writhing, crying, moaning on the bed beneath him, she begged him to take her, but he kept her on the edge for what seemed like forever, until she had to crawl away, the feelings so intense.

"You don't know what you do to me," she gasped.

He climbed over her again, laying his hard male body across hers, fitting himself between her legs. With his lips so close to hers that she could almost taste herself on him, he whispered, "You can never imagine what you do to me." He kissed her, so sweet, so reverent. "I love how you come for me."

He nudged her core, and just the tip of him slipped inside. She arched into the pleasure. "I love how you fill me."

He nuzzled her neck, kissed her there. "I love how sweet you are, how smart you are, how talented you are."

She drew her legs up, locked her ankles around him, pulled him the tiniest bit deeper. "I love how you take care of all your artists. How you take care of Dylan. How you take care of me."

"I love how you love me." Then, without another word, just a smile on his lips and a fire in his eyes, he thrust deep.

She arched into the pillow, closed her eyes, took all of him, until he was fully seated and still once again.

She could only whisper, "Don't stop. Don't ever stop."

"I'll never stop," he promised her. "I'll love you forever."

He withdrew, slowly, achingly, grazing that sweet spot inside her. Then he took her with short, tantalizing strokes, their bodies melding together as she fell closer to the edge.

"I love you," she whispered.

Without warning, he plunged deep again. And again. Her fire burned hotter, her body screaming for release. Then she lost herself in the pleasure.

Lost herself in him.

He knew the moment she came, her body clamping down on him, dragging him in. He took her hard then, the way he knew she loved. Circling his hips, he ground against her, inside her, loving the way she felt around him, her scent invading him, her skin like silk against him.

Until finally she squeezed him so tightly he couldn't hold back another moment.

He gave her everything—his heart, his soul, his essence, his love.

He eased his weight off her and cradled her in his arms. He couldn't say how long they lay there afterward. But when he opened his eyes, the sunbeams had moved across the bed.

She'd made him lose his mind. He'd never lost it with anyone but her.

The comforter was soft beneath his body, her skin smooth against his. The scent of their loving perfumed the air.

He realized she was awake when she swirled her fingers in his chest hair, her words whispering across his skin. "Where do we go from here?"

"I love you," he said, as if that were answer enough.

"And I love you." Both of them knew it wasn't an answer to the question she'd asked.

He exhaled, his gaze on the sunlight across the wall. "You're the anonymous artist who isn't anonymous anymore. And I have this platform that won't work the way I planned. Let's see how we're going to make that all work."

Her hair brushed his chest as she looked up at him. "You're already planning lecturers to help with the emotional side."

He sighed. "But can I do more?"

She stroked his face with one hand. "You've provided a beautiful, safe place. But maybe they need to do some of the work themselves. What about establishing pods in each of your warehouses? Like a potters' pod and a painters' pod? Where they can talk things through together."

There he went again—taking everything on himself, as if he were the only one who could get things done. But she was right. His people were capable. "I'll suggest that, then let them run with the idea." He laughed, joy bubbling up. "Damn, we're such a freaking good team. You have notions that never occurred to me."

She nuzzled his chest. "You're still the smartest man I know."

He snorted. "If I was so smart, I would have found you years ago, when you were Lynx."

"If you had, I wouldn't be the same painter I am today. Our pasts shape us, and we're the ones who have to run with it," she said, echoing him.

"You would have become the woman and artist you are no matter what happened." At the smile on her face, he knew how much his words meant to her. "But what will San Holo do now?"

She didn't pretend not to understand. "I guess I've always been afraid my parents would see what I was doing and crush my work like they did before. Being anonymous allowed me to do whatever I wanted. I never had to come face-to-face with someone who said they hated it."

"But now you have fans," he said gently. "They want to hear from you."

"But do I want to do appearances and interviews?" She shrugged. "I'm a little terrified of that."

He tipped her chin, forcing her to look at him again. "You can take on whatever you put your mind to." He tapped her chest. "In your heart, you know that."

"But do I *want* to?"

"If you want to remain anonymous, I'm behind you one hundred percent." He would back her no matter what she chose.

"But how can I do that since Hugo's given everyone my name?" She pointed at her phone on the side table as it pinged with another text. "My phone's been blowing up."

"You could paint under another name," he suggested, knowing even as he spoke that it wasn't the answer.

"But that's starting over again like I did after Hugo stole Lynx."

She was already talking herself out of anonymity, so he played devil's advocate. "Then *be* San Holo. Just refuse to do interviews and ignore social media."

"Or I could have Adrian say Hugo's claims are total bollocks." Her Britishisms were starting to come out.

Clay had to say it. "What about walking the walk? Especially after everything you told Dylan and Gareth?"

SASKIA ROLLED ONTO HER BACK, feeling the loss of his warmth immediately. Lovemaking with Clay was the most amazing of her life. And she wanted him in her life forever.

But that life was changing fast, and not only because Hugo had outed her. Fear suddenly roiled in her belly. "I'm afraid. I have to admit that. Own it."

He didn't touch her. She wished he would. But if he did, she'd never get all the words out. "You're right about walking the walk. But I'm still afraid of getting screwed over by the people I love and trust." She looked at him. "Not you. In any way imaginable. But it's like a little kid who almost drowned and is terrified of the water after that. Even though she's learned how to swim and will never come close to drowning again."

He gathered her into his arms once more. "I get the analogy. You don't have to make a decision right now. You have time to think about it."

She gazed into his eyes, her heart filling up with him. "I love your generosity. I love how you think of everyone else before yourself. I love *you*."

They clung to each other, and he whispered, "I can't let Hugo Lewis get away with hurting you again. Do you understand that?"

She answered in that same reverent whisper, "Absolutely."

"I'm going to reclaim your art for you."

She shook her head, her hair cascading over his chest. "A lot of it doesn't even exist anymore."

"But you had canvases, right, just like you do now?"

She nodded. He knew so well how she worked.

"It's your name that's most important." After a long exhale, he said, "Let's talk to Adrian. And Gareth. Together, the four of us will figure out how to recover what Hugo stole from you."

Oddly, she found she didn't care that much about Hugo anymore. If he hadn't screwed her over, she wouldn't be San Holo. If she hadn't become San Holo, she wouldn't have found Clay.

And finding Clay was the most important thing she'd ever done.

CHAPTER TWENTY-TWO

*A*s the Saturday afternoon sun crept across Adrian's office, she hugged Saskia and murmured for her ears only, "I'm so sorry. I know how much this hurts."

Adrian hated the way Hugo had used her friend, all those years ago as well as now. He hadn't revealed her identity out of magnanimity. He was simply trying to regain some of the value of his art. Especially the crap he'd painted since he'd torn Saskia's world to bits.

But this was what Adrian had wanted for Saskia all along —to be public. To step out of her nighttime shadows and claim her name and her art.

Holding Saskia away from her, hands on her shoulders, she said for everyone to hear, "Are you okay?"

From the glow on Saskia's face, Adrian could see she was fine. Better than fine. Amazing. Because of Clay.

Having arrived a few minutes before Saskia and Clay, who'd called for the meeting, Gareth Tate was already seated in a chair. "How the hell did Hugo Lewis even know San Holo was here in San Francisco?"

"The latest mural," Clay said.

But Gareth shook his head. The man was gorgeous, his clothing impeccable, his body toned to a fine edge. Under other circumstances, Adrian might drool.

"I get that," he said. "But how did he know *Saskia* was San Holo?"

Adrian took responsibility. "There was a photo of you two in the gossip columns." She fluttered a hand at Clay and Saskia. "I tried to have it quashed. But not everyone took it down."

Saskia gasped just as Adrian knew she would. "Why didn't you tell me?"

Adrian could have said that Saskia was so obsessed with Clay that she hadn't answered Adrian's texts or calls, especially since Hugo's press conference. But she couldn't blame Saskia. After all, she was the agent. She hired the publicists. "Honestly, I had no idea Hugo would put two and two together. That you were here. And so was San Holo. Ergo, you must be the same person."

Clay came to her rescue. "It's spilled milk. Let's clean it up before it turns sour."

Adrian pointed to the sofa. "Have a seat, and we'll plan our strategy."

Saskia and Clay sat together, hands linked, while Gareth dragged his chair to the opposite side of the coffee table. Rolling her desk chair closer, Adrian sat next to him. He smelled delicious.

With Gareth already briefed on Hugo's machinations, Clay jumped in. "I intend to neutralize Lewis and get Saskia's art back."

The lawyer asked, "First of all—Saskia, why didn't you go up against him before? Especially right after he claimed your name?"

Even as Saskia opened her mouth, Adrian stepped in, speaking mainly to her friend. "When Hugo stole your art and you had to start over, your name wasn't as well known in the art world. You were good, and you were growing, but you weren't quite there yet." She turned to Gareth. "Neither of us thought we could win if we went up against Hugo."

Saskia held tight to Clay's hand. "I have to admit I felt beaten. I didn't want anything more to do with him, especially not a long legal fight."

Gareth nodded briefly. Clay put his arm around Saskia's shoulders, giving her comfort. But her friend had her own strength now.

Adrian looked at Saskia. "As San Holo, you have a lot more clout than you did five years ago." She took a deep breath, hoping Saskia was ready to hear this. "If you embrace that he outed you, you could come out publicly and say that his art prior to five years ago is yours."

Saskia swallowed hard, as if it hurt.

Clay stared Adrian down. "He'll just call Saskia a liar."

Gareth stepped in. "We have to look at the legal ramifications of taking him on that way. Hugo could sue her for defamation."

But Adrian was already shaking her head. "It's not defamation if it's true."

Clay leaned forward, his elbows on his knees. "But how do we prove it?"

Adrian felt like doing a happy dance. Her idea was brilliant. "The fleur-de-lis."

They all looked at Saskia. Clay asked, "Were you hiding the fleur-de-lis in your work even then?"

Saskia had signed *Lynx* on every mural and canvas. Just as she put a small SH on her San Holo work once that name became known. Those initials and the fleur-de-lis were hidden in the artwork itself, which made it a great boon for anyone finding them.

Adrian smiled at Saskia. "Why don't you tell them, friend?"

"In addition to signing *Lynx* on each piece, I also hid a small lynx somewhere, like I do now with the fleur-de-lis. The Eurasian lynx had become extinct in England, and they were talking about reintroducing it. I felt it was a fitting image."

Adrian detected the gleam in Clay's gaze. More than admiration for Saskia's intelligence and her art, it was pure love.

For a moment, Adrian ached for what she didn't have. But she couldn't think about that now. Especially not with handsome Gareth Tate sitting next to her.

Clay said, "Hugo doesn't know about the lynx?"

Saskia shook her head, her smile growing. "I never told anyone." She turned that smile on Adrian. "Except my best friend."

Adrian grinned. "Who was forever sworn to secrecy."

"With San Holo, I used the fleur-de-lis as a gimmick, hiding it along with my initials, but letting people know it was there somewhere. It got them to really *look* at each piece."

Clay gazed at the woman Adrian was absolutely sure he loved. "Smart move. Can you remember where the lynxes are in the existing murals and canvases that he claimed from you?"

Saskia rolled her eyes. "Of course."

Adrian could almost see the elation jumping out of Clay. "Then we'll challenge him. If he were the true artist, he'd be able to find them all. When he can't, you'll show that you can. Which makes you the artist and not him."

Gareth got into the scheme too. "He probably thinks she was using the fleur-de-lis even then. He'll search the art for that and never even see the lynx."

Adrian had to agree. "That would be just like him," she said, a snide note in her tone. "He always did take the easy route. He's too cocky by far." She speared her best friend with a look. "And he never valued your ingenuity."

Clay sat back, a half-smile crooking his mouth. "Then that's the plan."

Adrian had to say it. "It means you can't hide anymore."

After a quick breath, Saskia said, "I know."

Clay drew her in, his fingers caressing her cheek. "We'll only do it this way if you're totally okay with it. I'm one hundred percent behind whatever you decide."

Adrian almost loved him herself for giving Saskia that option.

But her friend didn't back away. "Challenging Hugo forces me to speak out instead of letting him speak for me." This time when she swallowed, it didn't seem hard at all. "I've been hiding for five years, all because of Hugo and my parents." She sat straighter against the love of her life. "I'm not going to hide anymore." She put her hand on Clay's arm. "I'm going to walk the walk." To Gareth, she added, "I told you and Dylan that you both need to accept criticism. Not only survive it, but also learn from it if there's anything valid. I need to let people throw it all at me too. Being anonymous, I could ignore reviews because nobody ever said anything to my face." She took a deep breath that seemed to fill her with confidence as much as Clay's arm around her did. "I will own my art in front of everyone."

Clay kissed her soundly. Adrian wanted to clap. Gareth actually did.

Then Adrian had to be the bearer of potentially bad news. "There is a downside. If you come out of seclusion, you have to be prepared for the possibility your art might drop in value. Or even become worthless."

Clay started to speak, but Saskia stopped him. "Go on," she said.

"A big part of what people pay for is the allure of your anonymity." With their eyes on her, Adrian pursed her lips. Thought for a moment. "Even as I'm saying that, I'm realizing you're not anonymous right now because Hugo has already outed you. I know it's only been a day, but your work's value hasn't dropped at all. Honestly, I don't think you've needed to be anonymous for a long time. Your name is big. You keep on producing. You're not like Hugo, who stole someone else's art only to find his own couldn't live up to what he'd claimed. You're one of the best in the world, and it's long past time for you to claim your crown."

Once again, Clay kissed Saskia as Gareth applauded. Adrian smiled. "Do what you love, and the money will come."

Clay's eyes glowed. "Everything could explode for you. Especially when we prove that all of Hugo's art is derivative of yours."

Adrian couldn't help adding, "Since the initial buzz, I have to say the women of the art world are cheering you on. They're starting up a whole debate about how unfair it is that they have to hide behind male pseudonyms." She laughed. "Then there are the misogynistic art critics having a cow that the artist they've been praising all these years is actually a woman. So yeah, I take back what I said. This will make you even more valuable."

Gareth chuckled. "The battle of the sexes."

She wanted to cheer him for that.

But because he was a lawyer, he had to say, "Since all the art you painted as Lynx was purchased legitimately, with Hugo acting as your agent, it might not be possible to reclaim those canvases."

Saskia shook her head. "I don't want them back. Those

people paid for them. I just want everyone to know I painted them, not Hugo."

"It could turn out to be just like Taylor Swift," Clay said.

Saskia looked at him while Adrian knew exactly what he referred to. She let him explain. "After she got big, she wanted to buy back the master recordings for her first albums, but the label wouldn't sell them to her. Taking advantage of a loophole in her contract, she rerecorded all those songs and albums and put them out herself. Those rerecordings are even bigger than the old ones. Any old albums became virtually worthless."

Gareth nodded, a wry smile on his sexy lips. "The value of your work could skyrocket. The patrons who bought it will love you."

Ooh, he was good. Very good. And handsome. And sexy. Adrian's temperature shot up so fast she almost had to fan herself.

But she had to maintain decorum. "Since we're all in agreement," she said, "I'll call a press conference."

Clay looked at Saskia. "You okay with that?" When she nodded, even smiled, Clay jumped to his feet and punched the air. "We're going to nail this creep."

Adrian would have broken out a bottle of bubbly, but a knock rattled the door. Who the hell could that be on a Saturday?

Saskia, being closest, went to answer it. She stood stock still, holding the door open with a white-knuckled grip.

Then Adrian saw them. A nattily dressed couple somewhere in their early sixties, a purse hanging over the woman's forearm as though she were Queen Elizabeth.

Saskia whispered in incredulity, or horror, "Mum? Dad?"

The bloodsucking vampires had arrived right on cue.

CHAPTER TWENTY-THREE

*H*er father's hair had gone completely gray, and his shoulders, which he'd always held erect, seemed stooped, his height diminished. But her mother hadn't changed at all, her hair dark and lustrous like Saskia's, her face still carved in stark, unforgiving lines. But, on a closer look, Saskia saw gray roots sprouting from the part in her long hair. Saskia had the irreverent thought that she looked like Elvira, the campy vampire movie queen.

Voice familiar yet more gravelly than she remembered, her father said, "Oh my dear, all these years, we've never known where you were. But the moment we saw that press conference, we had to come."

Even as they stood on one side of the threshold and she on the other, his words stunned her. So did her thoughts. *Oh my God, they're here. They finally love me.*

Maybe they'd recognized how they'd abandoned her, leaving her to fend for herself. Maybe they understood now how badly they'd scarred her. Then she'd fallen prey to Hugo. She'd been desperate for love, and he'd spouted so many pretty words in the beginning. About how perfect she was.

All the words she'd wanted her parents to say. Now they were here. Finally. After all the years she'd felt so abandoned.

"We're stunned at what you've accomplished." Her father spread his hands. "It doesn't seem possible. How could you have made so much money from your *art?*" he asked, the last bit said with the slightest sneer. As if he could barely use the word *art* to describe what she did, what she loved.

Her stomach plummeted, past the floors, through the basement, down to the very ground the building stood on, taking with it all her hope. Because he still didn't care about her. It was only about her art, which was now surpassing theirs. They wanted to reconnect only because their fame was on the wane, while hers was rising. It wasn't as if she hadn't looked them up on the internet over the years. They were still famous, but the art world didn't clamor for *their* art the way it once had. Her parents were relics.

And they were here to use her.

She ached deep in her bones, in her soul, maybe even worse than on the day they'd kicked her out. Because now she'd admitted how badly she wanted to please them, even after all these years. She wanted them to throw their arms around her and tell her she was amazing, that they'd been wrong, that they were sorry.

Yet that subtle sneer in her father's voice crushed her magical thinking. They'd come for her fame and her money. Nothing more.

She sensed Clay move up beside her, felt his caring, his strength, his love. He drew a breath, opening his mouth to speak, to tell them to shove it where the sun didn't shine.

Stopping him with a hand on his arm, she said softly, "Don't. They're not worth it." She had to handle them herself, the way she hadn't been able to when she was young.

She spoke to her parents for the first time since they'd knocked on the door. "You need to go."

More words whispered in her mind. *Go crawl back under the rock you came from.* But she didn't say those words. Her parents weren't worth it.

Her father opened his mouth, more useless words pouring forth. "But we want to be here for you. Help you. Mentor you."

If only he'd said those words sixteen years ago. They would have meant the world to her. But they meant nothing now.

"I said, you need to go."

The great Julian Oliver puckered his lips and huffed out an annoyed breath. "You should know we've done a lot of thinking. Your mother and I would like to talk to you about what happened all those years ago." But he made no apologies.

Her mother didn't echo his words. In fact, she said nothing at all. Her expression hadn't changed during the entire exchange, her lips a grim line bisecting her face. No smile, not even a frown. Maybe she'd had Botox.

"We'll let you think it over," her father said. Then he handed her his card. Saskia reached out automatically to take it as he added, "Call us. We're staying at the Palace Hotel."

Just before her fingers touched the card stock, she hesitated. Then she withdrew as he let it go, and the card fell to the floor between them. "We don't have anything to talk about."

Her father didn't look down or bend to pick it up. "Please. Call us."

Then they turned together, her father's hand on her mother's elbow, their movements synchronized as if they were one unit. Saskia didn't move as they headed down the corridor to the elevator and their footsteps faded away.

Her father had looked back once, her mother not at all. Just as she hadn't spoken the entire time. Not one word.

Obviously, Patricia Oliver wasn't ready to admit she'd been wrong. She never would be.

Even if Saskia let them in, if she told them about her art and her life and what she'd been doing, after they got what they wanted, they would desert her.

But she would not let them suck her dry again.

CLAY ACHED FOR HER, but he was immensely proud of her too. He'd seen hope in the slight curve of her lips when she'd first seen them. He'd seen the hope die. Then she'd stoically sent them away. She had emotions about the episode, but she hadn't let them devastate her. She was tougher than that. Not hard, but tough.

After a deep breath and a long exhale, she said, "I just realized I've been mourning a relationship with my parents that I never actually had. All they care about is the money I make. They'll bleed me dry to get it."

He could see the intense emotion roiling inside her, but it was the emotion of release. Her parents had trampled her when they'd kicked her out—not just her art, *her*. Hugo Lewis had ripped her asunder all over again when he'd stolen her name.

But her suffering had made her a strong woman, tough enough to take all the blows thrown her way. That made her a very special woman indeed. The woman he loved.

He had to give her the words her parents wouldn't. "I'm so sorry. I know what your parents did was even worse than what Lewis did."

Behind him, Adrian snorted. "Hugo was a jerk. Your only mistake was not realizing it from the start."

Clay wrapped Saskia's hand in his. "You have to forgive yourself for that too."

All she'd ever wanted was someone's love and appreciation, the things she'd never gotten from her parents. It had made her an easy target for a man like Lewis.

A small smile creased the corners of Saskia's lips. "Hugo was a total douche." Then she squeezed his hand. "I'm sorry, but I really need to get out of here. I just—" She cut herself off, turning and dropping his hand. Then her boots echoed down the hallway as she strode away at a fast clip.

"I'm going after her," he said to Gareth and Adrian.

Adrian grabbed Saskia's bag off the couch and handed it to him. "Take care of her."

He would.

Part of him wanted to run after her parents and tear into them for what they'd done. But he'd figure out how to deal with them later.

Saskia needed him more right now.

Ahead, she took the stairs instead of the elevator, and he followed her down. As they stepped into the lobby below, her parents were just leaving through the outside door. Saskia stood for a moment, watching them.

Beautiful. Strong. His.

As the Olivers turned left on the crowded street, she crossed the lobby, opened the door, and turned right. Maybe it was an intentional separation, he couldn't tell, but she headed to the coffee shop. Clay was reminded of the day the self-driving car had almost mowed her down. The most important day of his life.

They entered the coffee shop, and she still hadn't said anything to him. At the counter, she ordered two flat whites, and when they were ready, she took a corner table.

Sitting beside her, he held her hand. He didn't ask if she was okay; he knew she was. Even if she was brimming with emotion that wanted to spill over, she was okay.

"I'm here," he murmured.

His heart broke for her as, despite her strength, everything she felt flooded out of her.

"They didn't come all that way for me." She tapped her fist to her chest. "They came to see what they could get out of me."

"They're parasites. You're the world-famous San Holo, bigger than they ever were, and they want to leech off your fame."

She sucked in a breath, and he feared for a moment that he'd hurt her. But when she spoke, he was surprised there wasn't a forlorn note in her voice, just a statement. "Why didn't they love me enough? What was wrong with me? Now, suddenly, I'm good enough for them because other people recognize my art?"

"There was always a piece of you that thought your parents were right—that you weren't good enough." He ached to make them pay for stripping away her self-confidence at such a young age. They'd stolen from her in ways even more harmful than Hugo had.

She swallowed as if her throat had suddenly gone dry. "They didn't think I was a real artist because I wasn't a classical painter." She huffed in a breath, held it, then let it out in a rush. "For just a moment, I wanted to tell them how much money I make and ask if I'm good enough now." She looked at him, her dark eyes piercing. "That's why I needed them to leave. Because I would rather die than say that. But at the same time, it means I have no family now."

He squeezed her hand. "But you do."

She nodded. "I'll always have Adrian. She's my family."

She wasn't getting it. He had to remind her. "I have two brothers and two sisters and the Mavericks as well. Without a doubt, they'll all bring you into the fold. You'll have more family than you know how to handle."

She clapped a hand to her mouth. "Oh my God. I'm meeting them all tomorrow at the birthday party."

He raised her hand to his lips, kissed her fragrant skin. "They'll love you the way you've never been loved before." Then he sat back, looked at her. "You want me to pack up your parents in wooden crates and ship them back to England?"

She laughed, then leaned over to kiss him. "You always know exactly what to say right when I need to hear it." As he relished the sweet taste of her on his lips, she said, "Let's go home to the warehouse." His home was her home. "You should make love to me so I forget about all this."

He would give her everything she asked for. Always.

ADRIAN STOMPED across the office and picked up the card Julian Oliver had left, a physical representation of Saskia's parents. She shredded it into tiny pieces and threw them in the rubbish bin. "She won't need this. I always knew her parents sucked, but now I see just how creepy they really are."

She turned back to Gareth, pasting a smile on her face. "All right, let's talk about your career."

He was right there, far closer than she'd realized.

The beautiful man cupped her face. "You're hard as nails when you go to bat for your clients. But you love them like family, and that means you're actually as soft as a marshmallow on the inside."

Then he kissed her.

She had one last thought before she sank into the heat of his arms around her.

I absolutely am a marshmallow. And right now, I'm going to melt all over you like s'mores.

CHAPTER TWENTY-FOUR

*S*askia had to admit that the birthday party, held at Dane Harrington's luxurious Napa resort, was a tad overwhelming. The Mavericks had taken over a large ballroom that opened onto a patio outside. Dane and Cammie had done wonders with the decorations. Banners stretched across the walls, streamers hung from the ceiling, and confetti sprinkled the tables.

Clay hadn't introduced her to everyone yet, though he had pointed out most of the Mavericks and the Harringtons. There were just so many of them. With the kids' birthdays, not to mention the babies, she wasn't sure she'd remember all their names.

As Clay wrapped his hand around hers, she named them off in her head. Noah and Jorge were the eldest, both eight years old. Noah was Matt Tremont's son, and Matt was married to Ari, who was Gideon Jones's sister. They had a nine-month-old, Penelope. Jorge belonged to Gideon and Rosie. Okay, got that. Then there were the twins, Keegan and… Savannah, that was it. A year old, the twins belonged to Evan and Paige Collins. Okay, check. Twins clearly ran in the family, as Evan's younger siblings, Tony and Kelsey, were also twins.

Dylan practically bounced over to them, dragging Gideon Jones with him. "Gideon, this is Saskia. She's actually San Holo." The fan-boy gleam in his eyes lit up his whole face.

The big man stuck out his hand. "Nice to meet you, Saskia San Holo." He was tall, blond, and as handsome as all the Mavericks and Harringtons.

"Just call me Saskia." She smiled. "I've heard all about your foundation. It sounds amazing."

Gideon actually blushed.

Dylan jumped in. "I haven't seen you for days, Gideon. So much has happened. I got totally trashed," he said as if it were a badge of honor. "But I handled it." His chest seemed to puff out. "Now I'm an even better artist. Saskia says so."

"He truly is," she agreed, glad he called her Saskia rather than San Holo. Saskia was her true self.

Clay squeezed her hand as if he'd read her thoughts.

"Thank you for all you're doing to help Dylan." Gideon ruffled the young man's hair affectionately. "I've always known he was brilliant."

"I absolutely second that." She looked at Clay, her heart wanting to burst into song. "So does Clay."

Dylan dragged Gideon away, heading for Rosie, Gideon's beautiful wife who was holding their nine-month-old daughter Isabella. Wow! She'd remembered two more names.

Appearing out of nowhere, Adrian hugged her, whispering, "Are you okay after the vampires' visit yesterday?"

Saskia hugged her back, holding on. "I'm perfect. And you're the best." Saskia was so glad Clay had thought to invite Adrian.

They smiled together as only two best friends could. "Back at ya. And this is your coming-out party, my darling."

"I had *that* at Hugo's press conference," Saskia said dryly.

Adrian wagged her finger. "But *you* weren't there." She looked pointedly at the birthday boys and girl. "They think it's their party. But it's really yours."

Gareth stood beside her. Though they didn't hold hands, there was something. Attraction, maybe? With that gleam in Adrian's eye when she looked at him, oh yes, something had happened. Saskia couldn't be happier.

Clay and Gareth man-hugged with backslaps. Then Clay hugged Adrian. "We're glad you made it."

It really was like family, just as Clay had said.

Then Adrian waved at one of the Mavericks. "Cal Danniger," she said, sotto voce.

The man headed over with Lyssa Spencer, who had their baby boy on her hip. Saskia knew Cal was a fan of her work, but her heart jumped into her throat, as though this might be a confrontation, especially since they were trailed by so many Maverick ladies. She suddenly felt spotlighted.

Clay snaked his arm across her back. Fortification.

Cal hugged Adrian, since they'd had so many dealings together.

Then he simply stared at Saskia for an excruciating moment, his face flushed, before he stuck out his hand. "It's great to meet you. I'm Cal Danniger. I—I—"

His beautiful wife Lyssa, youngest daughter of Susan and Bob Spencer, the Maverick matriarch and patriarch, stepped in for him. "He's trying to say he loves your work. We've got several of your prints, even some canvases."

Kelsey Collins, Evan's younger sister, said in a high voice, "Will you look at that? Cal is tongue-tied. That's so adorable." Her laughter ran through the crowd of ladies around them.

Cal collected himself and said, almost smoothly, "I saw your mural in the graffiti tunnel in London—" He scratched his temple. "Oh… about eighteen months ago."

Lyssa gazed at him with adoration. "You know exactly

how long ago it was, my darling." With the way they smiled at each other, Saskia was sure there was a story there.

"I've been following your art ever since," Cal said. "Your new piece in the Mission District is incredible."

Saskia felt a sweet thrill, almost as good as the thrill she got when Clay touched her. "Thank you. I'm glad you like it."

He jutted his chin at Clay. "This guy told me that you're both San Holo *and* Lynx."

Last night, Cal and Clay had talked over the ramifications of Hugo's press conference. Clay had told him how they planned to take care of Hugo.

"Now it makes perfect sense," Cal went on, "why Lynx's work took a sudden nosedive five years ago. I have a Lynx print from the old days." He blushed. "Would you show me where the lynx is?"

She felt as if she were standing on top of The Shard, London's tallest building. She finally had the recognition she'd always sought. The Mavericks seemed to hang on her every word, and yet, she was quaking inside.

Was this how it would feel when she came out to the press and took Hugo on? Could she handle that?

With Clay's support, she knew she could. "Certainly, I'll show you," she said, beaming at Cal. "Which canvas do you have?"

The talk went on from there, her anxiety lessening as the minutes ticked by. Eventually, the ladies around them dispersed, mostly because the three babies were fidgeting.

With that break in the crowd, a little woman pushing a walker decorated with streamers and spangles wheeled her way over. "My dear, I just had to meet you. Charlie has talked so much about your art."

Clay made the introductions. "This is Francine, Charlie Ballard's mother."

Saskia bent down to shake the woman's hand. "It's lovely to meet you, Francine."

Charlie Ballard joined them, a beautiful woman with fiery curls, her hand engulfed in that of Sebastian Montgomery, another tall, handsome Maverick.

Charlie hugged her. "I can't believe I actually get to meet the real San Holo."

Saskia laughed. "I can't believe I actually get to meet the real Charlie Ballard." Then she prattled like a superfan. "*The Discus Thrower* is out of this world. I've never seen anything so exactly perfect for a space."

Charlie seemed to beam. Saskia was sure she was beaming too. Then she turned to Sebastian. "You're an amazing artist in your own right. I've seen your drawings. They're brilliant."

He smiled almost shyly. "Thank you. But Charlie's the real star." He wrapped his arm around her shoulders, pulling her close.

Saskia thought they were shining stars together.

As the party went on, the warmth of the Maverick-and-Harrington clan filled her up. Each and every one made an effort to meet her, to welcome her, to bring her into their fold. These two groups had become one big, close-knit family.

She'd been afraid Clay's brothers and sisters might be more wary of her, but they surrounded her with good cheer.

Her anxiety faded when his brother Troy, a couple of years older than Clay, drawled, "Thank God we were able to talk Clay off the ledge at the family mastermind."

His older sister Ava nudged him in the ribs. "He was almost there on his own," she admonished. The beautiful, statuesque redhead tucked her hand into the crook of Ransom Yates's elbow. Older than most of the Harringtons, Ava's beau was still ruggedly good-looking.

Troy, tall, dark, and handsome like all his brothers, looked down his nose at Ava, a glint of humor in his eyes. He snorted. "He was so far from seeing the light." Then he turned to Saskia. "I give you all the credit for getting Clay to understand that criticism can be good for anyone endeavoring to reach a big goal. Like diving. If the coaches hadn't critiqued my every move and suggested ways I could do things better, I never would have made it to the Olympics." He threw an arm around Clay's neck, drawing him in for a brotherly hug. "I'm proud of you, little brother, for providing tools to handle the rigors of the artistic life. Your guest lecturers and workshops sound remarkable."

Clay ran his hand down Saskia's back. "I never would've thought of them without Saskia." He pulled her close to kiss her sweetly in front of his family. "Thank you for making me see."

She wanted to melt against him in a puddle of goo.

Susan Spencer stepped into the group. "I hate to break up this wonderful conversation, but I'd love to whisk Saskia away for a heart-to-heart." After the nods and smiles, as if they'd all had their own heart-to-hearts with Susan, she looped her arm through Saskia's and drew her away. "I hope you don't mind, dear."

Susan was a lovely woman, somewhere in her fifties, wearing her beautiful cap of silver hair like a crown. She deserved a crown after raising all these wonderful Mavericks. Except for Daniel and Lyssa, they weren't her natural children, but she had taken them into her care when they were preteens—taught them, supported them, admired them. Saskia recognized the love shining out of her eyes as she looked at each of her boys.

"We haven't had a chance to talk yet." She patted Saskia's arm. "We're just so glad you've become one of us."

Though Saskia wanted to gush, she toned it down. "You

all make me feel like I *am* one of you, even though Clay and I have only been dating for a couple of weeks."

Susan wagged a finger. "It isn't the length of time. It's the depth. The connection I see flowing between the two of you is unbreakable."

"Thank you," Saskia said in a small voice, tears pricking her eyes. "That means so much to me." Susan would never know how much. They were the words of approval she'd wished for from her own mother.

"I must confess…" Susan bumped her shoulder lightly. "Even though I have so many creative people in my family, I hadn't been aware of your art before. But when I heard the other day that you were coming to the party, I had to look you up. I was overcome by the beauty and feeling imbued in your work. I'm so glad you decided to tell the world who you are."

If only her father, or especially her mother, had spoken of her work like that yesterday, instead of going directly to the money. If only they'd welcomed her as Susan Spencer had, as all the Mavericks and Harringtons had, Saskia would have opened her arms to them.

Susan was the wise woman of the Mavericks. Just as Fernsby knew when to say the perfect thing, Susan seemed to know just the right thing to help a person find his or her path.

Impulsively, she hugged the Maverick matriarch. "Thank you so much. Honestly, you don't know how much I needed to hear that."

Susan feathered the hair back from Saskia's face. "I only say what I believe, my dear."

That made Susan's words all the more heartwarming and accepting.

CHAPTER TWENTY-FIVE

*T*he moment Susan Spencer whisked Saskia away, Clay found himself drawn into the fun, laughter, and games with the kids out on the tiled patio, which was warm with spring sunshine.

Laughing, he remarked to Ari Tremont, "I can't believe how fast these babies crawl."

Ari grabbed Penelope before she disappeared off the patio. "I said I'd never have a baby gate. But I was so wrong. You have to keep them corralled. At least in the classroom, you can close the door." She was a kindergarten teacher, and he knew she had to be excellent at it.

It struck him that it had been more than half an hour since he'd last seen Saskia with Susan, who was now speaking with Fernsby.

He went in search of the woman he adored and found her on a bench out in the resort's garden. Sitting beside her, he draped his arm over her shoulders. "Hey babe, why are you out here all alone?"

She closed her eyes, breathed in deeply, then looked at him. "Spending time with your family is amazing. You're all so loving and supportive." She hooked a thumb over her shoulder at the patio crowded with Harringtons and Mavericks "You're all one big, beautiful, happy, loving family."

He stroked her hair. "Yeah, we are."

She sighed. "It makes me think more about my parents."

Guilt wormed through him. Maybe it had been too soon to bring her here after what happened yesterday. His heart hurt for her. For the way her parents had shown up again like ticks, trying to burrow back into her life. "What are you thinking?"

He rubbed her shoulder, letting her know he was here no matter what.

"Today, I've seen what real family love is like, how Susan and Bob Spencer are beacons of light for everyone. My parents made me feel like they owned my talent because they *allowed* me to be born. Then they kicked me out because I wanted to paint my way instead of theirs." She shuddered.

He dropped a kiss on her hair, even as his heart ached for her.

She gazed up at him, her eyes shiny with tears, but something more too. With strength and resolve. "Yesterday, when my father asked only about the money I made, all I wanted to do was scream at them both." She sighed. "But I've had time to think about it. Should I go see them at their hotel? Should I write them a letter telling them how I feel? Should I try to fix things with them? This afternoon, being around your wonderful family, I find I don't want to hate them anymore. I don't even want to be angry with them. They are who they are, and they'll never change. I can accept that. I think I can even forgive them."

He leaned his forehead against hers. "I know you can. You're the strongest person I know."

She pulled back far enough to meet his eyes. "I can forgive." She pursed her lips. "But what I've decided is that I can't ever be a part of that kind of family again. I have to let them go. They're toxic. I don't want that in my life. Forgiving them, then letting them go is the best thing for me." Though tears glittered in her eyes, she didn't let them stop her.

He was so damned proud of her. "I fully support your decision. I wish more than anything they could see how amazing you are. But they'll never see past their own egos. None of us need people like that in our lives."

She dipped her head, nodded.

He dropped a kiss on her beautiful lips. "If you ever change your mind and want to see them, I'll be by your side every second. Whatever you need."

She wrapped her arms around him, her voice a choked whisper. "All I need is to be free. All I want is to love you and to make your family my family."

He held her tightly enough to show her he would never let her go. "I love you. Now and always."

THEY RETURNED JUST in time for cake.

Saskia had made her momentous decision. Truly, she was free. Free to love Clay, to find happiness, to throw her all into her art.

With the children seated at the birthday table with balloons tied to each chair, Fernsby and Gabby Harrington, Clay's youngest sister, carried out trays of cakes. Fernsby claimed the honor of setting one small cake in front of Savannah and another for Keegan.

Evan Collins, tall and handsome like all the Mavericks, ran a hand through his tawny hair as he leaned over his twins. "They each get their own cake?" He looked at Fernsby his gaze wide-eyed—and terrified?—behind his glasses.

Fernsby, being himself, which Saskia was getting used to, drawled, "It's a smash cake, sir."

Evan reared back as the rest of the adults stepped forward to listen. "What the heck is a smash cake?"

Fernsby seemed to smile, barely. Then he pointed as Keegan smashed his little fist into his cake and shoveled chocolate into his mouth.

Savannah plunged her whole face into her cake, then popped back up with cream icing and sponge cake all over her face, her smile wide beneath the mess.

A pretty woman with auburn hair, their mother Paige giggled. "I hope *you're* giving them baths, Fernsby."

Fernsby remained impassively stoic. "Have no fear, dear lady."

Clay whispered against Saskia's hair, his warmth shooting thrills through her body, "Fernsby tries to keep it a secret, but he loves babies and small children."

"And small dogs," she added as Dane and Cammie's dachshund jumped around at his feet, obviously waiting for his own treat.

"Where's *my* smash cake?" Noah cried, Jorge echoing him.

Fernsby answered, "Gabrielle has them."

Gabby set down two small cakes in front of the boys. They both hooted with giddy yelps, though Jorge looked at his mother, waiting until Rosie gave a nearly imperceptible nod.

Then the two boys threw themselves at their cakes, burying their faces, while the crowd of Mavericks and Harringtons clapped.

Bob Spencer, beloved father of the Maverick clan, guffawed and cheered them on. "You go, boys!"

"Jeremy, where are you, my dear boy?" Fernsby called.

The young man stepped forward, waving a hand. "Here I am."

Harper Franconi's younger brother—Saskia *was* remembering all the family ties—appeared to be in his early twenties, with beautiful blue eyes. Clay had told her that he'd been hit by a car when he was young that had left him more childlike than adult.

"Sit," Fernsby said with a flourish. Jeremy sat next to Noah.

Then Gabby trotted over with another smash cake.

"But it's not my birthday," Jeremy said with openmouthed wonder.

"You are, nevertheless, special," Fernsby intoned.

Jeremy looked as if he might cry for joy. Then he plunged into his cake and came up gobbling frosting and red velvet.

Will Franconi put his arm around his wife as Harper mouthed, "Thank you," to Fernsby and Gabby.

Saskia put her lips to Clay's ear. "What incredible fun." There was astonishing freedom in smashing your face into a cake.

Without anyone having noticed they'd gone, Gabby and Fernsby reappeared with a two-tiered cake, setting it on another table laden with silverware and plates. Then Fernsby announced, "The adults have their own cake." He wagged his finger. "But no smashing."

"The bottom layer is my vegan devil's food," Gabby told the crowd.

Fernsby muttered under his breath, though still quite audibly, "Most likely inedible."

Susan Spencer slipped her hand through the crook of Fernsby's elbow and said in an equally audible whisper, "Don't be jealous, Fernsby."

The tall man patted her hand, gazing down at her with admiration, and maybe even reverence. "There must always be a bit of envy if we are both to stay on our toes." Then Fernsby announced in a booming voice, "I have also made devil's food cake for the top layer, but mine will give you the full complement of butter, eggs, and sugar your bodies require."

Saskia had heard all about the rivalry between the two bakers—one vegan and one who steadfastly declared that butter and eggs were the staff of life.

A stampede of Mavericks bore down on the cake table.

Clay secured a piece of each layer and brought them back to Saskia to share. She had to admit that both cakes were equally delicious. Together, they demolished both pieces.

A shout rent the air. "What are you doing, woman?" Daniel Spencer scraped cake off his face and looked at his beloved with mouth agape.

Tasha whipped her long, dark hair over her shoulder. "I thought we needed our own smash cake."

"Oh my God," Saskia whispered just before Daniel wiped his cake-covered hand down Tasha's face.

She squealed. And laughed. Then he smeared cake and icing between them as he kissed her clean.

Then it was a free-for-all, cake flying, shrieks and laughter filling the air like music, every Maverick kissing their lover, licking away frosting and cake and acting like children.

Although children didn't kiss like *that*.

"Too bad we ate all of ours," Saskia whispered in Clay's ear.

"I can get us some more." He winked. "I'd love nothing more than to lick it off every part of your body."

She shivered with desire. Then, looking at the food fight, she smiled, her heart full for the first time ever. "I think I love your family almost as much as I love you."

FERNSBY STOOD with Susan beside the sad remains of his beautiful cake, their arms linked as they surveyed the damage her Mavericks had wrought.

"I do believe, dear lady, that your brood was even worse than the children."

She laughed. The adults' tiered cake was in far worse shape now than the smash cakes. "What about your brood? Your wonderful Harringtons were no better than my Mavericks."

He almost smiled. Just a little, just for her. Because she was such a special lady whom he admired with all his shriveled heart. "Agreed. Our broods can be atrociously juvenile at times," he drawled.

Yet he'd stood back and applauded, if only in his mind, as Dane threw cake in Cammie's hair. Then she'd licked cake and whipped cream from his face. And Ava and Ransom had been close to steamy.

It had been a delirious melee. Fernsby, of course, had maintained decorum, not wishing to dirty either his hands or his pristine suit.

What a beautiful, boisterous bunch they were, all these Mavericks and Harringtons. His heart actually swelled.

Susan gazed beyond the untidy table at her delightful brood. "I used to be the one they always came to. But, my dear Fernsby, you are startlingly good at handing out advice without them even realizing they've been advised."

He wanted to crow at her compliment. Though it was undeniably true, it held so much more weight coming from the incomparable Susan Spencer. "Thank you, Susan. But we all know you are the heart of this family."

She squeezed his arm, leaning a little closer. "How about if we share that heart, you and I?"

He couldn't help but say, "I find that immensely pleasing, my dear sweet lady."

She winked. "If there's anything in your life that you'd like to talk over, I'm always here for you."

The image of a certain woman from long ago came suddenly to Fernsby.

As though she could pluck that very image from his mind, Susan said, "Anything. Absolutely anything."

Something inside him crumbled. "You're very good at seeing straight into someone's soul, aren't you?"

She just smiled. Such an endearing smile. A lovely woman indeed.

"One day, dear Susan, you and I will get smashingly drunk." He bared his teeth in what he hoped was a smile. "And I will tell you all my secrets."

She beamed back at him. "I can't wait."

CHAPTER TWENTY-SIX

*S*askia was shaking in her boots. Literally. She stared at the video monitor in the small room in which she, Clay, Adrian, and Gareth were sequestered. "Look at all those people."

She balled her fists, her nails digging into her palms.

Adrian had gone a few steps bigger and better than a press conference and booked a morning talk show. Hugo had outed her on Friday, and now, on Tuesday, she would out him.

If she didn't faint from terror first.

Adrian threw her arms around Saskia and whispered, "You'll be amazing. Just answer the questions the way we talked about. The audience will love you." She held Saskia at arm's length. "The whole country, even the world, is going to love you."

Clay wrapped an arm around her shoulders and held her tightly, imbuing her with the strength she needed. "You've got this."

With Clay by her side, as well as Adrian and Gareth, she truly did.

They were in the green room of the popular morning show *Good Morning USA*, supplied with delicious snacks and drinks and a TV monitor airing the show in progress.

Adrian had arranged the interview wicked fast, since it was hot news on the heels of Hugo's press conference. It didn't hurt that Sebastian Montgomery owned the TV network that aired the morning show. Saskia had the fourth and final slot, and number three, the woman who'd started her own line of chemical-free vegan cosmetics with only five ingredients, was just finishing up.

The camera panned the audience, highlighting faces she recognized—art dealers, agents, art journalists—all waiting with bated breath for what she had to say.

Then she saw them, taking up the first three rows center stage.

On an oddly choked breath, she murmured, "They're here. All the Mavericks and Harringtons."

Clay nuzzled her hair with a kiss. "Of course they are. They all support you."

Dylan was out there, too, seated next to Gideon, as well as Susan and Bob Spencer, along with Fernsby sitting tall, straight, and immobile, his mouth a grim line. She'd come to suspect that was merely a veneer, and there was a lot more to Fernsby that lay beneath the surface.

"I'm going to cry," she whispered.

Adrian shook her finger. "I am not bringing that makeup artist in here again."

She'd had her makeup done, but she wore her favorite sweater, leggings, and boots. No point in dressing up when she was revealing her true self.

When the producer opened the door and said, "You're on after the commercial break," Saskia's knees turned to jelly.

Clay leaned close to whisper, "You can do this."

She *would* do it. Every interview after this would be easier.

The lights onstage were monstrous, blinding her to the audience, though that could be a good thing. She shook hands with the show's hosts, Wren Gardner and Steve Stevenson.

Wren led her to a chair. "We're so happy to have you with us, Saskia Oliver." She added casually, as she took her seat, "Or shall we call you San Holo?"

"Thank you. I'm so glad to be on your show." She feared her voice sounded weak, so she said more strongly, "Just call me Saskia. All my friends do."

They wanted her to explain street art, to give a little of her history, to say why she'd always been anonymous. She didn't reveal her personal issues—that she'd done it to hide from Hugo and her parents.

But what she said was still the truth. "Two reasons, Wren. First, I like the autonomy it gives me, allowing me to do whatever I want. Also, the art world, and especially street art, is very male-oriented. So, many female artists use pseudonyms or just their initials."

Someone in the audience called, "You go, girl." Cheers followed.

Then the questioning got intense. Wren asked, "Why do you think Hugo Lewis decided to tell the world who you are?"

Because Hugo is a jealous jerk who can't stand that I'm bigger than he is, especially after he stole my work.

But she said what she'd practiced with Adrian and Clay. "I knew Hugo many years ago. Our relationship ended badly. I believe he outed me as payback for the way things ended between us."

Wren Gardner went on relentlessly. "But how did he know that you, Saskia Oliver, are actually San Holo?"

Saskia gave the simple answer. "He knows my style. Even though it's changed over the past five years, there are still elements that are uniquely me. When he saw my latest piece in San Francisco and also learned that I was here, he assumed the connection."

Wren nodded thoughtfully for her audience. "I've also looked at your early work, and your style has changed. But there are still things I recognize. The way you render people's faces, for example. The way your work is very inclusive."

"Yes," Saskia agreed. "Hugo had a lot of time to study it. In fact, most of the pieces he claims are his works are actually mine."

The entire television studio fell silent. Wren Gardner's mouth dropped open in shock.

Being a professional, she recovered quickly, especially when it hit her that she had an even bigger scoop than she'd thought possible. Her voice, however, was calm. "How could Hugo Lewis claim your work?"

Saskia went on to explain, just as she'd practiced. "Like San Holo, I was painting anonymously when I first met Hugo. I called myself Lynx."

A collective gasp rose from the audience. The Mavericks knew, but no one else had.

Saskia continued smoothly, in her element now. "It was very easy for Hugo to say all my murals were his because there was no real person's name on them."

Wren's brow furrowed. She didn't miss a trick. "But is this something you can prove?"

The four of them—she, Clay, Adrian, and Gareth—had planned this meticulously. Hugo's payback time. "In the same way San Holo puts a hidden symbol in every work, so did Lynx."

She looked straight into the studio audience, even though she couldn't see past the lights. She knew where he was sitting. Sebastian had called Clay on his cell to tell him while they were in the green room. Saskia spoke directly to Hugo. "Hugo, why don't you find the hidden symbol in each piece of art you claim is yours?"

She could feel every head turn, searching. A spotlight lit up the audience, centered right on Hugo.

Originally, they'd planned to make the challenge through the camera. But Hugo had set himself up by joining the live audience, which made it so much better. All the butterflies she'd felt flying around in her stomach simply flew away. She was in control.

"When you can't," she called, "I'll be happy to show everyone myself." She held up an envelope. "This contains photos of all the artwork I created prior to five years ago. The work I—" She tapped her chest. "—signed with the name Lynx. I've circled where my hidden symbol is on every piece." She handed Wren the envelope.

The talk show host was practically foaming at the mouth. Her show's ratings would go through the roof. Opening the envelope, she pulled out the first photograph, studied it only a moment. "Ladies and gentlemen, we have a challenge here. Hugo Lewis, are you up to it?"

Hugo looked around him, red-faced, flustered, his mouth working but no words coming out.

Saskia hoped he'd scurry off like the scum he was, muttering like a madman.

But once he found his voice, Hugo stood. "I'll meet that challenge." People moved out of his way as he strode down the steps of the studio audience. He'd gained weight and lost hair, his face florid in the harsh lights.

Wren's grin stretched ear to ear, showing off her brilliantly white teeth as she home in on Hugo. "Let's choose Lynx's most famous piece, *The Merry-Go-Round*."

On the big screen behind them, the producer put up the image, which was readily available on the internet. In it, kids of all races played happily together, their hair whipping out as the merry-go-round seemed to move faster and faster in a slight blur.

For just a moment, Saskia's stomach lurched. Was it possible Hugo had figured out her lynx symbol?

He climbed onto the soundstage, the camera following him as he stalked to the big screen. The art had no background, just dirt beneath the merry-go-round, then white space.

Hugo didn't point out the symbol immediately. In fact, he seemed to be scanning every inch.

Wren, with a hint of sarcasm, said, "Are you having trouble finding it, Hugo?"

He didn't turn but flapped a hand at her. "This is one of my earliest pieces, and I'm trying to remember exactly where I put the fleur-de-lis."

He'd been so confident Saskia would never challenge him that he hadn't bothered to look for a symbol. Maybe hadn't even thought of it. And he was so damned linear, believing she would have used the same symbol when she became San Holo.

Wren turned to Saskia and raised one brow. "A fleur-de-lis? But I thought—" She didn't finish.

Instead, she said, "San Holo, or Lynx, as the case may be, can you find the symbol for us?"

Smiling, triumph bubbling through her, Saskia slipped out of her chair, walked to the screen, and stood next to Hugo. Just stood there for a long moment. *Drumroll, please.* Then she pointed to a little girl whose pigtails flew out behind her in the wind. "There."

The screen zoomed in on the spot Saskia pointed to.

Wren put the tip of a perfectly manicured nail to her bottom lip. "But gosh…" Sarcasm dripped off each word. "It's not a fleur-de-lis at all. It's a lynx."

Hugo staggered back three steps.

Wren asked, "Shouldn't you know that, Hugo Lewis, since you've called yourself Lynx for five years?"

The studio audience erupted, and the technicians turned the lights on him. A man cried out, "Holy heck, I own a Lynx print. And now to find out it's stolen?"

Another man yelled, "Crap! I bought a piece of art he did three years ago, and now it's worthless."

Even Cal Danniger leaped into the fray. "Thank goodness my Lynx print is one of the early works." He winked at Saskia.

Wren cupped a hand over her microphone, speaking aside to Saskia alone. "Hugo is going to be bombarded by angry art investors who bought something he painted rather than one of the earlier pieces he claimed from you. Because his stuff in the last five years is crap."

Cal spoke up again. "I don't feel good about keeping that print since it was stolen from you."

Saskia waved down all the shouts. "Of course you'll keep it. You paid for it. It's yours." The studio lights adjusted so she could see, and she gazed at the audience as a whole, even those watching on TV. "If you own one of Lynx's early works, all I ask is that you let me add my fleur-de-lis and my initials."

Hugo had never actually put his signature on those paintings, since he claimed to be Lynx.

"No one has to pay me more or give it back," she declared. "Because it belongs to you, the art lover. That's what artists do—they create, then they put it out in the world for all of you to enjoy. I'm just so glad you loved my early work."

259

She glanced into the wings where Clay stood and knew he'd recognize what she'd told Dylan. That you created, then you let it go. Whether the world loved it or trashed it.

From this moment on, she would be able to take whatever anyone said.

She'd forgotten all about Hugo, until suddenly he hissed at her, "You think you're so freaking magnanimous. But I've outed you, and your art won't be worth a shilling. Just like it was worth nothing before I found you. Then your pretty-boy billionaire boyfriend will dump you like a shot when he sees how worthless you are."

Saskia's lapel mic picked up every word and broadcast Hugo's ugliness to the world.

But she smiled at him. "I believe this audience sees things differently. It's time you got off the stage."

Shooting her a last glare, Hugo slunk away, disappearing into the wings instead of returning to his seat.

Steve Stevenson, who'd allowed Wren to handle most of the questions, asked, "Why didn't you challenge Hugo when he first claimed your work?"

It was the question everyone would ask. Saskia gave the true answer. "Because I was young. I let him control everything. When I found out what he'd done, I was too heartbroken to fight him. Instead, I became San Holo and made myself better than I ever was before."

The audience jumped to their feet, their applause thunderous. Wren Gardner hugged her. Then Steve Stevenson said, "Oops, we missed our commercial break. Gotta go, folks."

The cameras stopped rolling, and Clay rushed out to hug her. Adrian wiped tears from her cheeks. Then the Maverick-and-Harrington clan rushed the stage with hugs and attagirls.

Dylan whispered in her ear, "You're the best, San Holo, or Lynx, or whoever you want to be."

Then, amid them all, Clay wrapped his arm around her shoulders to pull her close.

She'd never felt so special or so loved in her entire life.

EPILOGUE

Two weeks later

Though most of the Mavericks owned private jets, they'd had to rent a plane that would fly the entire contingent of Mavericks and Harringtons to Las Vegas.

Clay and Saskia sat over the wing. "How did Ava even know what Charlie and Sebastian were planning?" Saskia wanted to know. Just this morning, the couple had left for a quick trip to Las Vegas to get married. Without a single Maverick in attendance.

There was no way the Mavericks would let that happen.

Clay nuzzled Saskia's neck, trying to steal kisses from the most beautiful woman in the world, but the plane was too crowded for furtive smooching. He was therefore forced to answer her question. "Francine figured it out. She lives in one of Ava's eldercare facilities."

The jet engines roared, and the chatter among the Mavericks and Harringtons was almost as loud. Two flight attendants made their way through the large cabin, handing out champagne, juice, and water. Susan and Bob Spencer were seated toward the front in seats facing Matt and Ari Tremont, who cradled nine-month-old Penelope. The twins, Noah, and Jorge were in the rear lounge area, which had been converted into a playroom. Even Jeremy and Dylan had gone back to entertain the kids.

Saskia nudged Clay. "Tell me the whole story."

"Ava was on one of her regular visits to Francine's facility."

"Then Francine must be one of her favorites," Saskia guessed.

Ava was CEO of Harrington Community Care International and flew out to her other facilities at least twice a year. But in the Bay Area, she visited monthly and was even known to paint the nails of her favorite ladies. Ransom also took time out of his busy chef-extraordinaire schedule to accompany Ava and help paint the ladies' nails.

"Funny how everything is connected," Clay mused. "Ava had no idea Francine was Charlie's mother before we all fell in with the Mavericks. Anyway, suspecting something was going on, Francine told Ava that Charlie and Sebastian were going on a short jaunt, after which they'd have a massive party." He smiled, looking a couple of rows up at Francine, who was seated with Ava and Ransom. "Francine was sure they were eloping, because Charlie wouldn't want a lot of fuss."

"But honestly, how did Ava figure out it was Las Vegas?"

Clay chuckled. "My devious older brother. Dane was able to find out their flight plan."

Thus, the Maverick group was on a mission to make sure they were in attendance at Charlie and Sebastian's elopement.

Clay looked up as Will Franconi made a beeline for

Adrian, Gareth by her side. Gareth was taking a leave of absence from his law firm to do some painting. Clay couldn't be happier that his friend had rediscovered his creativity, though he suspected Gareth had never lost it, simply buried it beneath everyone else's needs. And this thing with Adrian? A match made in heaven.

Will's voice carried through the plane despite the jet engines. "Adrian, give us the update on Hugo Lewis."

Clay was sure they'd all done an internet search on the man, but it was good to have a group update.

Adrian damn near beamed as she told them the news. "I'm happy to say that Hugo has disappeared from the art scene. Completely." She dusted her hands together as if she were erasing him. "Once he failed Saskia's challenge to find the symbol that was supposedly in *his* paintings, he slipped away into the weeds like the weasel he is."

A massive round of applause pounded Clay's ears as he snuggled Saskia closer. "I'm so glad," he murmured.

Adrian stood and made her way to Saskia. "The art world is begging you to tell them where all the lynx symbols are in your early work. Collectors are clamoring for your San Holo prints too." She laughed, her eyes glittering. "I've never seen so many zeros written after a number on a check. I was completely misguided when I suggested anonymity bumped up the price of art. Your stuff is hotter than ever, Saskia." She drew her friend up into a tight embrace.

Stepping back, Adrian pointed at Clay. "A little birdie told me that another mural with a fleur-de-lis has popped up in New York." She arched one eyebrow. "Weren't you two just there?"

Clay had stood at the end of that New York alley all night while she'd worked, despite her dry tone when she'd said, *I've been doing this on my own for years.*

But she was his now. He wouldn't stop worrying that something might happen to her out there alone at night.

The crowd raised their glasses in a toast, and a voice rang out, whose he wasn't sure. "To Saskia, San Holo, and her bravery."

Adrian leaned over to hug him, murmuring, "Thank you for keeping her safe. I never told her, but I've always worried about her hanging out in dark alleys."

He hugged her back. Then he looked at his beautiful Saskia. "She'll never be alone again."

He meant that in so many more ways than one.

———

SASKIA DIDN'T FEEL EVEN a twinge of embarrassment or nerves. Where before there'd been only herself and Adrian, this was her family now. Just like Clay was her family.

Her heart melted at the hug Clay gave her friend. Love and acceptance. Saskia could have cried for the genuineness and kindness of the man she'd fallen in love with.

After that sweet tête-à-tête with Clay, Adrian took Gareth's hand and raised her voice. "Another hot notice in the art world is that Gareth Tate will have a gallery showing in Carmel-by-the-Sea, the date still to be determined."

Gareth was working furiously on new canvases. He'd turned the spare bedroom of his San Francisco flat into a studio. Though Clay had offered him space at the warehouse, he'd politely declined. "I want to be able to get up in the middle of the night and paint when inspiration strikes."

He also didn't want to be away from Adrian too long. Though they weren't living together, they spent nights at his place or hers, and he had art supplies in Adrian's spare room too. It was a match made in heaven, to quote Clay.

Gareth would place his new work in the show, but Saskia,

Adrian, and Clay had talked him into unearthing his old paintings as well. Because they were brilliant.

Adrian added, "Movie star Smith Sullivan and his wife, Valentina, are eager to attend. But most of all, we'd love for all of you to come. I'll update you on exactly when as soon as we know."

Clay called loudly, "Looks like I need to find a new lawyer, dammit."

The cabin erupted in laughter. They all knew Gareth should never have been a lawyer in the first place.

Saskia hugged Gareth. "I am so happy for you."

His smile was true in a way she was sure his smiles of the past ten years hadn't been. "I'm happy for you and my best friend Clay."

Now *that* felt like an opening; Saskia had her own announcement. "Listen up, everyone." She raised her hand for their attention. "For those of you who don't know, we've decided to make the mural on Clay's warehouse a collaborative effort. We'll start work right after Clay and I get back from our drive across Europe in his new sports car." They would also stop in London for a reading retreat and still be back in time for Gareth's show.

Cheers rose up. Had Fernsby actually winked at her? No, that couldn't be possible.

"Rosie, Sebastian, Dylan, and Gareth will be working with San Holo on the mural." Her smile felt as wide as the Grand Canyon. "And Charlie will add her metal art."

Francine waved frantically, and the Mavericks parted for her to speak. "Please tell me Charlie's not going to put Zanti Misfits all over it. Those little creatures are terrifying." Everyone laughed. Saskia would have to ask Clay later about these Zanti Misfits. They might be a fabulous addition to the mural.

She finished her announcement with, "Once the mural is

completed, we'll have a grand opening party and invite all of San Francisco."

A cacophony of clapping rattled the plane as Saskia mouthed to Clay, "I love you."

He mouthed back, "I love you more."

She felt giddy with happiness "I love you even more."

The game set her skin on fire. They often played it in bed, each trying to outdo the other with how much pleasure they could give.

She sent thanks into the heavens above for the out-of-control robotaxi that had literally thrown her into Clay's arms.

With Clay, she'd finally learned how to trust more, fear less. And love with everything in her.

TROY'S BROTHER Dane had done the research to figure out exactly where Charlie and Sebastian had gone. It wasn't as if Sebastian had tried to cover their tracks. Maybe he thought no one would be the wiser until they returned and had their big bash.

But then he shouldn't have underestimated the passel of Mavericks and Harringtons and their vast resources.

Although, without Francine Ballard's insight, they *would* have been none the wiser.

Troy readied himself, adjusting the massive jewel-encrusted silver buckle at his waist, straightening his embroidered jacket, and slicking back his Elvis do.

After changing into their outfits on the plane, the gang gathered outside the Las Vegas chapel, Gideon using military-style hand gestures for the countdown. *Three, two, one.* Then he flung open the door, and the entire Maverick clan charged inside.

The Elvis Chapel was perfectly tacky, with a cutout of the King playing a pink guitar up there on the dais with the bride and groom. A photographer flashed pictures while a short man in a white tux trimmed in gold brocade stood before the happy couple. Sebastian towered over Charlie, who was radiant in an emerald gown that made her red-gold curls shimmer.

Snapping a picture, the photographer caught the couple in mid-gape as they surveyed their surprise guests.

The Mavericks had dressed in the flashy Elvis garb appropriate for the occasion. Even Dylan got in on the act, wearing an electric-blue jumpsuit contrasting with his very pink embarrassed blush. Jeremy was decked out in a gold-studded black jumpsuit, its wide bell bottom pants lined in gold. The ladies wore poodle skirts and tight sweaters. Though Saskia had gone for lime-green leggings and a yellow crop top reminiscent of Ann-Margret in the movie *Viva Las Vegas*.

Clay hadn't taken his eyes off her.

The Spencers had dressed in snowy white, Bob in a tux and Susan in an elegant, slim-fitting cocktail dress à la Audrey Hepburn. Francine, also wearing white, had tied shimmery multicolored ribbons to her walker.

The only one not a slave to Elvis fashion was Fernsby, wearing his usual black suit and stern expression and holding T. Rex—oops, Lord Rexford.

Daniel Spencer stood with legs spread, arms akimbo. "Did you two really think you could get married without all of us here?"

Charlie recovered quickly, arching one eyebrow. "You're late. We had to go ahead without you." Then she smiled at the officiant. "Now that our family have arrived, you may proceed," she said in a prim, authoritative voice as if she were a British princess.

The officiant was so nervous at being surrounded by so many Elvises and poodle skirts that he fumbled through the usual lines as though he couldn't get to the final one fast enough. "I now pronounce you husband and wife," came out almost as one word.

Tony Collins called out, "Kiss the bride, dammit."

In a theatrical gesture that made the ladies titter, Sebastian bent Charlie backward over his arm and planted a kiss on her that was fast becoming steamy until Francine piped up, "Get a room, you two."

The entire group burst into applause. Troy noted that even Fernsby applauded, though he'd had nothing to do with matchmaking *that* couple.

The thought made Troy tremble. He prayed Fernsby wouldn't look at him.

As the party moved outside to the chapel's fake lawn, Troy sidled up to Gabby, who wore a pink skirt patterned with party poodles.

"When we connected with the Mavericks," he said in a low voice, "I didn't know our family was also going to catch the virus."

Gabby fluffed her blond ponytail high on her head. "What virus?"

Troy jutted his chin at their lovestruck siblings, Dane, Ava, and Clay. "The true love bug."

Tipping her head down, she studied him through her eyelashes. "Are you saying you're not on board with true love?"

He shrugged. "I'm happy for them, don't get me wrong. But you should be the next one, not me."

Gabby laughed her pretty laugh. Troy adored his sisters. "You do realize now you've said that, you've jinxed yourself. You'll definitely be next."

A waiter carrying flutes of champagne mysteriously

appeared—who'd arranged that, he had no idea—and Troy grabbed a glass, downing it in one gulp. "Since we're in Vegas, are you ready to put money on that?"

Gabby's grin could rival that of an evil wizard. "A million bucks says you fall in love before I do."

He'd never been one to back down on a family wager. "Loser donates a million to a charity of the winner's choice."

Troy held out his hand, and they shook on it.

Little did she know he had a secret weapon—the contact info for a very exclusive matchmaker who had a one hundred percent success rate. Troy's friend had recently used the woman and was now blissfully wed.

This would be the easiest, fastest million he'd ever made. Gabby wouldn't know what hit her when he set the billionaire matchmaker on her.

WITH EARS LIKE A FOX, Fernsby heard every word of the wager.

He had no trouble discerning Troy's thoughts. The dear young man thought this would be an easy win.

He had another thing coming.

Fernsby raised Lord Rexford to whisper in the mini dachshund's ear, "I know exactly who it's going to be. But let them have their little wager."

When they both finally saw him, he pointed two fingers from his eyes to Troy's. When Gabrielle grinned, he repeated the gesture at her.

I'm watching you, his fingers said. *And I have plans.*

To his delight, they both turned pale.

Oh yes, he had plans. For both of them. And his plans always worked out.

Of course they did. Because he was Fernsby.

Thank you so much for reading PAINTED IN LOVE! I hope you loved Clay and Saskia.

The next Maverick Billionaire – TEMPTED IN LOVE -- will be released soon! Until then, please sign up for our new release newsletters to be notified as soon as new Maverick Billionaires are released.

Sign up for Bella Andre's New Release Newsletter at http://BellaAndre.com/Newsletter

Sign up for Jennifer Skully's New Release Newsletter at http://bit.ly/SkullyNews

ALSO BY BELLA ANDRE

Check out the Family Tree for the Maverick Billionaires!

Don't miss out on any books in this romantic and sexy bestselling series!

https://bellaandre.com/the-mavericks-family-tree/

Ready for more? Dive into another bestselling contemporary romance series from Bella Andre today!

(Note: While Bella's books can easily be read as a stand-alone stories, you'll likely enjoy reading her other books too.)

THE SULLIVANS

In Bella Andre's #1 worldwide bestselling, sexy, emotional and funny contemporary romance series, each member of the Sullivan family will eventually find true love…usually where he or she least expects it.

The San Francisco Sullivans: Start with THE LOOK OF LOVE

The Seattle Sullivans: Start with THE WAY YOU LOOK TONIGHT

The New York Sullivans: Start with NOW THAT I'VE FOUND YOU

The Maine Sullivans: Start with YOUR LOVE IS MINE

The London Sullivans: Start with AS LONG AS I HAVE YOU

———

THE MAVERICK BILLIONAIRES

Meet the Maverick Billionaires—sexy, self-made men from the wrong side of town who survived hell together and now have everything they ever wanted. But when each Maverick falls head-over-heels for an incredible woman he never saw coming, he will soon find that true love is the only thing he ever really needed...

Start with BREATHLESS IN LOVE

THE DAVENPORTS

Meet the Davenport family! Six brothers and sisters who call beautiful Carmel-by-the-Sea in California home. They're all successful and passionate -- and waiting for the perfect partner in love and life.

Start with CALIFORNIA DREAMING

FOUR WEDDINGS AND A FIASCO and MARRIED IN MALIBU

The staff of San Francisco and Malibu's premiere wedding venues have always made their client's dreams come true...now it's their turn. (Note: The "Four Weddings and a Fiasco" series and the "Married in Malibu" spin-off series are fun, flirty and romantic-- without the steamy scenes.)

For "Four Weddings and a Fiasco" start with THE WEDDING GIFT

For "Married in Malibu" start with THE BEACH WEDDING

THE WALKER ISLAND SERIES

Come for a visit to Walker Island where you'll find stunning Pacific Northwest ocean views, men too intriguing to resist...and five close-knit sisters who are each about to find their one true love. (Note: This series is fun, flirty and romantic--without the steamy scenes.)

Start with BE MY LOVE

THE MORRISONS

Sexy, sweet and addicting is what the six Morrison siblings - and their love stories - are all about!

Start with KISS ME LIKE THIS

ALSO BY JENNIFER SKULLY

Once Again Series

Let the Once Again series whisk you away for tantalizing summer reading where you can travel to the locales of your dreams with later-in-life heroines who find romance and love in fabulous faraway places.

Start with DREAMING OF PROVENCE

Return to Love

In the quirky small town of Cottonmouth, gossip spreads faster than a cold virus, and love and murder make for unexpectedly hilarious bedfellows. Laugh out loud with the citizens of Cottonmouth when they all get in on trying to crack the case!

Start with SHE'S GOTTA BE MINE

Mystery of Love

In a town full of eccentric characters and eyebrow-raising antics, love and murder go hand in hand—usually in the most awkward, hilarious ways possible. A quirky accountant, a lady who thinks she's psychic, a woman who talks to animals, a funeral home director, oh my!

Start with DROP DEAD GORGEOUS

Love After Hours

In a world of high stakes and even higher heels, power, passion, and ambition collide. These sexy executives dominate the boardroom by day and fall for each other by night. And love is the most unpredictable deal of all. Don't miss this crossover series *Naughty After Hours*.

Start with DESIRE ACTUALLY

ALSO BY JASMINE HAYNES

Naughty After Hours

Run a bath, pour in the bubbles, uncork the champagne, open the box of chocolates, and sit back to enjoy some racy reading in these super-spicy workplace romances. Don't miss the crossover series *Love After Hours*.

Start with REVENGE

Max Starr Series

A ghost, a psychic, and one very hunky detective, all tied up with murder and mayhem. Max Starr has developed an annoying penchant for being possessed by the spirits of murdered women. To exorcize them, Max must unmask their killers. with help from the ghost of her late husband Cameron and very hunky Detective Witt Long.

Start with DEAD TO THE MAX

Lesson After Hours

A sexy workplace romance series with a hunky high school principal thrown in (really, a high school principal can be *very* hunky!)

Starts with PAST MIDNIGHT

Courtesans Tales

An exclusive and secret agency, its clients are rich, powerful, and influential people. And everyone who's ever had the pleasure of a date with a courtesan will agree, the fantasy is worth every penny. And sometimes it changes your life.

Starts with THE GIRLFRIEND EXPERIENCE

Castle Inc

Castle Inc, a family-run business. He wants to run the company, and he wants her. And that's just the beginning.

Starts with THE FORTUNE HUNTER

The Jackson Brothers

A heart-wrenching saga about a family torn apart by tragedy... Three years ago, the eldest Jackson brother died in a work accident. And nothing has been the same since for the Jackson family. They lost their heart and soul, even as matriarch Evelyn tries to keep them together. But things are changing and the family will either find their way back to each other. Or they'll be torn asunder.

Starts with SOMEBODY'S LOVER

Open Invitation

Enclosed: your invitation to The Club, elegant, classy, sexy, every woman's fantasy, every man's desire. And where love is waiting for them.

Start with INVITATION TO SEDUCTION

Prescott Twins

Identical twins and the two special men who fall for them.

Start with DOUBLE THE PLEASURE

Wives & Neighbors

Two wives, two husbands, and a little hanky-panky. What could go wrong?

Start with WIVES & NEIGHBORS

Take Your Pleasure Duo

A duo of super-sexy tales...

Start with TAKE YOUR PLEASURE

ABOUT THE AUTHORS

ABOUT BELLA ANDRE

Having sold more than 10 million books, Bella Andre's novels have been #1 bestsellers around the world and have appeared on the *New York Times* and *USA Today* bestseller lists 93 times. She has been the #1 Ranked Author on a top 10 list that included Nora Roberts, JK Rowling, James Patterson and Stephen King.

Known for "sensual, empowered stories enveloped in heady romance" (Publishers Weekly), her books have been Cosmopolitan Magazine "Red Hot Reads" twice and have been translated into ten languages. She is a graduate of Stanford University and has won the Award of Excellence in romantic fiction. The Washington Post called her "One of the top writers in America" and she has been featured by Entertainment Weekly, NPR, USA Today, Forbes, The Wall Street Journal, and TIME Magazine.

Bella also writes the *New York Times* bestselling "Four Weddings and a Fiasco" series as Lucy Kevin. Her sweet contemporary romances also include the USA Today bestselling "Walker Island" and the "Married in Malibu" series.

If not behind her computer, you can find her reading her favorite authors, writing and performing songs, hiking, swimming or laughing with friends and family. Married with two children, Bella splits her time between the Northern California wine country, a log cabin in the Adirondack mountains of New York, a flat in London overlooking the

Thames, and a haven of tranquility in the beautiful ocean town of Carmel-by-the-Sea.

Check out the Family Tree for The Maverick Billionaires:
https://bellaandre.com/the-mavericks-family-tree/

Sign up for Bella's New Release newsletter:
www.bellaandre.com/Newsletter

Visit Bella's website for her complete booklist:
www.BellaAndre.com

Check out the Family Tree for The Sullivans:
BellaAndre.com/sullivan-family-tree

Learn the "Secrets Behind The Sullivans":
www.bellaandre.com/Secret

Connect with Bella Andre on Meta/Facebook:
https://www.facebook.com/authorbellaandre

Join Bella Andre's VIP reader group:
https://www.facebook.com/groups/bellaandrefans

Follow Bella Andre on Instagram:
instagram.com/bellaandrebooks

Follow Bella on TikTok:
https://tiktok.com/@bellaandrebooks

Follow Bella Andre on X:
https://x.com/bellaandre

ABOUT JENNIFER SKULLY

New York Times and *USA Today* bestselling author Jennifer Skully is a lover of contemporary romance, bringing you poignant tales peopled with characters that will make you laugh and make you cry. Look for *The Maverick Billionaires* written with Bella Andre, starting with *Breathless in Love*, along with Jennifer's new later-in-life holiday romance series, *Once Again*, where readers can travel to fabulous faraway locales. Up first is a trip to Provence in *Dreaming of Provence*.

Writing as Jasmine Haynes, Jennifer authors classy, sensual romance tales about real issues such as growing older, facing divorce, starting over. Her books have passion and heart and humor and happy endings, even if they aren't always traditional. She also writes gritty, paranormal mysteries in the Max Starr series. Having penned stories since the moment she learned to write, Jennifer now lives in the Redwoods of Northern California with her husband and their adorable nuisance of a cat who totally runs the household.

Newsletter signup: http://bit.ly/SkullyNews

Jennifer's Website: www.JenniferSkully.com

Blog: www.jasminehaynes.blogspot.com

Facebook: facebook.com/jasminehaynesauthor

X: twitter.com/jasminehaynes1

Made in United States
Troutdale, OR
06/20/2025

32268523R10173